To Daniel
from
Big Daddy.
June 1989.

FIRST
WICKET DOWN

FIRST
WICKET
DOWN

John Parker

W.H. ALLEN · LONDON
1987

Copyright © John Parker 1987

Printed and bound in Great Britain by
Mackays of Chatham Ltd, Chatham, Kent
for the Publishers W. H. Allen & Co. Plc
44 Hill Street, London WIX 8LB

ISBN 0 491 03155 6

For Margaret

ENGLAND

Alexander, Philip (Middlesex). Wicketkeeper. Aged 34. R/h bat. 65 caps, total runs 1,398, ave 28.99, two centuries, h/s 123 v India, 23 st, 98 c. Career h/s 123, 113 st, 546 c. Married, 3 daughters. Nickname: Great. No 9.

Bowyer-Smith, Christopher James Alan (Cambridge U and Gloucestershire). Aged 25. L/h seamer, l/h bat. 12 caps, h/s 24* v Australia, b/b 5–45 v Pakistan, 32 wickets. Career best: 56 and 8–36. Average outfielder. Single. Nickname: Jabs. No 11.

Broadbent, Geoffrey (Yorkshire). Captain. Aged 36. R/h bat. 78 caps, 23 as captain, total runs 3,789, ave 43.22, seven centuries, h/s 198 v India. Career best: 212. Slip specialist. Married, no children. Nickname: Badger. No 5.

Carter, Vincent John (Essex). Aged 21. 6ft 2in. R/h fast bowler, r/h bat. One cap. Career best: 44 and 7–32. Good outfielder. Single. Nickname: Vince. No 10.

Coetzee, Boris (Worcestershire). Aged 28. Born Natal. R/h bat, outfielder. 35 caps, total runs 2,390, ave 34.54, three centuries, h/s 156* v New Zealand. Career best: 230. Deep field, fine throw. Married, no children. Nickname: Cagey. Middle order.

Graham, Peter (Derbyshire). Aged 26. Born Zambia. L/h bat. 34 caps, total runs 1,832, ave 33.65, 14 centuries, h/s 265 v Australia. Career best: 286. Average fielder. Single. Nickname: Dingdong. No 3 or 4.

Mandell, Percy Quinton (Kent). Aged 33. R/h bat, l/h orthodox spinner. 22 caps, total runs 980, ave 32.11, h/s 100 v Australia, b/b 5–67 v Pakistan. Best all-round: 100 and 4–44 v Australia. Career best: 132 and 8–23. Brilliant cover fielder. Married, 2 sons, 1 daughter. Nickname: Peekue. No 7.

Prettyman, Anthony Brighouse (Oxford U and Surrey). Aged 30. R/h opening bat, r/h med bowler. 8 caps, total runs 456, ave 52.56, h/s 99 v West Indies, b/b 4–51 v West Indies. Career best: 298, bowling 5–19. Gully specialist. Single. Nickname: Sweetie. Opening bat, prefers No 1.

Spencer, David Austin (Northamptonshire). Aged 30. R/h bat, r/h seamer. 52 caps, total runs 3,693, ave 38.63, 235 wickets, ave 34.66, four centuries, h/s 125 v West Indies, b/b 7–49 v New Zealand, best all-round 102 and 6–117 v Sri Lanka. Career best: 176 and 8–65. Good fielder, any position. Married, one son. Nickname: Monkey. No 6.

Williamson, Frederick Arthur (Lancashire). Aged 31. R/h opening bat. 43 caps, total runs 1,908, ave 36.89, h/s 176 v New Zealand. Career best: 203 v Oxford U. Close fielder. Married, one daughter. Nickname: Diamond. No 2.

Woodman, John George (Middlesex). Aged 28. R/h bat and off-spinner. 6 caps, h/s 33 b/b 4–48 v West Indies. Career best: 85 and 7–42. Moderate fielder. Single. Nickname: Chopper. No 8.

Wetherby, Richard (Oxford U and Sussex). 12th man. Aged 22. R/h bat and cover fielder. No caps. Career h/s 144 v Yorkshire. Single.

Anderson, Roland. Manager. Aged 54. Former captain of Lancashire; played 10 times for England. Former Test selector. Successful publican. Married, two daughters, four grandchildren.

AUSTRALIA

Comberton, Charles Bright (Queensland). Aged 24. R/h bat, occasional r/h off-breaks. 23 caps, total runs 1,765, ave 32, h/s 184 v New Zealand. Career best: 231 and 4–61. Single. Nickname: Shiner. No 4.

Foster, Paul Collier (New South Wales). Aged 20. L/h bat, brilliant fielder. 4 caps, total runs 428, ave 107, two centuries, h/s 186 v India. Career best: 233. Single. Nickname: Collie. No 3.

Imrie, Bartram Victor (Western Australia). Vice-captain. Aged 31. R/h opening bat. 35 caps, total runs 2,879, ave 46.18, five centuries, h/s 142* v Pakistan. Career best: 349 v Tasmania. Competent fielder, any position. Single. Nickname: Wrecker. No 2.

Jones, Gary (New South Wales). Aged 24. R/h fast bowler, r/h bat. 14 caps, 53 wickets, ave 21.43, b/b 7–43 v England, h/s 12*. Career best: 8–65 and 34. Married, no children. Nickname: Ginger. No. 11.

MacPhail, Roger Philip Denzil (South Australia and Cambridge U). Aged 23. R/h bat, l/h spinner. 4 caps, total runs 370, ave 47.58, h/s 158 v India (career best), 34 wickets, ave 28.33, b/b 6–57 v India (career best). Married, no children. Nickname: Toffee. No 5.

Martin, Michael (Tasmania). Aged 24. R/h fast-medium bowler, r/h bat. 6 caps, total runs 112, 22 wickets, ave 34.73, b/b 5–42 v New Zealand, h/s 40. Career best: 62 and 7–53. Single. Nickname: Knife. No 10.

Rose, Brian Frederick (New South Wales). Aged 28. Wicket-keeper, r/h bat. 38 caps, total runs 2,003, ave 29.68, 27 st, 109 c, h/s 126* v England. Career best: 143. Married, 2 children. Nickname: Fingers. No 8.

Smart, Sydney Simon (Queensland). Aged 23. R/h bat, r/h off-spinner. 14 caps, total runs 1,087, ave 37.97, h/s 135 v New Zealand, 58 wickets, ave 25.45, b/b 6–81 v West Indies. Career best: 139 and 7–19. Single. Nickname: Sissie. No 6.

Viljoen, George (South Australia). Aged 32. R/h fast-medium bowler, r/h bat. 16 caps, total runs 952, ave 34.62, 61 wickets, ave 30.36, b/b 6–52 v England, h/s 96*. Career best: 111. Married, no children. Nickname: Both. No 7.

Viner, Jack (New South Wales). Captain. Aged 36. L/h opening bat. 79 caps, total runs 10,431, ave 43.95, 13 centuries, h/s 212 v England. Career best: 265. Married, 2 children. Nickname: Wino. No 1.

Walters, Neale (Western Australia). Aged 20. R/h fast bowler, r/h bat. No caps. Career best: 6–37 and 33. Single. Nickname: Wally. No 9.

Golander, Bruce (Western Australia). 12th man. Aged 23. No caps. R/h bat, occasional off-spinner. H/s 111 v Victoria. Nickname: Golly. Single.

Cousins, Griffiths. Manager. Aged 43. Former opening bat for Tasmania, now chicken-breeder in New South Wales. Divorced. No children.

Chapter 1

The First Day

Jack Viner, the Australian cricket captain, died in bright sunlight at precisely five minutes past eleven on June 12, watched closely by eleven members of the England cricket team, his fellow opening batsman, Bart Imrie, and two umpires. Some 23,562 paying spectators at the Second Test match at Lord's also saw him die, from distances of upwards of 90 yards and, from the visitors' balcony in the pavilion, so did the other 15 members of the Australian touring team, their manager and their coach. A further 4,500,000 television viewers perhaps had the best sight of the event which shocked two nations, because David Phillips, the cameraman 40ft up in the cherrypicker at the Nursery End had been told to go in close on the batsman for the fifth ball of the first over of the day; and in any case they were afforded the opportunity of studying innumerable playbacks, in slow motion and up to speed, with the inevitable stop-frame of the moment when Viner's knees buckled and the bright red ball cannoned with sickening force into his right cheekbone.

More than two million aficionados listened avidly to the description of the event on Radio Three, holding their breath in horror as the bland voice of the nation's favourite radio commentator rose from its customary slick sing-song into genuine, if temporary alarm. '. . . He's turning at the end of his run-up . . . the familiar shuffle . . . he's lengthening his stride . . . Viner waits, motionless like any great batsman . . . in comes Carter . . . It's short . . . Viner's hit in the face . . . he's falling . . . onto the wicket . . . my God, he's fallen onto the wicket . . . he's just lying there on top of the broken stumps . . . God, he's knocked out, I hope he's all right . . . They're all crowding round, Imrie was the first, then Carter . . . He seems to be just lying there, I can't see

. . . Well, whether he's hurt or not, he's out, isn't he, Charles? . . . What d'you say? He still isn't moving? No, I can just see Carter lifting his head . . . Wait while I get the glasses on him . . . What? Oh, yes, I'm a fool, we can see it better on the monitor . . . Must say he's looking very groggy, though I can't see very much . . . the cricketers are in the way . . . There's umpire Goodie, too, and the skipper's signalling to the pavilion . . . Here comes Doc Wright, the physio . . . he's running, and a couple of St John Ambulance people, very smart in their uniform. They've got a stretcher. It could be very serious for Australia, this . . . their captain hurt in the very first over of the Test . . . I wonder . . . Doc Wright's bending over Viner. The players are standing back . . . Wright's giving him the kiss of life . . . yes, yes he is! . . . How exciting! . . . Now they're loading him onto a stretcher, Viner, I mean, not Doc Wright . . . and little Ollie Smith is carrying his bat and gloves . . . Doc Wright's got a blanket from somewhere and put it over him, very sensible, that, in cases like this . . . Well, you have to expect everything and anything in cricket . . . I hope he's not badly hurt but we'll bring you news just as soon as we know how serious the injury is. Now, here's Charles Montfort. Monters, you played Test cricket for many years, ha ha, forty, I believe. Ha ha, Simon de Montforty. Ha ha. Tests, I mean, not years. Let's have your expert view on the dramatic start to this Lord's Test, and of course you might begin right away by telling us what you think about an experienced batsman, like Viner, who refuses to wear a helmet . . . Charles Montfort . . .'

Sixty miles due south of Lord's Cricket Ground Detective Sergeant Ambrose Light – his colleagues inevitably called him Amber – flicked the switch on his car radio and sighed. He didn't mind cricket particularly, but it irked him that his favourite Radio Three switched over to the Test match at a time when he had a tedious drive back to London to contend with. The M23 he could manage, he thought, but he did not need the bland oiled voice of Scott Marston or the slightly fatuous pomposities of Charles Montfort to accompany it. He set his conscious mind to concentrate on the road, while his policeman's brain continued to rake over the Brighton drugs case which had been his concern for the past three weeks. He had not been happy with the exhausted look in Chief Superintendent William Ashcroft's eyes as they'd moved in with the Brighton lads to take the flat overlooking the Marina. True, they'd found the stuff, more than £2 million worth of cocaine in neat little plastic bags. They'd arrested that precious pair in the act of weighing it out on a kitchen scale. But Ashcroft knew, and Light knew too, that had they acted more speedily on the tip Light had picked up in a Clapham pub, the haul would have been ten times the amount, and the big man they had missed altogether. They still had no inkling who he was. Old Bill, thought Light, was beginning to lose his touch.

The usual bottleneck in Streatham interrupted his reverie. Damn, he thought, I should have slipped up through Wallington, but then grinned as he recalled the old cabbie's motto: 'There's only one way through London. The wrong one.' He put his hand out to the radio again.

'. . . 23 for one wicket after an hour's play, Imrie on six and Foster, 11. Viner, of course, poor chap, was out hit wicket for nought, and he's off the field injured at the moment. We believe he's been taken to hospital. Wait a minute, I believe there's an official announcement . . .' The smooth voice died away and the hum of the great crowd grew perceptibly louder as the studio director at Broadcasting House gently boosted the power of his exterior microphones. The amplified tones of the Secretary of the Test and County Cricket Board reverberated gravely across the ground and into the car.

'Ladies and gentlemen, I regret to inform you that Jack Viner was found to be dead on arrival at the Middlesex Hospital.' The voice paused, as if the speaker was waiting for the crowd to react. There was a great collective intake of breath, as though a giant sighed. The voice went on, silencing the swelling murmur. 'I have no need to tell you how shocked we all are at Jack's death in these circumstances, and I know you will join with the TCCB and the whole England team in offering his family and of course the Australian team our deepest sympathy. We have consulted Bill Cousins, the Australian manager, and he has been on the telephone to the Australian Board in Sydney, and it has been agreed that the best course to follow in the distressing circumstances is to halt play for the moment. There will be a two-minute silence after which lunch will be taken and play will resume in one hour from now . . . Would you please all stand in silence for two minutes in memory of a fine cricketer and a great Australian captain.'

Up in the cherrypicker David Phillips pulled his parka more tightly around him and zoomed the lens of his videocamera slowly in on the white-clad cricketers on the field, standing awkwardly to attention as people do when showing public emotion.

'Go in on Carter. He's the big one, holding the ball. Quicker, man. You'll lose it.'

'Oh, piss off.' Phillips had nearly 30 years' experience behind him. 'Go teach your grannie to . . .'

The camera found the tall figure of Vince Carter, sideways on in the viewing screen, holding his arms behind his back in the army 'at ease' position, the bright red ball almost hidden in one large hand. But as the 1,000/1 zoom lens began to pick up the details – red stain on the right buttock of the whites where Carter polished the ball between each delivery, cream flannel shirt clinging to the body with sweat at the armpit, the outline of the singlet beneath – the focus moved up to the face.

'Go in. Go in close.' The director's voice in Phillips' earphone rose to a screech, and as the cameraman touched the button the face enlarged to fill the whole screen.

It was a good face, high in the brow and long in the chin, with fair hair matted with sweat, pushed back but still unruly. It was tanned, with little white lines at the eyes and at the side of the mouth now turned down with muscles taut at the corners. The camera picked up the beads of perspiration on the forehead and cruelly highlighted the tears coursing down the cheek. Suddenly, as though he was seeking solitude in the midst of 20,000 people, Vince Carter turned his back on the pavilion and looked up, full into the eye of Phillips' camera.

As if transfixed, the lens stared down at the man and the man stared unseeing back at the lens as the tears ran unchecked down his face, flashing silver in the sunlight. It was a shot which won Phillips the TV Cameraman of the Year award and the BBC the coveted Outside Broadcast Trophy, and it was to haunt both cameraman and bowler for the rest of their days.

'Thank you, ladies and gentlemen.' The voice over the Tannoy broke the spell. Broadbent, the England captain, moved across slowly to the Australian batsmen, standing with their protective helmets in their hands, and walked between them to the pavilion rails. There he stood back and led the England players in a brief, quiet round of applause, taken up by the silent members first and then rippling round the entire ground.

Detective Sergeant Light, easing the car past Kennington, home of London's other great cricket ground, had switched his radio across for the news headlines when the police set crackled authoritatively into life.

'X-ray calling Magpie. X-ray calling Magpie. Do you read? Over.'

Light leaned over to lift the grey microphone from its cradle.

'Magpie here, Shirley. What d'you want? I was just listening to the cricket . . . Over.'

'Funny you should say that, Magpie. You're wanted over at Lord's right away. Old Bill will meet you there. How soon can you make it? Over.'

Light glanced at the dashboard clock.

'What's the traffic report? Over.'

'Hang on a mo' . . . Oh yes, usual West End snarl-up at lunchtime. Nothing much else. Over.'

'All right. Shirley, I'm through Kennington. Say half an hour, with luck. Out.'

I wonder what Old Bill is doing at Lord's, Light thought. It can't be Jack Viner's death. There was nothing wrong with that, surely; it was simply a sporting misfortune. Although 15 years in the Force, seven of them in the CID and the last three with Chief Superintendent William Ashcroft had taught him that very many events were often not quite what they seemed.

He reflected that he had never been inside Lord's Cricket Ground, familiar though he was with its long grey brick walls from the outside. He'd often thought it looked like the outside of the nick. Although he had played some cricket as a boy, association football had claimed his leisure time until irregular hours and late nights found him more constantly at the snooker table than at Highbury or White Hart Lane. As a policeman on the beat he had had his share of crowd control, sitting glumly in the back of a badly-lit bus trying to read and keep warm while the match ran its course or until the strike pickets turned nasty. But for some reason he had never been called on for duty at a cricket match. His mind was still turning over what he had heard about, or read of, the traditional English game when he turned the car into St John's Wood Road. On his right a 12ft-high brick wall sturdy enough, indeed, to enclose a prison, ran alongside the pavement for some two hundred yards. Light could hear nothing over the hum of the traffic, but as he drove along slowly a sudden roar of sound welled into the car. I wonder what's happened, he thought as, indicator flicking, he waited to turn across the traffic towards the graceful wrought-iron gates that constitute the formal entrance to the greatest cricket ground in the world.

The Grace Gates were erected to honour the memory of Dr W. G. Grace, arguably the finest cricketer who ever lived, but anyone who has ever tried to pass through them while a Test match is in progress knows that the gates are established more as a barrier than as a means of ingress or egress. Light, a patient man by training, edged his car through a milling knot of a hundred or so people mostly male and Antipodean, who were endeavouring to gain entry to the ground and who were repeatedly repelled with surprising ease by an elderly man in a shabby white coat and an old-fashioned workman's cloth cap that had seen better days.

'Sorry, sir, not here. Paying customers along the road, if you please. No, sir. Not for a hundred fivers. Passes only. You can't come in if you haven't got a pass.' Every so often a suppliant would present a small piece of cardboard to be examined suspiciously, the great gate would be eased back a trifle, and the favoured one would sidle furtively through the reluctant gap to disappear into the throng inside.

Light's persistence and his ID card forced his car through the crowd until the front bumper touched the wrought-iron perpendicular bars of the gates. Leaning out of the car window he held up his card, face toward the guardian of the gate. The cloth cap shook vehemently from side to side and the mouth moved in an emphatic negative which Light could not hear but needed no lip-reading ability to interpret. The gates stayed closed. With difficulty, he elbowed the car door open and made his way along the bonnet.

'Police,' he shouted, pushing the card between the iron bars to within six inches of the gatekeeper's face. 'Let me in.'

'Can't come in wivart a pass.' The attendant knew every dodge in the book. He had held the Grace Gates against all comers for forty years and so far had never seen one over bowled nor one four

18

struck. His sport was racing. 'If yer police, get a pass. And yer can't bring that car in wivart a car pass,' he added as an after-thought.

Light looked into a pair of faded blue eyes set in a web of leathered wrinkles and realised why even the ebullient Australians had failed to carry the gate. Briefly, the arm of the law considered the representative of private authority and a newspaper clipping flickered across his memory. It was a knack he had.

'Look, ducky,' he said firmly, 'how can I have a pass when it's waiting for me inside? The Admiral will have your balls for break-fast if you hold us up.'

The stony eyes flickered.

'Oh, well. Why dincher say so before?'

With an effort he pulled the heavy gate open just far enough to admit Light's Rover. Light, who was expecting the human flood behind him to spill through the gap, saw in his rearview mirror that no one had even tried to cross the line of the gate. 'First door on the right under the arch,' the gatekeeper shouted through the open window.

'Thanks. Where do I put the car?'

The man grinned. 'Yer'll be lucky.'

As he inched his way forward through throngs of apparently aimless strollers, Light's trained eyes picked up the small hut-like building on his left, where white-clad minions lurked, handing out brown envelopes to the more privileged. Red brick and con-crete curved away to his right, with galleries at intervals, baking in the midday sun. A large notice proclaimed Q Stand. A line of men of varying ages shuffled towards an opening in the base of the stand, positive proof that all beer reaches most parts sooner or later. From a similar opening further along others emerged in a steady stream, some adjusting their dress but all with new spring in their step. Light thought it was appropriate at a cricket ground that one opening should be labelled 'In' and the other, 'Out'.

Another queue of men, interspersed with the occasional woman, waited patiently by a tiny moveable wooden hut where two well-scrubbed athletic youths wore navy blue blazers self-consciously and dispensed scorecards at 25p a time with an indif-ferent air. There was a queue for flat cushions, maroon and green; a queue for ice-cream; and even a queue for the expensive lunches at

19

the Banqueting Suite. Not for the first time, Light marvelled at the patience of the British sports follower. He had time to take in a flash of green between two buildings on his right, with white figures moving in the distance, and an unexpectedly pretty rose garden with low brick walls on his left before he drove quietly along the back of the great pavilion; past the modest headquarters of the Middlesex County Cricket Club (not, as he learned later, to be confused with the legendary MCC); past the Real Tennis court; past the cut-out hardboard effigy of W. G. Grace advertising the Cricket Museum, to double-park under the shade of a huge plane tree. Here the narrow roadway opened out as the Warner Stand curved away massively to the right. Modest notices declaring 'No Parking' and 'Special Car Passes Only' had failed to prevent a cluster of vehicles from overflowing from a tiny area tucked away to the left on to the pedestrian precinct, and another white-coated official, be-capped and belligerent, descended on Light.

'Yer can't park' ere.'

Light tried his ID card again.

'Police. Inquiring into the murder,' he added facetiously. 'Where can I find the Admiral?' Once more the magic worked. The man stared at him, then pointed back to the pavilion.

'Second door on the left. And yer won't be allowed in like that.'

Light paid no attention. With a muttered 'Ta' he began to make his way through a cackle of small boys trying to catch a glimpse of their heroes through the rear entrance to the pavilion. They could see nothing past the middle-aged men showing their bright scarlet membership cards to yet another attendant.

'Sorry, sir, members only,' Light heard, and the politely pushing queue opened a little to allow a red-faced enthusiast to back out of the door. This time Light was ready with his card and a sharp: 'Where can I find the Admiral?' The man looked back at him stolidly.

'Sorry, sir,' he said politely. 'I can't let you go in like that.'

'Like what?' Light said with some heat. 'I'm on duty and I'm going to see my boss. He's with the Admiral.'

'Sorry sir, but no one's allowed into the pavilion during a Test match unless he is wearing a tie. Not even if he was the Prince of Wales.'

Light was speechless. He had paid £80 at Simpson's for his blue

20

silk shirt with its fashionable roll-neck collar. He'd had tea at the Ritz (once) wearing it. He shook his ID firmly under the attendant's nose and tapped him gently on the chest with a forefinger.

'Now you listen to me, ducky. I'm going in here, and if you try to stop me you'll be round at the station in two shakes on a charge of obstructing the police. Now. Where's the Admiral?'

At last the majesty of the law held sway. The doorman flushed.

'Oh well, all right. I'm just doing my job,' he said defensively. 'Sorry, sir. Up the steps, turn right, along through the bar, up the steps in front of you and you'll find the Admiral's office. But you can't go in the bar without a tie . . .'

Light did not wait to argue further. He went up the short flight of steps two at a time and turned right through a wide doorway into the Long Bar. He was met by smoke, heat and a high noise level that beat at his eardrums as he elbowed his way along the length of the bar. He ignored the curious glances and the occasional hand on his arm.

'I say, old boy . . .'

'Can't come in here like that, old man . . .'

'Dash it, the man hasn't a tie . . . bad show.'

'Sorry,' said Light, pushing his way through. 'Police . . . on duty . . . excuse me, sir.' With some emphasis on the 'sir'. The red and yellow ties fell back and Light strode through the door at the far end, up another flight of wooden steps and into a tiny foyer empty except for a two-foot counter of polished mahogany and a bell-push. A half-glassed door opened as Light sounded the bell and a fuzz of red hair hiding green button eyes proclaimed the first female he had encountered since entering the ground.

'Yer Sergeant Light,' said the hair in broad Cockney. 'We was waitin' fer yer. Come on.' She rounded the counter and opened another door Light had not noticed.

'How did you know?'

'Wot? Oo yer was? Easy. The old copper said as you wouldn't be dressed proper.' She looked at Light's roll-down collar. 'Come on. They're waitin' fer yer.'

She led the way up yet another, narrower, flight of stairs and into a cramped office cluttered with files and filing cabinets. There were two desks, with in-trays and out-trays on one of them piled high with bulging files and papers. Behind it, looking out of place with his back to the grubby sashed window, sat a small upright figure who could have had no other background than nautical. The healthy brown-red of his tan spread evenly from his immaculate white collar to the crown of his head, interrupted only by a thin slash of a mouth, ice-blue eyes and Santa Claus eyebrows. The close-cropped white hair lay like a monk's crown round the sides of his head. He had the air of one accustomed to dominating the quarterdeck and much else besides; and as Light entered the little room the anchor buttons clicked metallically as the small man shot his cuff and glared at a large old-fashioned Rolex Oyster wristwatch. Light thought he looked a bit put out.

Seated comfortably in a capacious leather swivel chair at the bigger desk, whose expanse of gleaming mahogany bore only an unmarked blotting pad and a brass pen rack, was the large crumpled figure of Detective Chief Superintendent William Ashcroft, known with varying degrees of affection throughout the Metropolitan Police and a dozen other forces as Old Bill. He appeared quite undominated, and Light was not surprised that ten square yards of indifferent worsted should on this occasion be lit up by the scarlet and yellow of the MCC tie.

'Hallo, Amber,' said Ashcroft. 'What kept you? No, don't bother. We've got a tricky one here. By the way, meet the Admiral. It's murder.'

Unsure precisely to what, or to whom, his chief was referring, Light shook hands with Admiral (Rtd) Percival St John Rogers, hero of the Beira Patrol, the Falklands war and a number of the Royal Navy's more notable peacetime exploits, now running a taut ship as Comptroller of the Lord's Cricket Ground, its administration and its personnel.

Detective Sergeant Light stepped out of the gloom of the pavilion, blinking in the bright sunlight, and made his way to the seat the Admiral had pointed out to him. There was Lord's, the heart of cricket, laid open for his inspection before him with a Test match against Australia in progress. Even Light, who was not an emotional man, felt a tug at his stomach as he gazed down at the wide green acres.

'Get out and get the feel of it,' Old Bill had growled. 'You won't know what all this is about until you understand.' Light had demurred, suggesting that inspirational thinking of that sort was more in Old Bill's line, but the old man cut him short.

'Do me good to do some routine for once,' he said surprisingly. 'In any case, I'd be watching the match. You'll be more inclined to listen to what people are saying. Here, take these.' He thrust a large pair of Zeiss binoculars across the table, and Light found himself out of the door and on the wide steps before he could protest.

Now he looked about him with trained eyes, taking in his immediate surroundings before allowing his gaze to stray out-wards. He was seated on a white, freshly-painted wooden bench with curved wrought-iron supports, circa 1900. They reminded Light of Eastbourne seafront. Under his feet wide wooden board flooring had seen better days and in front of him, at an awkward height for viewing the cricket, an iron railing ran about a foot above the top of the grey brick balcony wall. Behind him and above, more tiers of plank flooring carried more seating, all seem-ingly held together by its latest lick of white paint and bearing serried ranks of spectators, most of them in their fifties or older. Tucked away behind their legs under the seats were plastic carrier bags or holdalls, which Light assumed (correctly) to be carrying sandwiches and some form of liquid refreshment. Between Light and a small blocked-off section where the Independent Television News team filmed, intent only on the game, sat an elderly man with a clipped military moustache and a white starched collar fashionable in the 1930s. A slim tripod at his knee held steady a well-worn set of surplus government-issue field glasses.

'Good afternoon.' He returned Light's greeting politely but dismissively, briefly removing his attention from the game. Light shrugged mentally and switched his gaze to the panorama before him. It was not the conventional picture of Lord's, which displays the Victorian pavilion with its twin towers and tiered galleries, but it was imposing enough. Left and right, the stands curved away to enclose the mown green grass, every seat taken and every square foot occupied with the varied colours of humanity out for the day. Looking down to his right, Light could see the packed area in front of the Tavern, with its convoluted queues snaking their way to the various bars. Many of the men had removed their shirts, brown Australian tans mingling with the paler shades of English supporters and the coffee and chocolate of India and the Caribbean. Girls in coloured dresses, some wearing sun-hats, sprinkled the scene, and Light, who rather fancied his artistic know-how, mentally described it as an animated Pissarro, with tiny points of colour blending to make a brilliant whole.

The twin horns of the stands did not quite meet on the far side of the ground. Over the top of the light blue sightscreens ('I always thought they were white,' Light said to himself), he could see through the gap more grass and a line of nets, a few treetops. Well above the height of the stands the long arm of the cherrypicker stretched upwards, like a praying mantis, while at its tip the little railed platform, the cameraman and his equipment appeared from this distance to be a small hunched blob. Advertising hoardings abounded for the benefit of television viewers. Over on the left, under a venerable clock and in front of one of the older stands, the crowd had been permitted to stray onto the grass behind a rope laid on the ground to mark the boundary. Hundreds of spectators had taken advantage of this leniency on the part of the management to spread their rugs, open their hampers and to devour much cold chicken and smoked salmon, washed down with beer or wine or, in a few exclusive parties, with iced champagne.

On the roof of the big old stand on the left, running at right angles almost due east of the pavilion, the weathercock figure of Old Father Time stooped darkly over his wicket, as still and steady as the quiet south wind itself. Underneath him the figures of the scoreboard, operated by invisible hands, changed almost imperceptibly as the game made its leisurely progress. It took Light, who had left his appreciation of cricket behind in the fifth form, some time to decipher the meaning of all the figures.

Batsmen 2 and 3 he identified on his 25p scorecard as Bart Imrie and Collie Foster respectively. The scoreboard told him that Imrie, a household name on four continents, had scored 33 runs; his partner, making his debut at Lord's for Australia, was on 20, and that the score had reached 60 for one wicket. Last man, 0. Light worked out which batsman was facing the bowling by noticing the tiny bulb which lit up over the relevant number, and he also deduced that Vince Carter was bowling from the Pavilion End of the wicket, with David Spencer at the other, Nursery, end.

The row of figures, with S at the end, baffled him until he realised, again with the aid of more little bulbs, that they denoted the fielder in action, although whosoever's finger was on the buttons often lagged well behind what was happening.

Light's career depended on his ability to ask questions as well as to decipher the answers, and his thirst for knowledge was insatiable. He also did not like discrepancies. He waited until the end of an over brought a slight relaxation to the shoulders of his military-looking neighbour, indicated by a minuscule unstiffening of the spine.

'Excuse me, sir.' Light thought a little old-fashioned courtesy might be useful. 'Can you tell me why the score's on 60 when the batsmen's figures add up to only 53?'

Cool grey eyes took in Light's blue silk shirt, suede jacket and designer jeans with a momentary lifting of the eyebrows, but the clipped voice answered courteously enough.

'Oh, yes, it's obvious. You see, there are the extras – byes, no-balls and so on – which don't show up on the scoreboard.'

The eyebrows lowered slightly.

'Pardon my asking, but are you a member here?'

'No, sir. I'm working.' Light produced his ID card. The eyes flickered appreciatively.

'Ah, good. I was afraid the Club was relaxing its standards.' As if aware that this might have been construed as discourtesy, the military man added: 'No tie, don't you know. Can't afford to relax standards, particularly in these days. Excuse me.'

He turned back to his field glasses, moving them slightly along to follow the bowler's run-up, steadying them as the ball was delivered, then leaning back as it thudded harmlessly into the wicket-keeper's gloves.

'Good ball!' he called softly to himself, clapping his hands gently three times. Light heard an appreciative frisson ripple through the crowd around and below him.

'What was so good about that ball?' he inquired, once his neighbour had settled down again. 'It seemed like any other ball to me. How can you tell?'

'Ah, you're not a cricketer, then.' He implied this was an explanation, not a criticism. 'It's difficult to explain precisely if you don't play the game. It's in the blood, don't you see. Young Carter is keeping a damn good line and length on a slow wicket that doesn't suit him. That ball drew Imrie forward and beat him off the seam. He might have got a touch. That takes some doing to a batsman of Imrie's class, especially to make the ball move up the hill from this end.'

Light filed this indigestible piece of information away in his mind, hoping that at some stage all might become clear to him.

'Thanks. You must come here very often?'

'Wait a moment.'

The elderly soldier held up a hand like a traffic policeman and glued his eyes to the field glasses again. Light realised that it was perfectly possible to carry on a coherent conversation, provided one was prepared to allow for rhythmic intervals of undivided attention to the game. He decided it must be part of cricket's mystique, if not its charm. At least it provided one with the opportunity to contemplate one's reply before making it.

'Oh, good shot! Fine shot, sir!'

His elderly companion was halfway out of his seat, applauding vigorously this time. Imrie had stepped forward and, without seeming to use any effort, had sent it racing to the boundary in front of the Tavern. Three small boys fell over each other in their frenzied attempts to seize it first. The winner stood up grinning widely and holding his prize aloft, and then threw it as hard as he could roughly in the direction of long leg, who had given up the unequal chase along the boundary to cut off the ball. The applause swelled round the ground. Light's companion needed no prompting this time.

'Did you see that? What a shot! The on-drive to perfection. They say Ranji used to do that, but that was before my time, of course. Bradman I saw play it, and Neil Harvey. It's a true Australian stroke, you know. All right hand but beautiful timing. Jack Viner plays it – I mean used to play it – from outside the off stump.'

Light suggested mildly that such enthusiasm for an opponent's expertise might seem somewhat misdirected.

'Great heavens, no, man. It's the game, don't you see? The game! If you can play like that, it doesn't matter if you're on the side of Beelzebub.'

Light repeated his unanswered question.

'Come here often? Oh, I don't think so. Just once a year, for the Lord's Test. Wish I could do more, but my wife . . . I look forward to it every year, but it's been spoilt for me by that unfortunate injury to poor Viner. Bad show, that.'

'Did you see it happen?'

'Oh, I had the glasses on him all the time. He was back on to me, of course – this isn't too good a position when you've got a left-hander batting. Well, there was something about young Carter's run-up that told me it was going to be a special effort, don't you know. They all . . .' he waved a hand at the crowd '. . . they could all feel it, too. There was a kind of swell, and that noise they sometimes make. A chant, Car-ter, Car-ter, every time his right foot hit the ground and rising to a crescendo as he jumped. Yes, Carter jumped. He doesn't usually jump. He's a smoother bowler than that. More Lindwall than Lillee, don't you know.'

He broke off to applaud a neat cut for two.

'Where was I?. . . . oh, the run-up. Yes, he jumped. I don't have to move the glasses very far from this angle for the run-up, and I had Viner in focus all the time, at least his top half. His back was towards me and he was very still, as if he knew something was going to happen. But he always stood still. He isn't – wasn't – one of these new-fangled batsmen who wave their bat in the air while they're waiting for it to arrive.

'It all happened very fast, of course. His legs seemed to buckle and he seemed to fall into the ball. I couldn't see where it hit him – somewhere in the face, I think. It was almost as if he was mesmerised by it, but that often happens with a bouncer. The ball seems to follow the batsman no matter what he does to get out of the way. I did wonder momentarily if he'd had a heart attack before the ball arrived. It must be terrible for young Carter to know that he'd actually killed the Australian captain, though they didn't know it till later, of course. I think he's done very well in the circumstances.'

'Why didn't they abandon the game?'

The grey eyes looked at him in horror.

'Good God, man, you can't be serious. Abandon the game because a man's died? There would be a lynching. Look at all these people. The game is much more important than one man, or one man's life, for that matter.'

Light might have questioned the old man's morality, but he was in full reminiscent flood.

'Why, in '73 it was, or maybe '74, during one of the IRA

27

campaigns, there was a bomb scare. The police gave out a warning and asked the whole crowd to leave the ground and wait outside until they had a good look round. The crowd knew better. The whole crowd – every one of them – left the stands and came down onto the grass. Very quietly, perfectly orderly. Little Dickie Bird, the umpire, sat down on the wicket to make sure no one trampled on the square. And no one did. They wouldn't, at Lord's. After half an hour the police announced that they'd found nothing, and the game could go on. That was the day Boycott threw his wicket away . . .'

In the course of the next half hour Light learned a great deal about cricket and about his informant. Brigadier Milford's lifelong passion had been cricket, but the needs of his invalid wife in Kent curtailed his visits to Lord's these days. His son had greatly disappointed him by preferring money-making to cricket, and was currently amassing a fortune in Hong Kong, so the Brigadier had bequeathed his dwindling estate to ensure the future of the Lord's Cricket School.

Light made the suitable responses, excused himself and returned to the Admiral's office. There he found Chief Superintendent Ashcroft ensconced in the Admiral's chair listening to a red-faced man with groomed silver hair, who broke off as Light entered.

Ashcroft waved a vague hand.

'Oh, there you are, Amber. We've been waiting for you. This is Detective Sergeant Light, Walter.'

He did not bother further to introduce the visitor. Sir Walter Brownley, the Queen's surgeon, was too well-known and liked seeing his face in the newspapers too often for Light to mistake him for a nonentity.

'I'm sure you won't mind repeating what you've just been telling me?' said Ashcroft, with just enough rising inflection to make the statement a question. Cunning old sod, thought Light, he's got you to rights.

Patently, the great surgeon enjoyed an audience. He stroked his hands upwards, as though he was smoothing on surgical gloves before an operation. 'I saw it at once,' he said. 'As soon as the poor fellow was carried in. They took him to the physio treatment room, by the members' changing room. He was dead, of course. I thought, by George, that fellow Carter must be really quick. He – Viner that is – had the mark where he'd been hit by the ball on the right cheek.

28

You could see the imprint of the seam where he'd been hit by the ball. I felt the bruise, and the cheekbone seemed perfectly sound.'

He held up his hand, and studied the fingers – strong, spatulate, and sensitive.

'I thought, he can't be dead. I've been hit in the face myself by a cricket ball, and it's bloody painful, but not often lethal. Not on the cheekbone, anyway.'

Brownley paused and looked from Superintendent to Sergeant and back again. 'I thought he must have had a heart attack, or even an embolism. But it wasn't that. I found it at once. Viner wasn't killed by the ball. He'd been hit by a powerful object, like a round-headed hammer, just behind the right temple. His skull was crushed like an eggshell.'

There was a brief silence. The surgeon turned to Ashcroft. 'That's why I called the Commissioner, Bill, and asked for you. He's a personal friend. This isn't an ordinary murder. You're a member, and you understand the set-up. Somehow, someone out there killed Viner; and if we'd raised the alarm and screamed bloody murder over the Tannoy, all hell would have been let loose. Test match cancelled, crowd stampede, your man gone for ever. The Commissioner agreed, and so did the Home Office. They've announced the death, of course, but not how it happened.'

Ashcroft sighed. Its echoes rumbled in his chest.

'Murder will out, Walter,' he said. 'But I suppose if my masters decree it, I shall have to make the effort to keep it under wraps. There's no doubt, is there? No doubt at all?'

'Of the cause of death? Oh no, Heatherington's autopsy will confirm exactly what I've said. I expect he'll be able to tell you which blow came first, if not how it was delivered. Dammit, I was watching, along with everyone else. It looked like an ordinary sporting accident. If fatal. It's impossible.'

He bustled out, shaking his head. Ashcroft looked after him.

'One blessing,' he said. 'At least we'll have to keep a low profile here. You stay with me here, Amber. Thomas can set up an incident room at the Yard. He's good at it and it will save great big boots trampling on the members' sensibilities, let alone allowing women coppers into the pavilion. Ask him to get copies of the video coverage from both the BBC and ITN, and start a team looking through every foot of the whole day's play for anything suspicious or out of the ordinary. Thomas can make up the files on the players and team officials together for you to go through. And arrange with the managers of both teams that nobody leaves their hotel this evening. We'll have to talk to them. Not that they'll feel like gallivanting, especially the Australians. Off you go, you've got work to do. I'm going to watch some cricket.'

Light could have sworn that, for the first time on a case, he saw a glimmer of a smile on Old Bill's face.

On the way to the wicket after the tea interval two conversations took place. The first, between Geoffrey Broadbent, the England captain, and his young fast bowler, was unheard by anyone but its import was fairly obvious to the entire gathering as the two strolled, heads down, towards the bowler's mark at the Nursery End. Indeed Scott Marston and his colleagues on television were able to give their listeners a pretty accurate rendering of the captain's morale-boosting lecture to young Carter, without being able to lip-read. Possibly unwisely, England had placed much hope and trust on the broad shoulders of young Vince Carter, the first genuine fast bowler England had produced since John Snow had quit the game. During the lunch interval, and throughout the afternoon session of play, nothing Broadbent had said could eliminate Carter's memory of that ball crashing sickeningly into Viner's face, the horror of his body lying motionless on the broken stumps, or the shock of that announcement booming across the pitch.

'I did it. It was me.' The words ran round in his head as he trudged back to his mark. His run-up lost confidence, his speed fell away, his length and direction faltered. With the batsmen in similar mood, half-volleys were played back down the pitch, full tosses driven with care to the fielders, and eventually Broadbent was forced to send him down to deep third man to mull over his troubles. Now, on the long walk from the little slope in front of the pavilion, Broadbent, usually a kindly man, was intent in putting some fire back into his protégé's belly.

'Look, son,' he said, 'I know you bowled a bouncer deliberately. I should bloody well hope you did. But what happened wasn't your fault. It could have happened to anyone, any time.'

'But I did it. I killed him.'

'For Christ's sake, boy, stop whining. Now listen to me. I'm willing to bet a thousand pounds that you did no such thing. I was at slip, see, and I never took my eyes off him. He was going down when the ball hit him. He never made a move to get out of the way. I reckon the doctors will find he had a heart attack at the crease, like Ken Barrington did. You never killed him.'

Carter looked sideways at him, scraping at his mark in the turf with the studs of his boot.

'Are you sure, skip? Bloody sure?'

'Yep.'

Broadbent put all the conviction he could muster into his answer. But he wasn't sure; at first slip the batsman is only in the periphery of the fielder's vision. His whole attention is fixed on the outside edge of the bat. Only thus are possible the lightning reflexes necessary to catch a ball flying off the edge at over 100 mph. Did he imagine, or had he seen, Viner's knees buckle a fraction of a second before the ball crashed into the face?

'Of course I'm sure. How long d'you reckon I've been in this game, lad? Now get on with it, and no more pissing about. I want you warmed up before the new ball comes along in a couple of overs. These two buggers have been here far too long.'

In contrast to this semi-private conversation at least 100 MCC members were able later to give the police verbatim accounts of the laconic exchange between Bart Imrie and Collie Foster, the Australian batsmen who had defied the England bowlers until teatime dourly and with not a little luck. As they stood clonelike in their dark blue helmets and plastic faceguards at the door of the pavilion, waiting for the England team to straggle on to the field, the taller figure was heard to say in a distinctive Queensland whine: 'I'll go for the bastard Carter, Collie. You get after the slows.'

To which Foster, fresh into the international team after making nearly 900 runs for South Australia in the Sheffield Shield series just past, answered with the assurance of youth: 'Not if I get him first, cobber.'

From this it was rightly deduced that the Australians were disturbed by their slow progress at the crease, as well they might be in normal circumstances. The death of their captain had cast a pall over the whole team, and it said much for the character of both Imrie and Foster, not to mention their application, that no more wickets

31

had fallen in the long session after lunch. Imrie, in his thirties and a veteran of more than 30 Tests, had shouldered well his responsibility for the team, and the innings. As senior cricketer and vice-captain he had shown a dogged determination not to be shaken in his concentration or technique. His back-lift, never exaggerated, was reduced to a matter of inches. His long left leg stretched far down the pitch to kill the spin of the slow bowlers and to stifle their appeals for leg before. What runs he scored came off little deflections or nudges down the leg side or 'thick edges' through the slips area, played downwards off a limply held bat. On his day, Bart Imrie could hit with the best, as the more experienced England players knew well, but today he justified his occasional nickname, 'Barnacle'.

His example infected Foster, who had been hailed by the Australian press as the 'new Neil Harvey'. At 20, he was one of Australia's best prospects for years, a left-handed near-genius with the grace of David Gower and the power of David Hookes. Against his natural instincts, he too had got his nose down over the ball and resisted his inclination to hit every delivery to the far corners of the field, and he had survived. He'd had some luck. Percy Mandell had thought him plumb lbw to his quicker ball that came through with the arm and rapped the batsman on the left – rear – knee. The next ball was driven fiercely towards cover point a couple of inches off the ground, where Boris Coetzee flung himself far to his left and nearly brought off a dazzling catch but actually saved a certain four. After that little rush of blood, Foster had gone back into his shell and scored five more in the next 70 minutes.

Even so, his 45 was six runs more than Imrie had accumulated with his prodding bat, and at 98 for one wicket, the batsmen had managed to imbue the sunlit afternoon with a soporific quality which infected a good half of the big crowd and drove the commentators into the wildest reaches of their imaginations to divert their listeners' attention from the strokeless batting and uninspired bowling.

Now Broadbent jogged back to his position at first slip wondering if his words to Carter had had any effect. He was still pondering if he could have said anything more, crouching automatically into position as the bowler ran in, when the ball, pitching well up on the off stump, nicked off the edge of the driving bat and flew shoulder-high to Broadbent's right. It was a catch which nine times out of ten Broadbent, a fine slip fielder, would have taken automatically. Now, off guard, he snatched at it one-handed at the last moment and, furious, felt the sharp pain at the tip of his fourth finger as the ball ripped through his grasp. Wringing his hand, he turned to watch third man race round the boundary to pick up the ball, and return it to the wicketkeeper.

'Ooooh!' The crowd's reaction billowed skywards, breaking into sympathetic applause for the bowler and a popular captain whose mortification was unrelieved by the knowledge that he had dislocated the top joint of the fourth finger of his right hand. Grimacing, he jerked the finger back into its socket, ignoring the vicious stab of pain. He had done it so many times before in a 20-year career that such instant remedy came as second nature.

Carter, who had found only minimal reassurance from his captain's attempts to underplay the morning's tragedy, glared at him with the genuine anger of the frustrated fast bowler and stumped back to his mark, evil memories and doubting thoughts wiped from his mind. Fast bowlers rarely feel sympathy for slips who drop their catches. Broadbent, flushed and angry with himself, barely acknowledged the sympathetic 'hard luck, skip' from his fellow slips, who knew as well as he did that he had broken the cricketer's first two commandments: Keep your eye on the ball and your mind on the game.

Foster, the batsman, completing two easy runs and thanking an unidentified deity for his luck, returned to the crease and took guard again carefully. It was not often, he knew, that you got a let-off like that in a Test match, but those two runs had brought his score to 47, a stroke away from his 50. Dare he but look ahead, and he was halfway to a century.

Whether the encouraging words had spurred Carter to unsuspected heights, or whether the dropped catch had put fresh heart into Foster was impossible to say. But in the strange manner of a cricket match, that evening session was suddenly transformed into one of the most thrilling pieces of play ever seen in the long history of Lord's. Journalists and commentators scoured their repertoire of superlatives to do it justice; statisticians pawed over *Wisden* and *Playfair* for a comparable performance. Foster's name began to evoke the hallowed figures of the game – Botham, Dexter,

33

Harvey, even Bradman, while one elderly scribe, anchored in his Press box seat for 40 years or more, could be heard to mumble Macartney and Trumper. He had never seen either, of course, but such was his age and air of authority, no one dared to question his memory, let alone his veracity.

In the same way Vince Carter's fast bowling began to bring back memories of Lillee, Holding and Snow at their best. In the two-hour session under the westering sun he bowled 15 overs unchanged, each one seemingly faster and more accurate than the last, and took four wickets. So, at close of play Australia went off the field having scored a total of 255 for six wickets. In the final two hours they added 157 runs, compared with the 98 hit off the first four hours' play.

Foster did not add his name to the semi-immortals who have scored a century on their Test debut at Lord's, but after the dropped catch he took the fight single-handed to the England bowlers. Even Carter had no answer. A head-high bouncer was hooked fearlessly in front of his nose, the wrists rolling over in the classic manner and square leg helpless as the ball hit the fence not two yards from him before he could move. Spencer was smashed out of the attack by four consecutive fours, each executed with grace and timing. Bowyer-Smith's left-arm seamers, which had commanded exaggerated respect for most of the day, suffered the indignity of 27 runs, most of them to Foster, being hit off two overs, including a mighty six over extra cover which narrowly missed the plate glass of the hospitality box windows.

Imrie was out at 137, bowled by an unplayable break-back from Carter, who had just taken the new ball. It pitched two inches outside the off stump and hit leg. Imrie departed shaking his head, with 56 sturdy runs in the scorebook and a weight of responsibility to come. Foster, rejoicing in the tiring bowling, swept on until, on 98, he was dismissed by an astonishing piece of fielding.

Unworried by two short legs, he played a full-pitched ball from Carter hard towards mid-wicket off the full meat of the bat and set off automatically for the run. Eight feet from the bat Graham, diving to his right by instinct, fielded the ball cleanly and flicked it towards the wicket under his body as he fell. Foster stopped at full stretch a pace down the pitch and stared aghast as the ball hit his heel and cannoned gently back onto the wicket, softly removing the leg bail. He was out by a foot.

Charlie Comberton took over where he left off, after a quiet start during which he let MacPhail take the lead in trying to hit Carter off a length. MacPhail managed two streaky fours before a third ball, lifting sharply off a length, took the outside edge of the bat and Broadbent, stooping leisurely to his right, picked up the catch as though he were plucking daisies. To the roar of the crowd he flung the ball aloft and caught it as it came down. As the team crowded round to congratulate him on the catch, he said to the world at large: 'Funny, I didn't feel a thing,' and held out his purple swollen knuckle for inspection.

'Ah,' said Alexander, the wicketkeeper, who knew all about such matters. 'You only feel the ones you drop.'

Fifteen runs later Carter struck again. S. S. Smart – Sissie to his Australian colleagues – presented a straightforward catch to the keeper; and two balls later George Viljoen, thoroughbred Australian despite his Boer name, failed to spot the leg-cutter and lost his middle stump.

And that was that, apart from some cheerful hitting by Comberton and his new partner, Rose, as Carter tired and none of the other bowlers looked likely to take a wicket. Promptly at 6.30 pm the players trooped wearily off the field, led by a depressed-looking Carter, through the cigar-smoked pavilion and up the stairs to their traditional dressing-rooms.

But for some of them, and for the police, the day's work was far from complete as the crowds emptied soberly through the narrow exits, and the ground staff fussed over the pitch with brushes and light rollers, tucking it up under its covers for the night. The Admiral's small army of cleaners worked their way systematically through the stands to collect and remove some five tons of cans, plastic cartons, paper bags and old banana skins, liberally laced with cigarette-ends.

England v Australia (First Day)

Australia (First Innings)

J. Viner	hit wicket, b Carter	0
B.V. Imrie	b Carter	56
P.C. Foster	run out	98
C.B. Comberton	not out	47
R.P.D. MacPhail	c Broadbent, b Carter	16
S.S. Smart	c Alexander, b Carter	9
G. Viljoen	b Carter	0
B.F. Rose	not out	11
	Extras	18
	Total (for 6 wickets)	255

Fall of wickets: 1/0, 2/137, 3/178, 4/198, 5/213, 6/213

Bowling	O	M	R	W
V.J. Carter	25	8	59	5
D.A. Spencer	19	5	61	0
C.J.A. Bowyer-Smith	22	10	44	0
A.B. Prettyman	12	3	38	0
P.Q. Mandell	9	1	35	0

Chapter 2

The First Evening

While these events were drawing to a close out on the field, Detective Sergeant Light was busily doing the job he did best – acting as leg-man for his chief, who was perhaps not quite so busily sampling the balmy evening air and the cricket from the same seat Light had occupied earlier. At this height Ashcroft could allow his mind to rove over all aspects of the case as it appeared to him at this early stage, while his eyes drank in the familiar but ever-changing patterns of movement on the field. The white figures on the green grass were constantly on the move, but as ball followed ball and over followed over a rhythm and flow established themselves in the minds of players and spectators alike, disturbed only by the quick flurry of activity as a batsman struck a ball into the open spaces. The pattern dissolved, only to form again, ready for the next delivery. In many ways, Ashcroft thought, cricket was like the sea, unchanging in its changeability. His mind on metaphysics, he half watched a player, crossing the pitch between overs, stoop and pick up something – a stud from a boot, a piece of litter, perhaps – and put it in his pocket. By this time in a day's play, the quickening breeze often blew stray paper or plastic bags across the grass to the distraction of batsmen and fielders alike.

Light, following his instructions, telephoned the Yard and apologetically made the necessary arrangements with Detective Inspector Thomas for the incident room to be set up. Thomas laughed. 'Don't worry about me, Amber. You can have all the Lord's you want. Can't stand cricket. I'm a rugby man, myself.'

'You might not be quite so happy by the time you've finished that monitoring,' said Light. 'As I understand it, there are six cameras, each feeding all the time unless ordered off the air by the director, usually for a repair, and he switches them as he wants into the live feed which goes out on air. That means 42 hours of monitoring for you, and Old Bill wants the results by tomorrow morning. Hope you can find enough cricket experts to cope.'

'Oh, I think we'll be all right. I've got half the section cricket team here. Have you any idea what the old man is looking for?'

'Not a clue. He merely said anything out of the ordinary. Good luck.'

'Thanks for nothing. I don't know what's ordinary on a cricket pitch. Ciao.'

Light hung up thinking that Thomas had a very generous spirit, and took the stairs two at a time towards the England dressing-room. At the top of the stair he paused. Outside the dressing-room a small man wearing a white sweatshirt and grey flannel slacks was talking on the public telephone attached to the wall. As he caught sight of Light the man turned away and leaned both elbows on the telephone box, cupping the receiver in two hands and speaking very close to the mouthpiece. In spite of the precaution, Light easily picked up snatches of conversation.

'. . . No, no, don't worry, Mrs Carter. There's nothing wrong with the boy. I've given him a thorough check over and so's the doctor . . . I know you saw him on telly . . . he was shocked, that's all . . . he'll be fine . . . If you look at the box now you'll see he's looking as well as ever . . . no, that's all right. I'll tell him you were on the phone. . . . Yes, I'll get him to call you, as soon as he can after the game . . . that's all right, Mrs Carter. 'Bye.'

He hung the receiver on its hook with an air of finality and turned to see Light looking at him inquiringly. He held up a hand before Light could speak, like a policeman on point duty.

'No, don't ask me. I've got nothing to say.' His eyes cast around with something like desperation. 'It's too bad. Too bad. They should really stop you fellows . . .'

Light grinned. 'Don't worry, I'm not Press.' He held out his ID card. The little man looked even more anxious.

'It's no good asking me anything. I'm just the physio. The manager's not here at the moment. I think he's gone to the President's box. Shall I tell him you called?'

Light let the absurdity pass. He spoke reassuringly. 'Oh, you're Mr Wright, are you? The one they all call Doc? There's nothing to be alarmed about. It's just routine. I'd like a few words.' He gestured towards the door.

'What? What? Oh, yes please. Do come in. Do come in.' He seemed to think that repetition might make up for a marked lack of enthusiasm for the idea. He opened the door, obsequiously.

Light was not sure afterwards what had impressed him most about the England dressing-room: the sheer tattiness, the smell or the state of chaos. He certainly had not expected the overpowering combination of stale sweat, embrocation, talcum powder and linseed oil which assailed his nostrils, while the room looked as though a bomb had exploded and no one had had time to clear up. It was also gloomy. A narrow glassed door opened onto the players' balcony, but the glass was dirty and it gave little useful light. In the right-hand corner of the room a second small window was half obscured by a pair of trousers hanging from its central catch. Wide wooden lockers round all four sides of the room were strewn with a miscellany of clothes and cricket gear, while above the chaos a row of double metal hooks held suspended suits, shirts and white trousers in varying stages of respectability. A large wooden table under a bare light bulb in the centre of the room carried two big cricket bags and two crates. The Foster's Lager was pristine, all 24 cans untouched, but large inroads had been made into the soft drinks.

The little man looked more confident on his home territory. 'I'm sorry. We're always in a bit of a mess.' He laughed, still nervous, and thrust aside a jumble of protectors, thigh pads and batting gloves to clear a space for Light to sit down on a locker. The high, prissy housewife's voice contrasted with the rippling muscles and taut tanned skin. 'What a terrible way to start a Test match. And at Lord's, of all places. But it was just as well it wasn't one of our lads. I knew he was dead, you know. I tried to revive him out there on the pitch, but there wasn't a flicker. I thought the best thing to do was to carry him off as though he was just injured. It would never do to have a man die on the pitch at Lord's . . .' his voice trailed off.

'Why not?' Light asked. 'People don't usually choose where to die, you know.'

'Well, think of all those spectators. And the scandal. It can't be good for cricket,' said the little man earnestly. 'I thought the quieter we could keep it the better, for the time being at least. And you never know. I'm not a doctor. Sir Walter, the surgeon, you know, thought so too. He knew Viner was dead the moment he saw him on the stretcher. And he hustled us upstairs out of the way of the members and told us all to keep our mouths shut. He seemed to think there was something wrong. About Viner's death, I mean. Was there?'

'How did Viner die?' Light asked curiously, ignoring the question. 'You must know a good bit about medicine in your job. Is it usual for a cricket ball to kill a man?'

'Well,' Wright sounded almost intelligent. 'Believe it or not, I've never actually seen a dead man in my life until today. Except on television. I deal with live bodies, not dead ones. I know the theory, of course, but I'm no doctor. Your pathologists will tell you far more than I can.'

'But you were there less than a minute after Viner was hit. Your impressions must be just as important, if not more so.'

The little man swelled.

'Well.' Most of his sentences seemed to begin with the word. 'Well. I think he must have had a heart attack or a stroke brought on as a result of being struck by the ball. Carter's quick, you know. But I don't think being hit on the cheek would have killed him. He might have had a secondary embolism. I don't know.'

'What about Carter? I understand he's taken it pretty hard, from what I heard you saying over the phone.' Light did not apologise.

'Just now? Yes, that's true. But his mother was being stupid, hysterical. She said she'd seen him on the television and she was sure there was something wrong with him. Se said: why did he look so terrified? She almost screamed it at me. I told her it was all the shock of learning over the Tannoy that Viner was dead. It could have happened to anyone.'

'Was Carter terrified?'

'I think it was shock. All through lunch he wouldn't eat a thing, just kept muttering to himself as how he'd done it, how it was his fault. You know. "But I did it on purpose" sort of rubbish. And after lunch he went to pieces, bowled a load of crap. I asked Badger to have a word with him after tea. Seems to have done him a bit of good.' He jerked his head towards the balcony as a crowd roar

40

swept into the dressing-room. 'That's another wicket. You can tell by the noise the crowd makes, even if you can't see anything. Anyway, Vince kept on and on about it, and I suggested Badger should try tough tactics. Bully him a bit, you know. It could have happened to anyone. It wouldn't do him any good to mope. A fast bowler must have the killer instinct, as the Press call it. Oh, sorry.'

Light grinned at him. 'Don't mind me. I'm only a copper,' he said. 'Look, do me a favour. Show me where young Carter's camped in this pigsty, and then turn your back for a minute or two. Go and talk to those legs I can see on the balcony and keep them there. I want to do something that's not strictly in judges' rules.'

'Ooh. Is there really something wrong, then?' Wright's round face twinkled inquisitively.

'There might be. But you didn't hear it from me. And it's not for broadcasting.' He grinned again, conspiratorially. Small brown eyes looked back knowingly. 'You scratch my back, I'll scratch yours,' Light added for good measure to seal the unwritten pact. His ability to spot and enlist an informer was one of his lesser talents.

'Over in the corner, there. It's that old leather bag with the brass label and that rather neater pile. The end two pegs. The blazer with the Essex badge on it. This is only Vince's second Test and he hasn't had time to be measured for his England colours yet. I fixed him up with a sweater, though.'

'Thanks.' Light went over to the clothes indicated. Wright hesitated, reluctant to miss anything, and then went to the balcony door without looking back, shutting it behind him and leaning on it. Light could see his mouth moving. He ran his hands expertly through the jacket and trousers arranged neatly on a hanger.

There was little to excite his interest. The blazer yielded a slim wallet containing £15 in five-pound notes, a Barclaycard and a plastic slip in red and white informing the reader that Vincent John Carter was willing to be a kidney donor in the event of his premature decease. There was a packet of Peter Stuyvesant cigarettes in the outer pocket, a slim gold ballpoint pen and half a dozen letters, apparently from fans.

Light turned his attention to the long leather cricket bag, creased with age but well-kept, and with 'V.J. CARTER' stamped on a small old-fashioned brass plate. Delving under the neatly packed cricket gear Light found a sweater, five cricket shirts and four pairs of flannels, all new, some still in their wrappings. Under them his probing fingers felt the sharp edge of a thick envelope, folded back as though it had been hurriedly thrust into hiding. Light drew out a common brown envelope, its flap not properly secured as though someone had dabbed a hasty tongue at it before sticking it down, leaving most of the glue unmoistened. He eased it open, and riffled through a number of £50 notes, pristine from the mint. Whistling gently to himself. Light made a mental note of the number sequence – £2,500 in all. He stuck down the envelope again and slipped it back under the shirts. Beside them was a carton of Stuyvesant cigarettes, opened with one packet missing. Light made sure of everything was as it had been before he began, and went over to open the balcony door. He tapped the physiotherapist on the shoulder.

'Thanks again, doc.'

'Don't mention it. Did you find anything interesting?'

'I'll be in touch.' He paused. 'Do many of the team smoke?'

'Far too many and far too much.' Wright grimaced. 'We keep telling them they're ruining their health but it makes no difference. Cricketers aren't special, sergeant. They smoke and drink and fornicate like everyone else. They're young men and they play hard on the field and off it. You can't blame them. At least when they get to Test level they can afford it.'

He looked round at the field as a great roar welled up from the crowd.

'Well bowled, Vince.' He clapped his hands together softly in a curiously private gesture. 'That young man,' he said to Light, 'gets through 40 a day even though he spends six hours a day on the field, sometimes. He doesn't drink much, though, not like some I could mention.'

'Drugs?'

'Vince? Good Lord, no. There isn't much of that in cricket, especially since all the fuss a few years ago. Booze, though, that's a different thing. Carter's not like most fast bowlers, who can get through ten pints after a day in the field and not feel a thing. But everyone has their fads. Badger Broadbent, the skipper, doesn't drink or smoke, except maybe a half pint at the end of the day. He won't even take orange juice on the field. When the twelfth man takes the drinks out you'll notice there's always a glass of water for the skipper.'

Light was diverted.

'Doesn't like orange juice. Why?'

'Well, he says you can never tell whether it's Outspan or not. From South Africa, you know. Badger's wife's a Cape Coloured and he won't have anything to do with apartheid, or the Boers, as he calls them. Jack Viner's – sorry, was – just the same. Jack married an Abo girl and they've got two of the prettiest kids you've ever seen. He was always dead set against apartheid and the South Africans. He's refused to play there for years and won't have anything to do with these rebel tours. He nearly quit cricket altogether because Kepler Wessels was allowed to play for Australia, but then Kepler never had a thought in his head except for cricket. At any rate, Jack's done more than anyone to prevent the Cricket Council allowing South Africa back into Test cricket. It was like a religion to him.'

Light stemmed the flow, took his leave at last and digested what he had discovered on his way to find the manager of the England team. He had learnt that Roland Anderson was a respected figure, a former Lancashire captain and briefly a Test player, remarkable for the fact that he held the all-round record for runs scored and wickets taken in the history of matches between the white rose of Yorkshire and the red one of Lancashire, an obscure statistic which for some reason had caught the fancy of Press and public and earned him the soubriquet of Rosey. The less charitable commentators, usually Yorkshiremen, liked to point out that the nickname was particularly apt, as Anderson's preference for strong ale had over the years established in his countenance a ruddy glow, reinforced by the climatic vagaries of the cricketer's life. He was regarded as a shrewd judge of a player and one of the best managers England had found since the system started. On difficult tours to Australia and the West Indies he had established himself as something of a diplomat as well, despite having an extremely sharp tongue on occasions.

Having negotiated a passage past yet another monosyllabic member of the Lord's ground staff, Light climbed the concrete steps at the back of Q stand and tracked down Anderson in the

43

President's box. Lord Holmbush's entertainment there on Test match days had become something of a legend, and an invitation bearing his Lordship's crest of crossed bats on a field vert was prized in certain circles only slightly behind a summons to the Palace. The box itself was crowded with a number of middle-aged men, most sporting an MCC tie or cravat, with a sprinkling of green Australian blazers, and most carrying that air of benevolent prosperity that the English upper class have appropriated to themselves. Light, who rarely felt out of place anywhere, overcame the impression that everyone in the box was three inches taller than himself, and showed his ID to the beetle-browed aristocrat he knew from his pictures to be Lord Holmbush, President of the MCC.

'Police, eh? You want Anderson?' He raised an imperious voice. 'Anderson? Ah, there you are. Come over here a moment, would you mind.' It was not a question. Lord Holmbush was accustomed to being obeyed. He turned to Light. 'Not in here, eh? Shockin' business, this. Be discreet, eh?' He turned a fierce blue glare on Light and then turned his back on him. Light tugged at a tuft of hair over his brow behind the broad back and looked up to see Anderson grinning at him.

'Let's go outside,' the manager said without introduction. On the narrow balcony overlooking St John's Wood Road, he added: 'Don't mind old Huffer. He's always like that. He's shy. He can't think of anything to say. But he's all there, and his heart's in the right place. You're police, aren't you?'

He held out a hand, and Light introduced himself.

'We don't want to barge about disturbing things,' he explained. 'But in any case of sudden death we have to make routine inquiries, for the Coroner, you know.'

Anderson studied him.

'They don't usually send the Yard in to a sporting mischance,' he said reflectively. 'It's something I've never seen before, and I've been around a bit. Anything wrong? Really wrong, I mean. Look, Sergeant, I'll do anything I can to help, but I've got a job to do, just as you have. I can't have size 11 boots clumping around the dressing-rooms upsetting the players. There's a Test match on.'

'Don't worry, Mr Anderson. I only take eights. But my boss, Chief Superintendent Ashcroft, would like to drop into the dressing-room when they come off the field at the end of the day. Just to get the atmosphere, like.'

'Chief Superintendent? They are taking it seriously, then. It's a bit odd. Jack Viner dies after a bang in the face and suddenly we have the bigwigs from Scotland Yard on our necks. What is all this? Why all the secrecy?'

Light couldn't say. He asked instead who had access to the dressing-rooms while a match was in progress.

'Anybody, really. The doors are supposed to be kept on the latch but more or less anyone can get in. But it's generally accepted that the Press won't be welcome, and here, at least, the security is pretty formidable. The lads don't welcome visitors. They want a bit of privacy.'

'I mean, could someone get in and pinch stuff?'

'Not in the batting side's room. There's always someone about. It would be easier while the team was fielding – they're all out on the pitch except for the twelfth man, and he's got to keep an eye on the game, in case he's needed. The doors are supposed to be kept locked when there's no one around. But that doesn't often happen. I'm usually in the England team room, and it'll be the same for Griff Cousins and the Aussies, you'll find. It's open house, really. But I wouldn't go in there for an intellectual conversation. Does your Chief Superintendent know his cricket?'

'He's revelling in it. It's the first time he's been able to see a Test in 20 years, he says. He's a member here, too. He'd like a word with you now, if you're free.'

'Good.'

Light led the way back into the pavilion. This time the fact he was talking to the England manager got him past the doorman without difficulty, but he made a mental note to acquire a pass. And a tie.

There was no one in the outer room or the Admiral's office. Light sat down in the Admiral's chair and waved Anderson to a seat. The manager whistled softly.

'What's up?' he asked.

'You'd better ask the Super. If you don't mind waiting here, I'll fetch him.'

He found Ashcroft seated peaceably where he had left him, watching the closing minutes of the day's play. With some

45

reluctance, the Chief Superintendent allowed himself to be briefed swiftly and heaved his bulk off the seat.

'What's he like, this Anderson? Never held with managers myself.'

'Fifty-ish. Weatherbeaten. Good tailor, but not stylish. Red-faced. Experienced. He's pretty shrewd. Smelt a rat already. Keeps asking questions.'

'Does he know anything?'

'I don't think I'd know if he did, sir. Here we are.'

He held the door open for Ashcroft. The England manager was sitting back in the chair, relaxed with his eyes closed, as if asleep. He opened them, rose without haste and held out his hand, suddenly alert.

'Ashcroft,' said the policeman. 'We've met before.'

Anderson looked inquiringly at the portly figure, the crumpled tweed and the brilliant tie. He hesitated. MCC members were always claiming acquaintance and this one appeared the archetype, right down to his fob watch. Then he caught sight of the grey eyes under the used leather face.

'Did we play cricket together?' It was the safest gambit.

'Thirty years ago. Middlesex seconds versus Lancashire at Blackpool. You bowled me out. I caught you. Both ducks. Lancashire won. Don't worry, I've that sort of memory.'

Anderson stared at him, grinning.

'Oh well, I suppose even a copper can play cricket. What's this all about? I think I'm entitled to know. How can I help you?'

'You can answer a few questions and then introduce me to the skipper in the dressing-room. As a friend and former cricketer. But first, I'm going to do something I shouldn't. I'm going to talk to you.' He turned to Light. 'And you, Amber, are going to listen. What you know about cricket would fill a whisky glass and I haven't been near it for too many years. Mr Anderson, I'm going to ask you to fill us both in with the background. Then we might know where to start. But I have to ask you to keep this conversation to yourself, at least for a day or two.'

'You mean there's something fishy about Viner's death and you want the smell kept under wraps while the Test is on?'

Ashcroft nodded approvingly.

'I suppose it's just what they'd do.' Anderson sounded both

tired and disgusted. 'Sit on it and hope it will make a noise like a hoop and roll away.'

'Oh, I don't suppose this one will go away, Mr Anderson. Murder doesn't, even for the MCC. But we might get along a little faster in this case without the assistance of the gentlemen of the Press.'

Anderson stared at him, white-faced. He hadn't heard anything after the word 'murder'. It shouted in his mind. He heard his own voice on a rising pitch he could not control.

'But that's impossible. You can't charge a fast bowler with murder. Young Carter's not to blame. Cricket isn't like rugby, where they'll kick a man's head in while he's on the ground. Even the socialists wouldn't accuse Carter of murder. For Christ's sake. It could have happened to anyone.'

'I'm not saying that we're charging anyone yet, Mr Anderson. There is something wrong about this death, but we won't know what it is until we have the pathologist's report in a day or two's time. Nothing is official.'

Ashcroft had not moved in his chair, nor had his tone changed. Yet Light could feel Anderson relaxing, leaning forward, anxious to help.

'What do you want to know?'

'Let's start with Viner. How well did you know him?'

'Pretty well. Cricket's a small world. I first met Jack when we all did over here. He was about 19, fresh out of college. He knocked on the door of Old Trafford and asked for a trial. Nobody'd ever heard of him and he hadn't got a track record. I was skipper of Lancashire at the time and we were going through one of our usual managerial crises and we didn't have a coach. I took him into the nets and liked what I saw.'

'Did you take him on?'

'Not at first. I asked him why he hadn't gone into club cricket in Aussie and he was a bit evasive. Then he blurted out that he'd married this Aborigine – or at least a girl with Aborigine blood – and they didn't like that back home. Just like South Africa, he said, only worse because of the hypocrisy. They didn't mind him joining, but they wouldn't have anything to do with his wife. I found out later that it wasn't really as bad as that. The Australian clubs – some of them at least – are male chauvinist

47

strongholds and shy at any woman coming near them. Anyway Jack felt he'd been frozen out of a couple of the leading clubs. Eventually his father, a wine-grower who also disapproved of black in-laws, gave Jack a cheque for £5,000 on condition he took Julie to England or, as he told me, the hell out of Australia. Jack didn't seem to mind as much as you'd think, and when he introduced me to Julie I saw why. She was – and is – the loveliest thing I've ever set eyes on. All honey. That was 15 years ago.' He sighed.

'Anyway, I told him he'd do better to start with a season or two in the Leagues before coming into the county stuff. I thought it would toughen him up. So I sent him along to Moseley with a heavy introduction and they took him on. He made a hundred in his first game for them and topped 1,900 that season. The next year he made a hundred in his first game for the county. He made over 5,000 runs in his first three seasons. Then South Australia asked him to go back for the Sheffield Shield season, with a house and a job on the side. He never looked back.'

'What was he like? As a person, I mean.'

'I liked him, but he always held strong opinions, particularly about apartheid, for obvious reasons. He was headstrong, too. He met Julie somewhere in the outback, didn't bother to tell his parents and married her within a week without them knowing. Now they've got two kids who dote – doted, dammit – on him.'

'As a captain?'

'Tough and ruthless, though usually pretty fair. He saved a series against us by batting all the last day for 70-odd runs on a plumb pitch; then in the next Test hit 98 before lunch and went on to 150 in under three hours. But he wouldn't have anything to do with anyone who sympathised with South Africa. He regarded apartheid as the greatest evil the world had ever seen, on a par with Hitler. He was quite fanatical about it. Wouldn't have anyone in the side – for South Australia after he was captain, or in the Australian team – anyone who'd so much as sniffed the breezes of Cape Town.

'He certainly knew how to get the most out of a rather mediocre side. In that he was a bit like our Badger – Broadbent, you know. They've captained against each other in two series so far, and this is the decider, as it were. Jack won the first over here four years ago and then two years ago Broadbent took the side to Australia and we won the rubber three-two. I went as manager and it was a bit hairy.'

'What do you mean?'

'Oh, the Press over there, you know. It's even worse than ours, if you can imagine it. They built the whole thing up into a grudge between the two of them, comparing their careers, their lives, the lot. The *Mirror*, I think it was, sneaked pictures of their wives in bikinis and ran a series asking readers to state which of the two they would prefer in bed. Badger and Jackie played up to it, of course, to help the publicity and snarled at each other in public. In private they always got on quite well, but it all became a bit of a strain, particularly as Julie and Belinda Broadbent loathe each other's guts.'

Anderson moved uncomfortably in his chair, feeling he had gone too far. Ashcroft slumped down, scratched the side of his nose.

'And Broadbent. Tell me about him.'

'Yorkshire as they come, and twice as stubborn. He's the first Yorkshireman to captain England since Illingworth – no, sorry, Geoff Boycott did that in New Zealand when Brearley broke his arm. He's put the guts back into England, but there's a growing feeling that he may be getting a bit past it. He hasn't scored a hundred for two years now and increasingly people are calling for his head. He can afford to go, too. He's had two benefits and made a lot of money on the side. I said he was a Yorkshireman. He bought a derelict farm in the North Riding somewhere and it turned out to be the precise site for the Magnum oilfield – second only to Wych Farm. It only came out when one of those investigative journalists spotted his name in the small print of a Magnum prospectus. Badger was livid. He hadn't even told his wife. He probably thought she'd blue the lot.'

'I understand she comes from South Africa.'

'Yes, Cape Town, originally. She was a dazzler, too. Badger fell for her when he was coaching in the Cape about ten years ago. But it hasn't been much of a marriage. Perhaps if they could have had kids . . . but Belinda made Badger have a vasectomy. Said she didn't want to bring any more half-castes into the world. Can't say I blame her. But Badger would have loved a son. That's why she and Julie have never seen eye to eye.'

Ashcroft stirred.

'What does a Test cricketer earn these days? Is he well off?'

49

'It depends what you mean. Compared with top tennis players and golfers, or soccer stars, no he isn't. But compared with the run-of-the-mill county cricketer, he doesn't do so badly at all.'

'How well?'

'Test cricketers are paid by match, unless they go on tour, when they all get the same, apart from the captain and vice-captain. At home they get £1,500 a match, plus £30 a day out of pocket expenses. All living paid, of course. So a regular player who's in the team for all five Tests this summer will pick up £7,500 plus another £750 cash expenses. Then there's share of win bonuses and man-of-the-match awards, which go into a players' pool. With the match fees for the one-day internationals, I doubt if a regular player will clear less than £15,000 for the summer, £12,000 for the winter tour and anything up to another £15,000 from their county. Plus free cars and whatever sponsorship they can pick up personally. Superstars can push it up to any amount you care to think of, but it doesn't last long – six or seven years at the most. The poor bloody county man grubs along on a three-year contract at eight to ten thousand for the summer and bugger-all for the winter. No wonder the poor sods snatch at the Krugerrand when it's dangled in front of their noses.'

'How does a Test player get paid? Physically, I mean.'

'Oh, the salary comes from the Board by cheque, usually midway through the game. To make sure you're there, I suppose. It's the manager's job to dish out the exes. I draw the money in envelopes from the office upstairs and hand it out in the evenings. It's like feeding time at the zoo. You'd think they'd never seen a fiver in their lives.'

'Why daily?'

'You'd be surprised. To stop them blowing the lot at once, of course. They're not all like Broadbent. You have to remember that even at this level many of the players are nothing more than overgrown boys. Half of them would booze it away and the other half would be down at the betting shop.' He paused. 'I suppose I'm exaggerating a bit. But not much. The average cricketer is about as responsible as a two-year-old. I expect you know that motor insurance companies place cricketers at the top of their bad risk tables. Worse than journalists.'

'So a manager is a sort of nursemaid, even at this level.'

'You can say that again. Where the youngsters are concerned, at any rate. Managers these days have to act as cricket coach, financial adviser, sex consultant, marriage guidance counsellor, press agent, PRO and even friend. As well as provide a shoulder to cry on when the umpire's been more obtuse than usual.' He grinned. 'I'm not complaining. It's a good life and it's much better than working.'

'What about perks? We read a great deal about sponsorship and so on.'

'For the players, you mean. The poor bloody manager doesn't get many perks, except a trip overseas now and again. It rather depends on each individual. The top ones, call them superstars if you like – Dave Spencer or Broadbent, the skipper, for example – often have one of the big agents working for them, and they'll be paying most of their tax at the 60 per cent rate. It's peripheral, of course – direct sponsorship, endorsements, TV appearances and so on. I doubt if anyone makes more than £25,000 a year directly out of the game. But the big boys will be pulling in anything upwards of £50,000. Badger keeps one firm of Yorkshire accountants busy for half the year – but then he's got business interests on the side. As many others have, too.'

'Their gear must be pretty expensive.'

'It is for club cricketers. But most pros, right from the start, will have their bats provided by one of the makers and if they make the grade in first-class cricket, they'll get all their gear free each year. Nabbing promising cricketers is a cut-throat business. A bit like "Opportunity Knocks". Anyone the least bit promising is signed up in their teens, not always to their advantage. I had to lean pretty heavily to extricate young Bowyer-Smith from his first so-called sponsor. The university graduates are the most gullible. He'd been signed up at Cambridge by Bats Beautiful for two bats, a tenner for every time he made 50 or took five wickets, and £25 for a hundred or eight wickets. When he came into the England side he'd made a total of £150 in three years – all from bowling. He didn't know what he'd signed up for, and was too scared to do anything about it. The sharks are swarming all over the Australians now, but you'd better see my opposite number, Griff Cousins, about that. He knows the score. He ought to. He's the agent for Robinson's down under. They're straight enough, but there are plenty of rogues about. Viner loathed them. I don't think he could have been bought by anyone.'

'Is Carter fixed up with anyone?'

'I'm pretty sure he is. Essex will have seen him all right. They're one of the best outfits in the business. There are plenty of batmakers in his area who'd be only too willing to help the lad. Fast bowlers of his calibre don't appear often. Now I think of it, I believe he's with Mumford Co at Maldon. They make balls as well.'

'What would he get out of it?'

'You'll have to ask him. He's young, and it won't be much, gear and about £200 a year, though it'll probably double if he stays in the England side. I'm glad for him. His father's dead and his mother's a district nurse, so the family hasn't got much money. There's a handicapped sister, too. They couldn't afford to come to the match here even though he sent them tickets. Mrs Carter couldn't get the time off from the local authority.'

'How has he taken Viner's death?'

'Pretty hard, but he'll get over it. He's young, and a sporting accident . . . cricket's a dangerous game.' He paused. 'You know Viner wasn't wearing a helmet?'

'Yes.' Ashcroft made no comment.

'He never did, you know. He made a fetish of it. Said cricket was a game to be played with the eyes and the bat, not the head. He always defied the pessimists, who've turned out to be right, I suppose . . . It's not bloody football, he'd say. I admired him for it. I don't think he criticised other batsmen for using one, whatever he may have felt, but he refused to have a helmet used in the field. He said it was unfair. Anyone who fielded at silly point or short leg in one of his sides went in as close as he dared without protective equipment. No farting about with shinpads or boxes while Jack was in charge.'

He stopped abruptly, as though he had brought himself too swiftly into the present, and looked at his watch.

'Mr Ashcroft, if you've no more to ask me, I must go to the team. They'll be just about ready for me. There are the Press and TV interviews now, and they'll be wondering where I am. Badger will cope, but today especially it's my responsibility.'

To Light's surprise, Ashcroft merely nodded.

'Of course. Thank you for your help. Just one thing. It's too much to hope that the Press will ignore the police interest in Viner's death, but I would be obliged if you don't say anything to anyone of your suspicions, if you have any. We're making routine inquiries. We'll be round at your hotel later, to have a word with the captain. I'd be grateful if you'd ask him to be available at, say 9.30. After dinner, anyway. We may be a little late.'

'No one else?'

'I don't think so, thank you.'

The telephone rang, and Ashcroft waited until Anderson had closed the door behind him before picking up the receiver.

'Heatherington here, Bill. Your cricketer. You'll have it in writing in the morning, but I thought you'd like to know as soon as possible. Old Brownley's a bit pompous but he knows his stuff. The cricket ball didn't kill him, though it would have given him a mighty sore face and a lovely black eye for a few weeks. Cracked cheekbone. No, he was killed by a blow on the right temple by something heavy, small, and rounded, no more than an inch across. Like one of those hammers snobs – shoemenders – used to use. Or a slingshot. His skull was crushed. Death must have been instantaneous.'

Ashcroft said: 'And what about the chronology?'

The voice laughed softly.

'I knew you'd ask that. I can't really help you. The two blows certainly came within seconds of each other, but which was first I can't really say. I have ordered further tests, of course, but there's no guarantee of a positive diagnosis.'

'Can you hazard a guess?'

'Not in a court of law, you old buzzard. But strictly for your ears, it's my belief that he was dead when the cricket ball hit him, poor bloke. Bloody good bat, too. Awful thing to happen at Lord's. Must have woken up the Long Room at last. Happy hunting.'

'Thanks Alan. Do your best. Good night.'

He replaced the receiver and relayed the conversation to Light.

'Well, that's it. Two blows make it murder, whatever Heatherington's doubts about the sequence. And it will be public property by tomorrow, however hard Lord Holmbush tries to keep it dark. I don't suppose he'll mind too much, provided the

53

TCCB don't decide to call off the match. It should ensure full houses for the rest of the game, if not the series.'

Light was accustomed to the Ashcroft version of cynicism. It was usually directed against the Establishment, which was probably why the old man was not an Assistant Commissioner, at least.

'Why didn't you stop the manager going back to the team, sir? Wasn't it taking a chance? Surely he'll talk.'

'Probably he will, although he won't mean to. I rather expect him to. And in any case the murderer, if he's one of the team, will know what he's done, and will know we know, merely because we're here. Senior policemen, even detective sergeants, don't investigate sporting accidents as a rule. They send the bobby round from the local shop.'

Ashcroft positively twinkled. Light thought he looked rather like a rumpled garden gnome in Harris Tweed. He said, tentatively: 'But how it was done? Who would want to kill a man like Viner? And why? From all we've heard he was a popular captain who was respected for his ability and his integrity. Things may get pretty tough on the playing field but I can't imagine him being murdered by a cricketer.'

Ashcroft's black eyes flickered in their sockets.

'What a very English sentiment. I sympathise. But even Dorothy Sayers once cast a fine cricketer as the villain in one of her books,' he said. 'Fiction has often been the father of fact, Amber. But have you considered Carter? The bowler? The young man who wept and who bowled so erratically before tea and so well after it? And whose bag contains – or contained – £2,500 in £50 notes? An unlikely sum for such a young man to possess, even in these days of sponsorship. But still possible legally.'

'Possible, sir, but not probable. You're right. What about that loot? For services rendered? No one can tell me he could guarantee to hit a batsman on the head with a bouncer – even one without a helmet. And Viner is supposed to have been a fine player of fast bowling. The Brigadier told me that in the ordinary course of events he would have put that ball over the boundary without any problems. Which would confirm your theory about the two blows, sir.'

'I never theorise, Amber. I state the obvious. But we need more data upon which to do either. I propose to drop some stones into

54

two adjoining pools and watch where the ripples spread. You are one of the stones, Amber, if you will forgive the pun.'

'Not too precious, I hope, Sir.' Light had learned to humour his chief's moments of weakness.

'Good. Then off with you to the Australians and talk to them. Tell them Viner was murdered and watch for their reactions. Put all the usual questions, enemies and so on, and ask about his personal life, and about his peculiarities. He seems to have held very strong opinions. His team will be very shaken but I am sure they will be in the mood to talk. Especially to a sympathetic policeman who assures them that none of them could have murdered their captain. It was physically impossible for them to have done so. You'll find them in the Waldorf Hotel about an hour from now. I don't suppose any of them will feel like going out on the town tonight, but let me know who does. I envy you. They do a very good roast beef at the Waldorf. I will be doing the same at the Westmoreland. We shall compare notes in the morning. In the big Committee Room downstairs. I shall have the very great pleasure of asking Admiral St John Rogers to arrange it. With two thumping big coppers at the door.'

Light thought he had never looked more like a garden gnome.

The Westmoreland Hotel, situated at the east end of St John's Wood Road, opposite the Nursery End of Lord's, is one of the more comfortable modern plastic palaces and well accustomed to catering for England's cricketers and their sundry hangers-on when London plays host to a Test match. It is, of course, ideally convenient for Lord's but not for the Oval, which is at Kennington, south of the River Thames and so in a desert area as far as the hotel chains are concerned. By tradition, visiting teams are housed in the more baroque luxury of the Waldorf Hotel, in the Aldwych, which is equidistantly inconvenient for both London's cricket grounds, but adjacent to the more sensuous attractions of the West End. Cynical writers have been known to suggest that this is a leftover from the days when international cricket came under the aegis of the MCC, and that the choice of the Aldwych was a ploy to seduce the naive young men from the Colonies into indulging in a surfeit of wine, women and song during the evenings and so turn out for the game not as fit as they might be. Meanwhile, the pure young gentlemen of England would be resting without temptation in the salubrious environs of St John's Wood. Certainly the Aldwych, were it ever to be so indiscreet, could tell many a tale of wine, women and raucous song, but the fact that this ploy, if ploy it was, has never seemed to work suggests that either the visitors have been less seducible than expected, or that the leafy avenues around the Westmoreland might hide other forms of off-duty amusement for the England stalwarts.

Light dodged a small gauntlet of Press and cameramen, held amiably at bay on the pavement by the Waldorf commissionaire, and was surprised to find none of the touring team in the bar. Its sole occupants, apart from the barman, were three people in deep conversation at a low table in the corner. Two large men dressed in well-fitting lounge suits were obviously subjecting the third, wearing a green tour jacket, to a heavy sales pitch, for they were emphasising vigorously points in a large folder on the table between them as he turned the pages. Light ordered a lager and chose a seat not directly in their line of sight. The man in the jacket did not seem to have his mind fully on what they were saying. Light studied the headlines of his evening newspaper – 'DEATH AT LORD'S', 'Carter bumper kills Aussie skipper' – and caught snatches of the conversation.

'. . . The very best hotels, of course . . . all found, naturally . . . fifty thousand, that's right . . . two hundred a day pocket money . . . Kruger National . . . Eight, we think . . . three Tests . . . six weeks . . . no, well, see what you can do . . .' The voices dropped and then the men were standing up, shaking hands. 'We'll be in touch. And the cigs will come down later tonight or in the morning. Totsiens.'

The large man left without a glance at Light. The man in the green jacket moved over to the bar. Light could see that he was small, even tiny, with delicate hands and feet. The wallaby emblem on his jacket seemed out of keeping, but his voice was a clipped Australian twang, almost a whine.

'Gimme a Foster's, mate. Reckon I've earned one, today. Room 109,' he added as an afterthought. He tossed the folder onto the bar as though in disgust, then pulled it back and leant an elbow on it, almost possessively. He drank deeply, emptying the glass in one draught. Light moved up alongside him at the bar. Close up, his deep tan was revealed to be a mass of freckles, splashed across the skin at the back of his hands, over his face and brow. Across the front of his head, a thin strand of light brown hair fought a losing battle with fast-approaching baldness.

'Excuse me, sir. Are you Mr Cousins?'

'Who wants him?'

'Detective Sergeant Light of New Scotland Yard.' Light held up his ID card. 'If you are Mr Cousins, I'd like a word with you, in private, if you don't mind.' He glanced at the barman.

'What the hell do you want now? Haven't we had enough goddam hassle today? I haven't been off the bloody phone since Wino was hit. Oh, OK, then, you'd better come up to the room,' he said grudgingly.

In the lift Light tried to soften the blow, but even to his ears his little speech sounded stilted.

'I know you've all had a shock today, Mr Cousins, and I'm very sorry. But I'm afraid that what I have to tell you is going to be even more of a blow.'

Cousins led the way out of the lift.

'You're not going to tell me they've cancelled the tour after all. Those bastards would do anything. Fuck them.'

'Which bastards, Mr Cousins?'

'Up there at Lord's, of course.' He opened the door of Room 109. 'Come in. Give me the worst.'

'I am instructed to tell you that Scotland Yard does not consider the death of Jack Viner to be accidental. We are conducting a murder investigation, Mr Cousins, and I must ask you some questions in connection with it.'

Cousins, in the act of placing the folder on the small table, swayed and would have fallen had not Light grabbed him firmly by the arm. The folder slipped to the carpet, some of its contents spilling out. Light bent down to pick them up, but Cousins lurched sideways, pushing him off balance.

'Sorry, sorry Inspector.' Cousins straightened up, hand over his mouth as though about to vomit. His brown eyes stared at Light, his freckles stood out against the underlying pallor of his skin. His

57

nose looked pinched. 'It's the shock. On top of everything. I need a drink. D'you mind?'

He gestured vaguely towards a small refrigerator in the corner of the room and collapsed wearily back into one of the two armchairs.

'Detective Sergeant,' Light corrected him, opening the refrigerator and fishing out an unopened half-bottle of brandy. 'This do?' He found a glass and handed Cousins a good two fingers. The glass rattled against his teeth as he drank greedily, dissolving into a spluttering attack of coughing. Light noticed that in spite of his distress, he had managed to pick up the dropped folder and place it on the table with some other papers.

'If it helps at all,' said Light, 'I am also authorised to tell you that there can be no question that any of your team or your party are under any suspicion of killing Jack Viner. The circumstances make it quite impossible for them to have done it personally, although that does not, of course, necessarily absolve them from complicity in the event.' And that sounds even more bloody pompous, he added to himself. We know you didn't do it but you could have fixed it, I should have said. Cousins took another deep sip at his brandy, more cautiously this time.

'I don't understand what you're saying. Somebody murdered Jack? You're bloody crazy. Jack was hit by a bastard cricket ball, that's all. You Poms are stark, raving, bonkers. Murdered, my arse. Wait until I tell this to the boys. They'll piss themselves.'

'You'd better pull yourself together and listen to me, Mr Cousins. I can't tell you how he was killed, but the autopsy has proved that he was killed deliberately. The formal announcement will be made tomorrow.'

Cousins did not seem to be listening. He sat up abruptly and laughed, a neighing sound.

'For Chrissake, d'you mean you load of wankers are going to charge that poor young bugger Carter with murder? Just because he hit Jack with a flamin' cricket ball? You must be out of your fuckin' minds.'

'We're not doing anything of the sort, Mr Cousins. Nobody is being charged with anything until our investigations are complete. It's no use being stroppy with me. I'm just doing my job, like you. Now. Are you ready to answer my questions?'

Cousins' mood changed abruptly as Light put on his police-man's voice.

'Oh, all right, Sergeant, I was only joking. Fire away. I don't think I can help you, but I'll try.'

'Thank you. It's really for background. Is this your first tour as manager?'

'Yep, it is, but I've been on tour before as coach and I came over eight years ago as part of the team. But I was hurt before the first Test and had to fly back. I was hit on the head in the nets by one of our quickies. Ironic, ain't it? No one charged anyone with tryin' to kill me.' He seemed much calmer now.

'Was Viner a good captain?'

'Yeah, great. Real great.' Cousins sat up and gazed earnestly at Light. 'Don't you let any bugger tell you different. He was bonzer, real bonzer. The boys'ud fly through fire for Jack. He'd got a cricket brain, y'know, just like Richie Benaud. He was the best skipper we've had since Chappell – Ian, not Greg. And the best bat too, by a long chalk. They say he could even spot the way a coin would spin – and allow for the wind.' He laughed sharply. There was a suspicion of moisture in his eyes, and for the first time Light felt and suppressed a flicker of compassion.

'Was he liked? As a captain? As a man?'

The brown eyes shifted.

'Oh, yeah, the blokes liked him all right. He could be tough, a right bastard, when he wanted to, but provided you did what he wanted on the field he was OK. He was respected, all right – just ask any England skipper. He'd give 'em nothing. Not even the time of day.' Cousins felt he had gone a little too far. 'I mean, he was OK off the field. Some of the Poms quite liked him. Badger did. Broadbent, I mean.'

'I gather he held strong opinions.'

'Christ, you can say that again, mate. He was that hot against apartheid and those rebel tours. Anyone who went on one of those was out, as far as he was concerned. O – u – t. He kept a list, you know, of anyone who went there to coach, who he worked for, how long, what he did, how much he earned, the lot. He used to send it to New York to the United Nations every year, and to that Sanroc outfit, to get them blacked. George Viljoen had to produce a pedigree proving he was dinky-di Oz, like a bloody dog. I thought

59

Jack went a bit over the top, myself. He even turned down two hundred thousand dollars, cash up front, to lead a tour like Goochie's. I ask you. One's got to make a living, hasn't one?'

On impulse, Light asked: 'What's that in the folder you were given?'

Cousins flushed under the freckles. He eased a finger under his collar.

'Nothing very much. Just a prospectus I was looking at. It's private . . . you know, business.'

'If it's nothing very much, Mr Cousins, you won't mind my looking at it.' Light had the folder in his hands and opened it as the little man started up in protest, his voice rising from a whine to a screech.

'You can't do that. It's mine. It's mine.' He reached out as if to grab the folder from Light's hands, then sank back into his chair, defeated. 'Oh, all right. Look at it, if you must. It's only a prospectus, like I said. Nothing's settled.'

Light thumbed through the glossy, beautifully illustrated pages. There were colour photographs of Newlands, Cape Town's cricket ground, reputed to be the most spectacular setting of any cricket ground in the world, the amazing bowl of the Wanderers in Johannesburg, plush hotels, scantily-clad girls, superb landscapes and pictures of wildlife. It looked like a millionaire's dream world. There was no script. The first page merely carried a message. 'All this can be yours free for two months a year – plus $100,000 cash in your pocket.'

'Very interesting. Not the sort of thing Jack Viner would have approved of, though, would he, Mr Cousins? Now he's out of the way, are you planning a little bit of private enterprise of your own, I wonder?'

Again the flush under the freckled skin. The knuckles turned white as the mobile fingers bit deep into the arms of the chair. Cousins opened his mouth to speak, but no words came out. Light said: 'I don't know what you're worrying about, Mr Cousins. There's nothing illegal about being offered a job, and I'm not here to question the morals of the case. But if this has a bearing on Viner's death, as it appears it must have, I must ask you about it.'

Cousins' complexion returned to its normal blotchiness as he let out a long breath.

'No, no, I see that,' he said. 'Sorry, Sarge. It's been so much of a bloody shock, and I've been on the telephone ever since it happened, trying to sort things out. And the Press, and the telly. I can see why they don't want to call off the Test, but I wish to Christ they had. Things would have been a damned sight easier for me, I can tell you. And now you. It's bloody murder all right,' he added bitterly. 'What d'you want to know?'

'Why are you so cagey about that?' Light indicated the folder. Cousins managed a short laugh.

'It's just that I can't believe that Jack isn't here. He'd have had my balls for breakfast if he'd got so much a sniff of this. He'd've had me thrown off the tour, straight, he would. And I couldn't afford it. It's my first tour, you see.' His voice rose again to a whine.

'But wouldn't the Board be just as hard on you if they found out?'

'Yeah, maybe, but they're a load of wankers. They wouldn't smell a cartload of shit until it hit them in the face. And by the time they find out this little lot it doesn't matter a fuck whether they know or not. It won't make any difference.' A thought struck him. 'I hope this won't go any farther, Sergeant, will it? I'll lose the lot if they think I've let it out before they're ready.' There was a heavy emphasis on 'they'.

'When will they be ready?'

'I don't know. This is only the start.'

'What happens next?'

'Can't say. It's up to them.' Cousins took a long pull at his drink. 'Mind if I smoke?' He pulled out a packet of Stuyvesant and lit up with a gold lighter, which he held out to Light. 'Not bad, eh, Sarge? Present from a fan.' He winked.

Light handed the lighter back. He said: 'Very nice. Who are those South Africans? Are they the bosses? How did they get in touch with you?'

Cousins shook his head. 'I don't know who they are, really. Hermann is the one with the mouth. Hennie just does what he's told. One of the telly boys introduced me to them at the first Press conference. He said they were something at the embassy. You won't bugger things up for me, will you Sarge?' The plea was more urgent this time.

'Don't worry, Mr Cousins. I haven't heard that anyone's doing anything illegal – yet.' He let the word linger on the air. 'But withholding information from the police in a murder investigation could well come into that category. Come on, man, you must have some sort of a clue. A telephone contact number, for instance.'

Reluctantly, Cousins dug into an inside pocket and brought out a small visiting card. On it was inscribed, in gold, 'Hermann Du Plooy. South African Ventures Ltd' and a telephone number Light recognised as that of one of the West End's better hotels. He handed back the card without comment. If Cousins was going to clam up, as he showed every sign of doing, there was no point in pressing the matter. He returned to easier ground.

'Was Viner a good family man?'

'I don't know. Nobody ever said anything, not even our Press. Which is even worse than yours.' He sounded proud of the fact. 'But then, Julie, his wife, keeps the kids away from cricket. She doesn't like it very much. Never comes to the ground, hardly ever turns up at a dinner, or whatever. Come to that, Jack doesn't – didn't – want her around, either. Not that the lads would mind. Julie's a humdinger. There ain't a player in Oz who wouldn't give a week's wages to get up her skirt. Even though she's an Abo.' He sketched a figure in the air with both hands and whistled softly.

'Has anyone ever tried?'

'No, not with Jack around, anyway. He'd have killed him. A Brit did, though, when England were touring a couple of years back. It was a party at Jack's house. I wasn't there, but everyone in the game heard what happened on the grapevine. The tale goes that one of the media guys tried to feel Julie up in the garden. Jack hauled him off and nearly throttled him. Then he chucked him in the pool and held him under the water. He'd have drowned if the boys hadn't jumped in and hauled Jack off.' His eyes shone with relish at his own story. 'Bloody fine way to end the party. The High Commissioner was there, and a helluva lot of high-ups, so it was all hushed up. The Pom got a bigger bollocking than Jack, come to think of it, for abusing hospitality, they said. He threatened to sue Jack for damages for assault, and Jack went for him again, and broke his nose. He was threatened with the sack, and he wasn't sent home only because it would have made a bigger stink, and there was a Test match on. He claimed Julie liked it, anyway. C'mon, Sarge, have a drink.' He held out the bottle. He seemed set for an evening's reminiscence. Light stood up hastily.

'Thanks all the same, Mr Cousins, I'm on duty. Let me know if anything develops. I'll be at Lord's tomorrow. In the main Committee Room.'

He pondered the story as he abandoned the lift and strolled slowly down the short flight of carpeted stairs. A swell of conviviality forced its way up on his senses, which identified it as coming from the lounge bar.

Light realised immediately that they had wrongly anticipated the Australian team's reaction to the loss of their captain, and that this was not the moment for him to obey his chief's instruction to inform them of a murder investigation. The bar was crowded with virile and vociferous young men in green blazers, liberally interspersed with girls of varying ages and degrees of insobriety. Light was impressed by how much larger, and yet more ordinary, the team seemed in real life compared with their appearance out on the cricket pitch. A large man in a grey suit was ordering a large round of drinks at the bar, and Light realised with interest that it was Du Plooy, the South African he had seen with Cousins in the same bar earlier. The man called Hennie was dispensing the drinks, easing his bulk delicately through the crush with both hands full of brimming glasses. He thrust his last glass of Scotch at Light and looked astonished when Light handed it back to him.

'No thank you. I'm not with your party.'

'What does that matter? Come and join us. Have a drink, yong. Don't you oggies drink nowadays?' The South African accent was very strong. Hennie shrugged his shoulders and headed back towards the bar for more supplies. Light saw his hand linger sensually on a shapely pair of buttocks in a tight-fitting yellow dress as he shoved past. Their owner paid no heed. Light saw a blonde head, and a pair of blue eyes he recognised flickered at him. He winked, and after a pause she detached herself from her large companion without haste and made her way across to him.

'Hullo, Renee,' he said. 'This is out of your way, isn't it?'

'If it isn't the dashing Amber. You're off your patch, too, my pet, aren't you? Thought you was with Old Bill these days? Or am I wrong?'

'Right, Renee, but not here. I thought the Market was more your scene?'

'Oh, it is. But someone suggested there might be more to be had out of sport. As well as sport.' She looked approvingly across at the two young cricketers she had been talking to. They were eyeing Light with obvious disfavour. 'It's like taking candy from kids, if you know what I mean.'

One of the players spoke in Du Plooy's ear. The big South African elbowed his way forcibly through the throng towards them. Light had time to draw the girl closely to him and whisper in her ear, 'Earn yourself a favour, love. The Park. Sunday. At ten.' He felt her nodding against his cheek. Then a strong hand gripped him by the arm and spun him round.

'What the fuck are you doing in my party?' Close up, Du Plooy was impressively powerful, with a massive Afrikaner's face set close down on his shoulders. Light's voice came out high and hesitant. 'N-nothing. I said I wasn't with you. Is this a private party? The manager didn't say the bar was closed.'

'Well it fucking well is, now. And who the hell are you, messing about with my girl?' He turned on Renee. 'Who is this little twerp?'

'Nobody. Just someone I knew. Don't hurt him, please, Hermann. He didn't mean any harm. His name's Smith.'

Renee contrived to look innocent and pleading, her eyes a wide blaze of blue. Du Plooy gave a bellow of laughter.

'Is that what he told you? Well, now, Mister Smith. It's time you were on your way. And don't cross my path again.' He prodded Light in the chest with a stiff forefinger, forcing him towards the exit. Light fell back, his face tight. He wondered: 'Shall I break it?' and thought the better of it as he stumbled out of the room and down the entrance stairs to the revolving door.

Light did not take kindly to being humiliated. But he had once been severely reprimanded by Detective Chief Superintendent Ashcroft for losing his patience, and he liked that even less. So as he strode round the Aldwych in search of a taxi, he forced himself to speculate whether Renee Stringer would meet him on Sunday in Hyde Park, as she used to in the days when they were both learning to work their very different beats on either side of the law. Renee still held that very feminine attraction for him, in spite of all he knew about her. The cab was halfway down Fleet Street when he remembered he had parked his car on a yellow line in the Aldwych and he didn't need a taxi after all. It was also humiliating to plead that he had changed his mind, pay off the cabbie and walk back. The dusk was balmy and the air warm. Light breathed deeply.

'I think you've earned yourself a proper drink, Amber,' he said out loud, and plunged into the Cock Tavern.

Chapter 3

The Second Day

Over the years, Detective Chief Superintendent Ashcroft had come to value a good breakfast beyond any other meal, largely because once the day was started, there was never any certainty that he would be able to eat again for the next 24 hours. It was also the only meal he ate at his large bare Islington flat. He never entertained there, and on his rare free evenings he was wont to sit slumped in front of his television set, a packet of fish and chips on his lap and a two-litre plastic bottle of beer from a supermarket on the floor within easy reach. In the morning, he liked to mull over the previous day's progress standing over the frying pan, savouring the inimitable odour of sizzling bacon, eggs, mushrooms and tomatoes; while the morning newspapers would be digested with the toast, butter and marmalade. Detective Sergeant Light, who was a jog-and-a-coffee man in the morning, usually arrived as late as he dared to avoid being pressed into plates full of calories and carbohydrates, delivered his report over the ritual pot of tea and thanked his stars that Old Bill did not smoke.

'Hmm,' was Ashcroft's first comment. 'So who are Du Plooy and Hennie?'

'The embassy say they don't know him, or anyone called Hennie. But then they always say that. The hotel says Du Plooy has been an occasional customer over the past few years. They say, stuffily, that they do not inquire what their guests do for a living. They implied that most of them don't need to do anything. But the floor housekeeper thinks he's into diamonds, or gold. No trouble. Tips well, if not lavishly. Pays by American Express. The bookings come via Amex too. He only takes a continental breakfast in his room at the hotel. They can't remember him dining there. If there's any sex it doesn't take place there. Sometimes he books in another man, like this time. A Mr Hendrick Van der Merwe. They're due to stay for a week, until next Thursday.'

'Well, we will have to talk to them. I suppose you wouldn't mind having the first go, as it were, at Mr Du Plooy, Amber?'

Light was experienced enough not to fall into the little trap.

'I don't think so, sir,' he said, grinning. 'Last night I'd have jumped at the chance, but this morning I think a less, well, prejudiced copper might be a better idea.'

'Good. What else?'

'We'll have to find out the name of the media guy who Viner nearly drowned, and if anyone else had made a pass at his wife before. Cousins, who's a nasty little piece of work, said he didn't know of anybody.'

'And there must be several cricketers whose careers have been affected one way or the other by this obsession with apartheid. It's a job for Thomas and his team, plus all the other routine. Is he in residence at Lord's?'

'He said he'd be in working order by nine,' Light replied. 'He's been in touch with Sydney through the night and they've been checking out the Australian team for us. And the officials, but they haven't come up with anything yet, apart from the fact that Cousins has been mixed up with some odd deals with cricket bats. Apparently they're quite big business. Nothing strictly illegal, they say, but one or two companies he's had his fingers in have come unstuck, and the fraud boys have been sniffing around. But as Cousins seems to have lost out each time there hasn't been much incentive to prosecute him. A bit like kicking a lame dog, they said.'

'Does that tally with your impression of the man?'

'I certainly think he smells like a loser, and I don't believe he has the brains or the guts to lay on a murder like this one. He doesn't give the impression of being able to manage the team either. But lame dogs can still bite.'

'Hmm.'

'Oh, yes, and Sydney says Mrs Julie Viner is flying to London tonight on Concorde. She'll be landing at Heathrow at eight o'clock tomorrow morning. She wants to take charge of her husband's body and arrange the funeral. Sydney said she was more angry than distressed at Viner's death. Said something to the effect

67

that the silly bugger had been asking for it. Then she refused to answer any questions and kicked them out of the house. A nice big one in Bondi. There's an au pair for the youngest kid who acts as a sort of housekeeper as well. Mrs Viner's well paid in her job and Jack Viner was pretty tight with his money, so the family will be all right. He had a sporting goods business in Newcastle. Not our Newcastle, the one on the New South Wales coast. They're looking into that as well. As he died on tour there'll be a big insurance payout.'

'Hmm. That it?'

'I think so, sir, apart from the fact that Inspector Thomas' team have gone through all the BBC's video coverage and they confirm the Brigadier's impression that Viner's legs had begun to buckle when he was hit by the ball. Otherwise, none of them could find anything out of the ordinary.'

'Hmm. Tell 'em to try again.'

Light took a swig at his mug of tea. It was only lukewarm. It was time Old Bill contributed. He said: 'How did you get on last night, sir?'

Ashcroft had had a most unsatisfactory evening, in so far as the investigation went, while thoroughly enjoying himself. It was a long time since he had been able to steep himself in cricket talk with a man he liked instinctively from the moment he went over to the table where the England manager, Anderson, was sipping his brandy with Geoffrey Broadbent, the England captain.

Anderson introduced them, finished his brandy and excused himself. 'I've told Badger you want to talk to him and he knows why. The others haven't been told yet. I'm going to do that now. See you later, I hope.' He left them without fuss.

'Ashcroft?' The captain looked at him curiously. 'Roly told me you were a cricketer yourself, once. There was an Ashdown who played for Kent once. Don't know an Ashcroft.'

'It might not seem possible, but I once bowled off-spinners for Middlesex Seconds. When I first joined the Force. But that was some time ago.'

'Policing doesn't seem to go with cricket, somehow. And you're a Detective Chief Superintendent. What's all this mystery about Jack's death? It was a bloody shock to us all, but it's pretty clear what did it. Young Vince is a bit down, of course, even though he bowled bloody well after I dropped Imrie. He reckons it was his fault.'

'At the moment we're not here to apportion blame, but to investigate a death. I'm sorry to tell you, Mr Broadbent, that Jack Viner's death is being treated by us as murder. The cricket ball did not kill him. Something else did.'

'Jesus Christ!' Broadbent sat up straight in his chair, knocking over his lager which he did not notice. 'Can you tell me anything more? Was he poisoned? Who did it? No, that's a stupid question. You wouldn't be here if you knew.'

'How do you know that, Mr Broadbent?'

'What? Oh, I see. It could have been one of us.'

'Indeed. Or more than one. But that is only speculation at the moment. We need to know a great deal more about the circumstances and the background to this case. We hope you can help us. And Mr Anderson here.' He turned to the manager, who had rejoined them. Anderson nodded.

'Of course. And I'm sure Badger will do all he can. Won't you, Badge?'

'I'd be glad to. I've never heard of a cricketer being murdered anywhere before, least of all at Lord's. It's unbelievable.' Broadbent's flat Yorkshire face matched his accent. He leaned forward, anxious to please.

'Superintendent, tell me what I can do to help?'

'First, you can answer a few questions, privately if you don't mind. Second, I'd like you, as skipper, or Mr Anderson, I don't mind which, to tell the team what I've just told you. I'll be there to field the questions, but I think the news would come better from you. It will obviously be a shock to them.'

Broadbent thought slowly, weighing up the situation. He turned to Anderson.

'This is your pigeon, Rosey, isn't it. My contract says I'm the boss but you deal with the Press and the public, and that's about right. I reckon police has been added to the list.'

He sounded relieved. Anderson nodded.

'Yes, I think that's the best way. You've got quite enough pressure to cope with as it is, Badger. Leave it to me. I'll call a general get-together for ten o'clock. Will that be suitable, Superintendent?'

He excused himself again and threaded his way round the tables, his shoulders rounded a little, his usually ruddy countenance pale. They watched his progress. Surprisingly, Broadbent spoke Ashcroft's thoughts aloud.

'It's a bit hard on Rosey,' he said. 'He loves the job, but they've placed him in an impossible position. He took us to Oz last time and we won the Ashes. Now unless we win them again, and better, he'll be out on his ear, murder or no murder. And he's just bought a new house, God knows how much he paid for it, in Hampstead of all places. It's about the same for me, personally, but Win's got money of her own and we don't need much.' He brought his gaze back to Ashcroft's face. 'Sorry. How can I help you? Ask away.'

'You were there when it happened, of course. From the beginning.'

Broadbent spoke slowly, thinking his way along the infinite lane of memory.

'Well, I won the toss and put them in. Not that it makes much difference in these days when the pitch is covered all the time before matches, but sometimes there's a bit of a nip in the Lord's pitch early on, on the first morning. I thought, or hoped, rather, that young Carter might be a bit of a surprise to them. They'd only seen him once before in the first Test and he wasn't too impressive on a slow pitch – Essex kept him out of their match at Chelmsford and Rosey persuaded the selectors not to put him in the MCC game. He's the fastest we've had since John Snow – but you know all this anyway.'

Ashcroft nodded.

'There was another reason, too. I didn't want him to brood too long so I didn't even open up the other end. Get him over the nerves fast, you know.'

'Mightn't he be intimidated? Viner had a big reputation.'

'I didn't think so. Young Vince is pretty cocky. It's what makes a good fast bowler. In any case, I knew Jack wouldn't take him apart in the first over, unless he bowled complete tripe. That wasn't Jack's style. He'd take a long hard look at anyone new. He'd even let full tosses alone down the leg-side at the start. Stop them if they're straight; leave them if they're crooked. That was Jack. We'll miss him.'

'So what happened?'

'Just what I expected, until that fifth ball. Not much. Carter bowled the first two pretty wide and wild, and Jack didn't even bother to lift his bat at them. The third was a better ball – not his fastest but short and on the stumps and Jack just played back, defensive. It got up a bit but Jack had all the time in the world. The next ball Jack left down the leg-side and I ran up to give Vince a bit of encouragement.'

'What did you tell him?'

Broadbent looked sheepish. 'I told him to bang one in a bit, if he felt like it. Anyone is a bit vulnerable early on if the ball starts flying about. I'm not squeamish. It's all part of cricket and everyone understands it. Not that Viner was likely to be intimidated. He never wore a helmet. He used to say he let the fast bowlers part his hair for him because he couldn't be bothered to comb it. Anyway, I told Carter to bounce him, and he did. He came galloping in like a racehorse and I saw the ball hit the pitch, short, and the next thing I knew was Jack going down onto the wicket. I appealed, of course, from instinct, but Carter carried straight on down the pitch. He was first to get to Jack, and he tried to lift his head. Vince was staring as though he'd been hit himself. I've never seen anyone so utterly, well, desperate. It takes a long time to tell, but it all happened so fast, we were all around Jack and I was trying to bring him round and calm Vince down at the same time. Then I signalled for Doc Wright and the stretcher. Jack hadn't come round, of course, and they all went off, and we got on with the game. Until that goddam announcement, of course. I wanted to call the whole thing off, but the bosses wouldn't let me. They kept muttering about keeping faith with the crowd, and about cash, and the sponsors, and none of it seemed to matter a monkey's.'

He added fiercely, 'I wish they had called the damned game off.' Then more slowly: 'But the boys need the cash, too.'

'Did you notice anything, anything that struck you as strange? Anything at all?'

'Well, it was odd that Jack didn't duck out of the way of the ball. No, not that, he never ducked. He played bumpers in the classic style, he swayed out of the way, keeping his eyes on them. Or he'd hook. He had the best hook in the game. He used to see the ball as early as Bradman, Jack did. But not then.'

'Anything else?'

'Vince's reaction was a bit over the top, but then he's only young. He recovered after tea when I dropped that catch. I'd had a word with him, but I don't think that made all that difference. He just got bloody mad. He'll be all right.'

'What did you say to him?'

'Oh, the usual flannel. It wasn't his fault, nobody could blame him, he mustn't blame himself. I told him Jack had probably had a heart attack, because I saw him start to fall as the ball was being bowled. All a load of crap, of course, but I did wonder afterwards. That was why I dropped that catch, thinking about it. All to the good, I suppose. Except it won't bring Jack back.'

Broadbent sighed. He sounded very weary.

'There was nothing else. Just a day's cricket. It only came alive in the evening. But that was a good session. For both teams. I guess we both needed it. But I still hope they'll cancel, now you say he's been murdered.'

'I don't think they will, from what I've been told, Mr Broadbent. The official view is apparently that cricket is more important than a death, or even a murder. It is a view shared by the Home Office, so the show must go on. It is not up to me to agree or disagree. You must make your own choice.'

'There's no choice, is there? Cricket's my job, and I'm one that does what he's told. I'd rather other people made those decisions,' said Broadbent resignedly. 'And people still think it's a game.'

'I'm told Viner held strong opinions, particularly about apartheid. Do you share those views?'

'Yes, of course I do, to some extent. You know about my wife, of course. She's Coloured too, from the Cape. But I think the way Jack goes about it is wrong. He gets people's backs up – people who are influential, or are in a position to help. We've often had words about it. I take the view that if people want to go to South Africa to coach, on what they call rebel tours, that's up to them and their consciences. I'm not sure whether the total ban is right, or will ever work.' He leaned forward, his Yorkshire accent broadening in his earnestness. 'Linda says Jack's too hard, almost like the black extremist politicians. That's why Julie can't get on wi' her. But Jack did go too far. It was a sort of crusade, for him, and not only in Australia. Julie helped him, of course. I don't know what she'll do now. All this banning. It doesn't improve the game in any way, I reckon, to throw good cricketers out of the team just because they've been to South Africa. It's made a bloody mess of the England side for years. There must be at least 20 players today who're unavailable for the team or tours because of the TCCB attitude. I know they shouldn't give way to blackmail – literally – but they think they'll kill cricket if they don't. And it's bloody big business these days. It would sink me if the game packed in. I don't know any other trade.'

'What about South African players playing over here?'

'That opens another can of beans. And here I go all the way with Jack. We don't need 'em and we don't want 'em, unless they live here for at least five years and go through the right procedures to get British citizenship. Then they can play anything they want. I don't reckon overseas players have done our cricket any good at all in the long run.'

'Not even the West Indians?'

'Not really, though I suppose they did bring in the crowds. No, we taught them how to bowl fast and they were so bloody good they bloody nigh ruined the game for us. I'm biased, of course. To be honest, they learned to cheat better than we did. From us. But all that's got nothing to do with Jack's death. Reckon I'd better tell the lads. If you don't mind.'

'That's fine, Mr Broadbent. Thanks for your help.'

Broadbent grinned shyly. 'Don't know about that, Superintendent. And will you please call me Bill, or even Badger. Everyone does. After all these years I don't know anyone called Mister Broadbent.' He went off to find Anderson, and in five minutes' time the players tropped from their several tables to assemble in the small television room set aside by the management for their use. There was some audible speculation on Ashcroft's identity as they sprawled into the easy chairs. Most of them looked bored and there was some resentment. They were not used to being cooped up for the evening and were busy saying so. Some carried in half-finished pints of beer, one or two had wine glasses and Ashcroft noticed that one of them, Spencer, was sipping from a generous brandy balloon.

Anderson was brief, and blunt.

'I'm sorry, everyone, to spoil your evening. It can't be helped. We were all shocked by Jack's death today, but I'm afraid there's worse to come. This is Detective Chief Superintendent Ashcroft from New Scotland Yard, and he's here because the police believe Jack Viner did not die naturally. They think he was murdered.'

One or two players gasped. Mandell, the off-spin bowler, one of the oldest members of the side, let out an abrupt, explosive laugh and then coughed, covering his mouth. Bowyer-Smith sighed, a long outpouring of breath that sounded like a sob. Carter sat still, white as a sheet, locking his hands together with fingers interlaced in his lap. He appeared to be about to vomit. Spencer, the all-rounder, voiced the disbelief apparent on several faces.

'Jesus Christ, Rosey, have you all gone mad? We all saw what happened. We were there. Bloody there. Wino bought it. Vince creamed him and he didn't even make a stroke. Did he?' He gestured around at his team-mates. Heads nodded in a chorus of agreement.

'That's right.'

'It bloody is, too.'

'Come off it, Rosey. Who d'you think you're kidding? If it's a joke, it's a shitty one.'

Broadbent said, forcefully: 'There's no joke about this lot. I think we'd better hear the Chief Superintendent. He's not here to mess about. This is something we don't know anything about, and a bloody good job too. So shut up and listen to him.'

They all looked at Ashcroft, who had busied himself with loading a pipe. He occasionally smoked one, not from habit but because he had found the homely gestures distracted the attention of his witnesses and disguised the essential aggression of any police interrogation; Light privately called it his Uncle Bulgaria role.

The cricketers watched him fumble for matches, and Spencer leaned forward to offer his cigarette lighter with a typically flamboyant flourish of the wrist. Ashcroft struggled to light it, and Spencer took it from his fingers and flicked it to life with professional ease.

'There you are, sir,' he said, almost apologetic for an elderly man's inability to cope with the modern gadget. 'If you turn it up, you'll find it won't burn your fingers.'

Ashcroft thanked him and found that indeed the lighter turned into a miniature blowtorch when upside down. He resembled more than ever a rumpled and beardless garden gnome. He waved away the cloud of smoke. He began without preamble or apology.

'Jack Viner was not killed by the cricket ball bowled by Carter. His skull was broken by another implement or projectile either immediately before or very soon after he was struck in the face. In view of the fact that it would have been virtually impossible for any of you to have hit him on the head with some form of blunt instrument without being seen by at least someone in the crowd or by the television cameras, we believe that the second possibility is most unlikely. The same and some further considerations may be said to rule you all out of direct participation, which may be of some relief to you. However, there may well be some questions that I or my team will want to put to you in the course of the next few days, and I hope we can have your full cooperation. The Home Office and the TCCB have agreed that the Test match should go on in as normal a manner as possible, and we shall try not to disrupt your normal day. If anyone has anything they can tell us that may have a bearing on the matter, I am here now, or there will be someone in the big Committee Room at Lord's from tomorrow morning. We should like to know particularly if any of you noticed anything strange or out of the ordinary during today's match.'

He paused and looked round the room slowly. He thought someone moved, but without exception they were leaning forward in their seats, their eyes fixed on him.

'If any of you have any questions, I'll try to answer them now, but I can't guarantee you a satisfactory answer.'

It was Ashcroft's experience that people often gave more away by the questions they asked than by their answers. But the cricketers seemed either too shocked by the situation or too weary after their day's efforts to respond. After a few desultory questions more concerned with the future of the match itself than the crime, he thanked them and prepared to leave. He was collecting his hat from the cloakroom when a broad Lancastrian voice stopped him.

'Excuse me, Mr Ashcroft, could I have a word with you?'

'Yes?' It was Williamson, the opening batsman, who had shown little reaction at the revelation of Viner's murder. His lined face with sad bloodhound eyes proclaimed that there was little that would ever surprise him.

'D'you think this might be what you're looking for?' he asked, holding out his hand. 'I found it just beside the pitch after tea. I stuck it in my pocket for luck. I thought it must have come off the mower.'

Ashcroft looked at the outstretched palm.

On it was a ball-bearing, measuring almost an inch in diameter.

'Go ahead, Amber. You can touch it. I took it down to the Yard last night in the faint hope it might show something. But Williamson had kept rolling it between his fingers, and after the afternoon in his pocket there were no traces of anything bar his fingerprints.'

'Dr Heatherington?'

'Oh, yes, this could have caused death all right. The effects are exactly consistent with the temple being hit by something of this size, although it could have been a hammer. Heatherington says it must have been a glancing blow from something travelling at around 200 miles an hour to do the damage it did. The skull was literally splintered. The remarkable thing was that the skin wasn't broken.'

'So there must have been some form of gun involved.'

Light's experience of picket duty had taught him that a ball-bearing fired from a catapult or a compressed air gun can severely dent or even pierce the thin sheet steel of a car or a coach, but he found it almost impossible to believe in a weapon that would be needed to fire a projectile the size and weight of the ball-bearing.

'It doesn't make sense, sir,' he protested. 'A bullet from a rifle, yes. But this? You'd need a young cannon, and no one's said anything about an explosion. And nobody could guarantee the accuracy needed.'

Ashcroft was at his most inscrutable.

'They're all difficulties that occur to me, but I don't think they are necessarily insurmountable,' he said on the short car journey to Lord's. 'I want you to go and talk to Armitage and the ballistics people. They should be able to help. No, I think I know how it was done. But who did it and why? Amber, they're the problems. Find the motive, and the motive will lead you to the murderer, they used to say. Let's get down to Lord's. I want to talk to your Mr

Cousins. And I want you to talk to Vincent Carter. You're more his age, and you might frighten him less. Remember the word his mother used to Wright on the telephone. Terrified. That is exactly how that young man looked last night, even after my qualified and quite dishonest assurance that none of them could have done it. Don't bring him down to the Committee Room – the incident room, I mean – it'll frighten him even more. Get Wright to give you the physiotherapy room, if no one's using it. It's not far from the dressing-room.'

Light turned into the rear entrance of the ground where an attendant took one look at Ashcroft's tie and waved them through.

'Right, sir. Do you think I should get a tie?'

'No, Amber, I think that would cause a lot more trouble than it would be worth.' Ashcroft's voice was missing its usual anonymity. 'They'd catch you. You don't look the part. It wouldn't do the Met much good to be accused of misrepresentation.'

'Can't you make me an instant member, sir? It shouldn't be too difficult.'

'Good God, Amber, there's a 40-year waiting list.'

'And I thought cricket was dead,' Light muttered to himself as, with some relief, he recognised the policeman who waved him into a ribboned-off parking space. 'Well, at least we're getting organised.' And the doorman at the pavilion recognised him and merely nodded. At the door to the England dressing-room he found Wright putting down the telephone.

'We mustn't keep meeting like this,' Light said. 'People will begin to talk.'

Doc Wright contrived to look flustered.

'Oh, it's you again. I've just been on to the bookies. Placing bets for the boys.'

'Bets? I didn't know cricketers placed bets. What on? I mean, on what?'

'Oh, anything. Horses. Dogs. Miss World. On the day's total of runs. On the declaration. On the Man of the Match. On the number of catches in an innings. Oh, on anything you can think of. If it moves, bet on it, that's the way they think.'

'All of them?'

'Well, no, I suppose not. The younger ones don't, so much. But

77

they soon learn, like they soon learn to drink. Or smoke,' he added bitterly, as though he'd lost any number of personal battles.

'Does Carter bet?'

'Not usually, but today he did ask me to put a pony on . . .' His voice stumbled slightly.

'On what?'

'Oh, sorry. On Lamplight in the 2.30 at Doncaster. I'd forgotten.' He sounded unconvincing, but Light affected not to notice.

'Twenty-five pounds is quite a lot for a young man to bet on a horse.'

'Oh, I don't know. They're often betting in fifties and hundreds. They get well paid for a Test, these days.' He sounded resentful, and Light asked, on a hunch: 'D'you get a commission? On the bets, I mean.'

Wright flushed.

'Yes, I suppose I do,' he said reluctantly. 'Not on the bets. Only on the winnings. Five per cent.'

'And a cut from the bookies, I suppose?'

'Well, they give me a sort of a present at the end of the season.'

'What do you mean by sort of a present?' Light persisted.

'Oh, it's nothing illegal, I assure you.' The little man sounded breathless. 'It might be a turkey at Christmas, or a few bottles of Scotch. Something like that. Nothing wrong with that, is there?' he asked defensively.

'It all depends. If it stops at that, then I don't suppose the law would notice. After all, a lot of people are coining it at both ends every day and nobody gives a tuppenny damn,' said Light casually. 'What your Mr Anderson would say is another matter, though, isn't it?'

'You won't tell anybody, will you, Sergeant? I . . . I can't afford to lose this job. I . . . I'm not as young as I used to to be.'

'Nor are we all,' said Light wearily. 'It's none of my business. But I would like to chat to young Carter, in private. How about lending me your treatment room for a quarter of an hour and telling Carter to slip in there for a moment? I don't think there's any need to tell anyone else, nor for me to mention anything to Mr Anderson, do you?'

'You're blackmailing me,' Wright said indignantly.

'Yes.'

Wright shook his head and went into the dressing-room. Light watched his retreating back and noted a substantial bulge in his hip pocket. It seemed as though playing both ends against the middle might be a profitable occupation. It might have something to do with the case, and it might not. He pocketed the key Wright handed round the door and received the whispered instruction, 'Nine-thirty, before they go out for a warm-up', with a nod. He had 15 minutes to spare, so he strolled slowly down the stairs to the newly set-up incident room. Detective Inspector Thomas greeted him with a broad grin, though there were lines under his eyes.

'Just in time for a cup of tea. I don't know what their lordships will say,' he said cheerfully, with a wave at the life-sized portraits of former presidents staring down sombrely from the panelled walls. 'We've brought in a kettle, and Morgan and Jones will be on the door in a minute, so we won't be disturbed. Morgan was the Pontypridd lock before he joined the Force, and Jones still turns out for London Welsh when they need a seventeen-stone prop.'

'How did you get on with the monitors, Tommy?'

'Nothing at all, boyo. We were at it until four this morning. No shortage of volunteers, though. We seem to have more cricketers than bobbies. There were even two WPCs. One of them scores regularly for her boyfriend's club and the other is actually a fast bowler. Or so she says. Bit of all right, too.' Thomas winked. 'With any luck she'll be down here to help. Old Bill's been in, and likes the set-up.' He indicated the six television monitor sets lined up on one of the long tables. 'The telephones will be in soon. The main thing is communications with Sydney. Old Bill asked me to pass on the message. They haven't traced the TV man who made a pass at Viner's wife, as nothing was reported and it was all hushed up. But they don't think it was an ITV man. The Beeb had a very strong crew out there, and ITV only had a news team, and they weren't invited to the party. Could you get on to it, he said. And Mrs Viner will be arriving at seven, not eight, tomorrow morning. Apparently the wind's behind Concorde, or they've found out it's downhill from down under.'

'Ha bloody ha. And what do you lot do while I'm wearing out my shoes?'

'Go over the videos again with a smaller toothcomb,' said Thomas, shuddering slightly. 'But so long as WPC Kingsley joins us at 11 am I won't mind too much. Good luck, Amber.'

Light located the head of the BBC's Outside Broadcast team in a small car park at the back of the pavilion, ensconced in the depths of a large dark green van from which sprouted a spaghetti junction of cables and aerials. There was a great deal of activity and some swearing, and Light gathered that supplying line feeds to the police operations room was the source of the annoyance. Inside the van a thin man uncoiled himself from in front of a battery of monitor screens.

'Hang on a minute,' he told Light. 'It's these bloody police. What they want duplicate feeds from everything for I'm buggered if I know. Bloody nuisance. And the crew are demanding double time because it's before they normally sign on. I'd tell them go and jump, but Shepherds Bush says no, pay up.'

He leaned forward into a tiny microphone.

'OK, Dave. That'll do for now. Come down off your perch and take a breather. There's over an hour before you need go up again. Have a wee or something.'

'OK, thanks.' The voice seemed loud in the confined space. There was a click, and a picture of groundsmen busily preparing the pitch for the day's play faded abruptly from one of the tiny monitors.

'Yes? Oh, police. Sorry about that.' He did not seem too perturbed. 'It's just that we've got far too much to do without all this extra. What can I do for you, Sergeant?'

Light explained his mission. The thin man laughed.

'A pass at Viner's wife? It could have been anybody. The only thing unusual about it is that he was caught before she got laid. Most of them go abroad with only one idea between their legs. I wasn't on that trip, worse luck, but someone will know. I'll find out for you by lunchtime.'

Light thanked him and returned to the pavilion. He knocked on the door of the physiotherapy treatment room and found Doc Wright inside, working on the back of a figure lying prone on the padded table and wearing only a pair of shorts.

'This is Carter,' said Wright, slapping the body on the shoulder. 'There's nothing wrong with him, but I thought it would attract less attention if I did it this way. Sit up, Vince, and meet the Detective Sergeant. He won't eat you. Put your shirt on. I'll leave you to it.'

He closed the door behind him. Light studied the young man as he pulled on a close-fitting white T-shirt. The first impression was of one of size in the small room. Carter was probably 6ft 2in tall and broad in proportion. His face was large, with widely-spaced grey eyes, a boxer's snub nose and a broad brow topped with close blond curls. But for all his fine physique, there was a suggestion of softness about the eyes which failed to meet Light's, and a curl to the upper lip which, Light judged, would send women wild. Under the tan, he looked desperately tired. He sat on the edge of the treatment table, staring down at his hands on his knees.

'What are you worried about, lad?' Light asked. 'Old Bill, I mean the Chief Superintendent, told you you were in the clear. But you don't look as if you slept all night.'

'I killed him. I know I did.' The voice carried no hope, no thought of reprieve.

'But why do you think so?' said Light. 'It seems perfectly straightforward. You weren't to know that anything was going to happen when you bowled that bouncer. I mean, Viner was a legitimate target, wasn't he? It's not as though he was tail-end Charlie. I'm told that normally he'd have hooked you out of the ground.'

Carter stirred.

'Not bloody likely. Not that early on, any road.'

'Why not? It's only your second Test match. He might have been wanting to hit you off form right away.'

'Not Viner. Not in a Test. He'd be too damn careful. That's what Badger told me, any road.'

'You don't normally bowl a bouncer in your first over, do you? I've been told you don't normally bowl them at all.'

'I doan't like it.' The Essex vowels broadened out. 'I 'it someone once. I thought I'd killed 'im. 'E went down, just like Wino. That's why I didn't want to do it, this time.'

'Didn't want to do what?'

'Cream 'im. Bounce 'im. Besides, 'e 'adn't got an 'elmet.'

'Does that make a difference?'

'I s'pose not, come to think of it. But it ain't so dangerous. I mean, you're not so likely to kill someone, are you?'

Carter paused, aghast at what he had said. Light gave him no time to recover, without altering the friendly tone of his questioning.

'Why did you bowl a bouncer at him, if you don't believe it's right?'

'Well, they was on at me. Badger, and Spence, and little Great.'

'Little who?'

'Great. That's Alexander. The keeper. Alexander the Great, see? He's great with the gloves, too, see?'

'Why were they on at you?'

'Oh, Badger said he wanted to unsettle them early on, before they got their eye in. Make them wonder, like, what the next ball would do. And Spence said to show them who was boss. He reckoned it was bloody cheek of Wino not to use a helmet, as if we was boys and not ready to play against the Aussies. And Great, well, he said . . .' he petered out.

'What did Great say?'

'Oh, it doesn't matter. Something about a bet.'

'He bet you couldn't deliver a bouncer?'

'Oh, no, nothing like that. He'd met these two geezers, in the pub, and they said they'd got a bet on with one of the bookies and they stood to win ten grand if they got it right. Said they'd see him right if he could arrange it. He told me.'

'What did he say?'

'He offered to cut me in. Half of a thousand. But it had to be a bloody good bouncer, and no messing. If I could hit him, so much the better.'

'So you agreed?'

'Well, it was bloody good money, and there didn't seem any harm in it. So I bounced 'im, and I 'it 'im, and he died. And it's all my fault . . .' His face twisted and he started to sob, thrusting his knuckles fiercely into his eyes.

'D'you know the men? Does Alexander?'

'N . . . no. I've never seen them. He said he just met them in the pub.'

'What did you do with the money?'

'I . . . er . . . put it on a horse. All of it. I won two and a half grand. Straight up. Ask the bookie.'

'What was the name of the horse?'

82

But Carter had had enough. He shook his head, and sat silent, motionless, staring down at his hands. Again the tears coursed down his cheeks. It was an exorcism. After a minute he looked up.

'It doesn't matter what you say. I'm guilty. I killed him.'

'What have you done with the money?'

'Nothing. It's in my bag. I wouldn't touch it with a bloody bargepole.'

'Have you said anything to Alexander about it? Or anyone else?'

'No, I haven't. But I'll have to tell Badger. He's the skipper. And Rosey. Then Great will think I've told on him.'

'I think I'd better take charge of that cash,' said Light. 'Just get the envelope and hand it to me through the door. I'll give you a receipt. You'll have to get ready soon. Sorry to have spoilt your massage.'

'Will I be charged?' Carter asked tremulously.

'It all depends. It's not up to me. I can't promise anything.'

Light waited until Carter returned with the brown envelope. He unwrapped and counted through the notes, wrote out a receipt for £2,500 in his notebook, tore out the sheet and handed it to Carter. With the money there was a small piece of white paper bearing, in sprawling capital letters: 'Great shot!' He thought it was not a very subtle attempt to get a man to convict himself.

On instinct he said, 'Don't worry. And good luck.'

'Silly young bugger,' he added to himself. After all, monstrous though it had seemed to Carter, there was nothing criminal in what he had done. Was there?

'I don't know why Old Bill had to send you down here. He knows the answer just as well as I do.' Chief Superintendent Charles Armitage looked fiercely across his desk, but Light, who knew him of old, declined to be intimidated. Armitage, for all his reputation at Bisley and his nickname of 'Hotshot', was known as one of the softest touches in the Metropolitan Police. There was very little he did not know about weapons of all kinds, and firearms in particular.

'I think he wants your expert guidance, sir,' said Light.

'Don't be a smarmy little sod.' Armitage was pleased. He took the ball-bearing Light had produced and balanced it on the palm of his hand, rolling it around in front of his eye. 'So what exactly do you want to know?'

'Whether this could kill a man in the middle of Lord's with all the world looking on, sir,' said Light. 'And if so, how? It wouldn't have been done on the pitch, so it must have been fired from somewhere in the crowd. But how would anyone guarantee accuracy at 100 yards plus? Old Bill – sorry sir, Detective Chief Superintendent Ashcroft – wants to know if it could have been fired from a sort of air gun, or a catapult, or something like a crossbow.'

Armitage took his time about replying. He looked closely at the ball-bearing again; then, Sherlock Holmes-like, he took a large magnifying glass from a drawer and peered through it. He sat back and rolled the ball-bearing gently across his blotter. He grinned fiercely at Light.

'Your answers are all yes,' he said. 'Yes, it could kill a man in the middle of a cricket pitch, or anywhere else for that matter, provided it was projected fast enough. Anything upwards of 100 miles an hour, I'd say. Yes, it could have been fired from the crowd, though your criminal would have to have had a first-class telescopic sight and a very steady hand and eye to guarantee the accuracy you want. He must have been noticed by someone. Yes, it could have been an air gun, or a catapult, or a crossbow, which is only an elaborate form of catapult, after all. Your problem is not how, but how on earth he managed it without being spotted.'

'Could you explain a bit more, sir?' But Armitage did not need prompting. He was riding his favourite hobby-horse.

'Let's take the air gun first, as it's the most likely. Weapons of such a large calibre aren't made commercially these days, but they were in use 200 years or so ago. I think some of Marlborough's troops used them during the Peninsular campaign. The main drawback was the high cost of manufacture compared with the normal gun of the time using powder and shot. Most light machine shops or even motor repair garages should be able to run up a weapon which could project this thing using a 2½ foot smooth or rifled breech-loading barrel with a high-pressure air reservoir fitted with a quick-release tap and a simple telescopic sight. With a high air pressure the trajectory would at 100 yards range be almost flat with still sufficient energy at the target to do extensive damage.'

He paused to draw breath, and Light asked, with some scepticism:

84

'But what about the accuracy? Surely you couldn't hit a man on the temple with a home-made air gun?'

'I could.' Armitage placed the emphasis on the pronoun. 'It wouldn't be a smooth bore, though. I'd need a rifled barrel, and because of its weight and also because it's made of steel I'd have to devise a sort of plastic or leather sabot – a sort of pouch – round the ball-bearing to obtain an air seal and also to take the rifling in the barrel. Steel's too hard. The sabot could be made to fall away after the ball-bearing left the muzzle of the barrel.'

'What about the crossbow?' asked Light. 'I think we can rule out the catapult because of the accuracy problem. Unless one of the cricketers had one in his pocket.'

'Precisely. But there is still the difficulty about being spotted. Even the modern crossbow made with carbon-fibre would be pretty unwieldy in a crowd. But it could easily be modified to fire a ball-bearing over the required distance. Some medieval types did fire stones and lead balls much farther than 100 yards. A number of modern crossbows firing small ball-bearings, about half this size, were made in the States during the 1950s and '60s, but they weren't as good for hunting as the usual crossbow bolts. You'd have to fix a leather or soft plastic pouch on the bowstring, which would have to be made of wire of some other form of nylon cord – not string. You'd also need a bolt groove fitted to the correct size and a top guide to hold the ball-bearing in the groove. The adjustment of the sight would have to be most exact to allow for the required range and the poor ballistics of the ball-bearing. Any crossbow has a low velocity and therefore a very curved trajectory over a distance The user would require good range estimation and a great deal of practice. That seems to me the main objection, but you'd have to weigh that against the fact that the bow itself could be obtained in many countries, including Britain, and the necessary modifications carried out on the kitchen table.'

While Light was pursuing the various missions entrusted to him by his superior, and a score or more Metropolitan policemen and women busied themselves in front of television monitor screens, at the keyboards of telex machines, or on long-distance telephone calls, Detective Chief Superintendent Ashcroft sent a message to the Australian dressing-room that he would be obliged if Mr Cousins would see him in the Committee Room at lunchtime, and allocated to himself the onerous task of watching the morning's cricket from the best and most exclusive vantage point Lord's could provide. The pair of large constables guarding the Committee Room door ensured that his concentration would not be disturbed while he watched the Australian innings disintegrate in the face of some supremely indifferent English bowling. Thirty years ago, Ashcroft said to himself in common with two hundred or more elderly gentlemen in the pavilion, he would have made a century himself against such a mediocre attack.

Having been informed by Light of his interview with Carter, Ashcroft was unsurprised to note that the young fast bowler did not take the field to finish the demolition of the Australian innings he had so ably begun the previous evening. A loudspeaker announcement in the Admiral's ringing tones informed him that Carter had torn a muscle in his side and was having treatment. Less public inquiries discovered that the bowler had simply refused to take the field, and was indeed closeted with Anderson, the manager, in some remote office far removed from the prying eyes of the Press. What Anderson said to him Ashcroft did not learn until later, but it was sufficient to persuade Carter to return to the field half an hour before lunch and even ask Broadbent if he could bowl. To which Broadbent replied unsympathetically, no he bloody well couldn't. Didn't he know the rule that a bowler who left the field, or did not appear on it at the start of any session, could not bowl again for at least the same length of time he had been absent? 'In any case,' added Broadbent, 'we're doing all right without you, thanks.' Broadbent wanted no prima donnas in HIS side, thank you very much. 'Deep third man this end, please, and long-on. Then you won't have to walk too far when the over changes.'

Indeed England were doing very nicely. Spencer, the all-rounder, who had bowled so wildly the day before, opened with his curving seamers in place of Carter and bowled Comberton, who had played so well the night before, middle stump with the fourth ball of his first over. Two overs later Alexander behind the wicket belied his 34 years and took off to his left, catching Martin one-handed from a leg-side snick and with his body horizontal to the ground. Immediately, Percy Mandell, who had been given some rough treatment by Foster the previous evening, found a loose piece of turf on the pitch and made the ball leap and turn at poor Jones, who fended it off with a glove and was both chagrined and secretly relieved to see the ball lob up into the hands of Woodman at short-leg. Even Chopper Woodman, said Spencer later, could have caught that one blindfold. And with both hands tied behind his back.

That brought the Australians to 271 for the loss of nine wickets, but then occurred one of those infuriating (to the fielding side) last wicket stands which provoke the most common of all cricket clichés – you never can tell.

Brian Rose, batting rather below his form at no. 8, and the 20-year old Walters, playing in his first Test and with a career-best score of 33 behind him, defied the England bowlers for nearly an hour while they added 39 to the scoreboard and took the total comfortably past the 300 mark. What was said in the Long Bar was unprintable until, on the stroke of lunch, Mandell induced a tremendous heave from Walters which took the top edge of the bat and ascended almost perpendicularly 50 or 60 feet into the blue sky before dropping neatly into Alexander's safe gloves. As Charles Montfort pointed out to his millions of listeners, it was only the twelfth time in history an England wicketkeeper had taken three wickets in six consecutive innings. So the players went into lunch with the game poised evenly, the Australian total at 310, while Ashcroft carefully unwrapped the expensive prawn sandwich PC Jones had bought for him from the Members' Bar ('because I though you looked hungry, sir') and awaited patiently the arrival of Griff Cousins. As he munched, he contemplated with some satisfaction the box of plastic-wrapped offerings provided by Scotland Yard.

In appearance, the Australian manager was even less prepossessing than Light's description of him. His sharp features had been blurred by a night's drinking and an unhealthy pallor underlay the tanned skin and the freckles. Light grey eyes shifted constantly about the room, taking in the banked television sets and the telephones. He had been drinking during the morning too, and the aura of alcohol hung round him like a nauseous blanket.

'What's all this?' he began belligerently. 'Some bloody rubbish about Wino being murdered? You Poms must be off your heads.'

'I don't think so, Mr Cousins,' Ashcroft said peaceably. 'Just a couple of questions, if you don't mind.'

Cousins visibly braced himself, but his anticipated ordeal did not materialise. Ashcroft, true to his word, asked him only two questions, both of them apparently innocuous.

'Can you tell me why Mrs Viner is so anxious to be here that she is taking Concorde tonight?'

'Because she's a cow. A bleedin' Abo cow.' The voice spat out, sudden and vicious. 'She's only coming to stir it up. She'll be a hundred times worse than ever Jack was . . .' His voice trailed off. He looked at Ashcroft, waiting for the inevitable. Once more he was disappointed.

'When you meet Mr Du Plooy at the Pandora tonight, would you please introduce me to him?'

Cousins looked blank, then as if he was about to deny any knowledge of anyone called Du Plooy, then recalled his meeting with Light the previous evening.

'You mustn't believe all you're told,' he blurted out. 'I've done nothing against the law. Your man told me. Sergeant, er, Light, whatsisname?'

'Then tell me more.'

'I can't. Gawdstruth I can't. They'd kill me.'

'So they might, Mr Cousins. But I don't want to keep you from your team. No doubt you'll want to talk tactics. I'll pick you up at eight o'clock at the Waldorf, if that will suit. I shall have a car.'

Cousins hesitated, then said, reluctantly, 'Oh, all right then,' and allowed himself to be shepherded from the Committee Room. On the threshold he paused, half-turning.

'. . . Er, er . . . make it 8.30.'

'Very well.'

Ashcroft followed him with his eyes, and nodded to Inspector Thomas.

'Two men. No. One man, one WPC. Less conspicuous. And don't lose him. Don't do anything. Just make sure he's still alive at 8.30 tonight.'

'Right you are, sir.' Inspector Thomas made it sound routine. 'Oh, sir. We've just heard from Forrester. That's the BBC man in charge. He says that he hasn't found out who it was who made a pass at Viner's wife, but there's a chap on the crew who might be able to help. It's the bloke up in the cherrypicker – Phillips, he's called. He isn't the guy we want, but he was on that last tour. He's a very experienced cameraman. Forrester says he'll bring him down if you're desperate, but he'd rather not until the end of play. There's no one else as good at the job up there. There's a 20-minute break at tea-time, but Royalty's inspecting the teams today and they want him safe up there in case it's the Queen.'

'All right, Thomas. We'll leave him safe up there. If you could get him to see me here at close of play. And thank Forrester for me. Ah, Amber, there you are. Tell me your news. Get him a cup of tea, Thomas, and one of those cheese sandwiches the Yard have so kindly provided us with. He looks starving.'

Between gulps of freshly-brewed tea and mouthfuls of a cardboard-like sandwich, Light reported his conversation with Armitage at the Yard.

'And so it looks to Armitage like a home-made air rifle,' he concluded.

'It would be reasonably easy for a DIY mechanic to construct, and if he was good he could make it accurate enough to hit a target exactly where he wanted to from the boundary. But how he could do it from the crowd without being seen, I just can't make out.'

'Oh, I know who murdered Jack Viner, Amber, and how. But not exactly why. We'll be interviewing him here at approximately 6.15 this evening, if I am not very much mistaken.'

But, for once, Detective Chief Superintendent Ashcroft was wrong.

It was the Queen. As the teams lined up in the afternoon shadow of the pavilion, she emerged escorted by Broadbent and Anderson for England and Bart Imrie and Cousins for Australia, with the figure of Lord Holmbush hovering anxiously in the background. Her bright yellow dress challenged the sun, still shining on nine-tenths of the ground.

The band of the Parachute Regiment materialised as if from the skies, although they had been there all day, to play the National Anthem, and up in the cherrypicker David Phillips touched his zoom button and slowly very slowly, the picture on BBC2 closed in on the familiar features and watched the curved smiling lips mouthing their friendly platitudes. Even at that distance, the viewer was able to identify the special sympathy and warmth she managed to convey to Imrie and his Australian team.

To Light's surprise, his chief was not watching the scene from the window, but had moved and was standing in front of a television monitor screen. For a moment, Light imagined that Ashcroft might just have been apprehensive, so still and intent was he on the little parade of tradition. But as the Queen disappeared up the steps leading into the pavilion and the players dispersed on to the field, Ashcroft turned away from the screen with something like a sigh.

'You didn't think . . . .?' Light left his question unasked.

'No, Amber, I did not. The range was far too great and that is not the object of this exercise. However, the possibilities of the situation did cross my mind for a second or two. She was warned, you know, and she still insisted on coming. But I want to tell you a story while we watch the closing overs. It will give you some idea of what we are up against.'

The afternoon's play had gone very much Australia's way, which was inclined to mar Detective Chief Superintendent Ashcroft's satisfaction in the progress of his case. He had watched with growing glumness an inept performance by England's early order with the bat, beginning in the first over when the experienced opening bat, Williamson, chased a fast outswinger from the strapping young Walters far outside the off-stump. Rose, the Australian wicketkeeper, in an effort as spectacular as Alexander's had been earlier in the day, took the ball inches from the ground a yard in front of Imrie, at first slip, rolled over twice with sheer exuberance and flung it high in the air.

Ashcroft's glumness deepened to positive depression four overs later when, with the score at 10, Walters tried what was intended to be a bouncer but turned into a medium-paced long hop. Graham, whose only scoring stroke had been a snick down the leg-side for four, welcomed it as manna from heaven and hooked it with all his might. Unfortunately for Graham, at such an early stage of an innings, a batsman's timing is suspect even if he is another Ian Botham. The ball flew high and wide towards the long-leg boundary with the crowd cheering it on but, instead of clearing the rope for a six, it dipped suddenly towards Comberton, fielding a couple of yards in from the boundary. 'Catch it!' came the scream from the whole Australian team as Comberton advanced two paces, then retreated, inching cautiously backward towards the boundary rope. The crowd fell silent as Comberton tensed, gathered himself and sprang, right arm stretched high and across his head to his left, in the manner of a baseball catcher. He judged his leap perfectly and rolled over with the force of the ball, his body not more than an inch inside the rope.

Lord's gasped, then burst into a roar of approval at a supreme piece of athleticism, while the umpire Goodie ran over to check for himself that the catch was fair, and that no part of Comberton's body had touched the rope. Comberton, meanwhile, as thrilled as he had ever been in a distinguished career, lay on his back on the grass temporarily exhausted by the explosive effort, holding the ball aloft in his right hand and savouring the applause.

Graham set out on his lonely walk back to the pavilion, the scoreboards already changed to accommodate his dismissal, barely heeding his skipper's 'Bloody fool' as they passed on the steps. Broadbent never minced his words, and he did not spare himself 45 minutes later when, after playing himself in with great care and seeing off the opening fast attack, he tried to cut one of Sissie Smart's seemingly innocuous off-spinners and unaccountably missed it completely. The one word he uttered was fortunately lost in the roar of the crowd as his off bail was neatly removed, but several million television viewers could lip read. Subsequently, and privately, Lord Holmbush told him that the BBC had passed on 243 letters of complaint, including one from the Archbishop of York, and that as England captain he should know better than to swear on television. 'We've almost managed to stop the spitting,' said his Lordship. 'Now you must set an example about the language.'

At 27 for three wickets, England's fortunes and the spirits of their supporters were at their lowest ebb, but two of the most experienced batsmen in the side began to set about putting things right. Prettyman, whose name and Oxford connections had held him back rather than helped him in the tough competitive world of county cricket, had only eight caps, but at 30 he was known as one of the most obstinate batsmen on the circuit, and a career-best innings of 298 for Surrey against a strong Worcestershire attack had forced him late into the England XI. Coetzee, a cricket immigrant from South Africa in the mould of Basil d'Oliveira, had nearly 500 Test runs to his credit, and a technique based on a short back-lift that gave the minimum encouragement to the bowlers.

It was slow going, though, for both players and spectators as the batsmen dug in, and in the dull two hours between lunch and tea England had mustered only 41 runs. But the pace of the cricket improved somewhat after tea and with it Ashcroft's humour. A boundary apiece to the batsmen in the first two overs, coupled with the news from Inspector Thomas that the Australian manager Cousins had made a couple of telephone calls and then left the ground and taken a minicab back to the Waldorf Hotel, seemed to agree with him.

'Just see they don't lose him,' he said, settling back in his uncomfortable armchair and waving Light to another. 'I can watch while we talk. You don't mind?'

Light was scarcely in a position to question his chief. In truth he found the afternoon's cricket thoroughly uninteresting, and welcomed the promised distraction of Ashcroft's reminiscences. The old detective was far removed from being the club bore. And, accustomed as he was to Ashcroft's methods, he was still impatient to learn why Ashcroft was so certain he had solved the case. As far as Light was concerned, it was full of leads that led off into the blue. Ashcroft began, his narrative interrupted from time to time by abrupt comments on a particular piece of play.

'It was before your time, about 25 years ago when I was still a sergeant in the CID. I was told off to keep an eye on a young fellow who'd come into the country from South Africa in, shall we say, questionable circumstances. His name was Keith – William Keith, or so he claimed, although he was known in some quarters as Keith Williams. He was a South African whose father emigrated there from Scotland after the war. He'd been educated in Durban and at the Witwatersrand University, and for a couple of years before UDI was a reporter on a paper in Salisbury. Then he moved to the *Star* in Johannesburg, where he had a bit of a reputation as a kaffir basher. He was a big fellow, and used to claim a fourth Dan in judo, as well as being an expert in karate and kung-fu. Not a chap to meet on a dark night, though as far as I know no one ever put the claims to the test. Oh, good shot, sir! . . .

'Where was I?'

'Karate expert, sir.'

'Oh, yes. Well, he arrived here on a British passport – as the son of a Scot he was entitled to one in those days – with a lurid story about how he'd escaped from the clutches of BOSS – the Bureau of State Security as it was known then – in a sort of James Bond chase across Namibia. It checked out. The *Star* carried a long report the week before about one of its reporters having been recruited to spy on white friends of the African National Congress and members of the liberal opposition. They did not name him, but everyone on the paper knew it was William Keith, or Keith Williams, as they knew him. He'd made sure of that by informing certain selected friends in confidence. The paper said he'd led BOSS on by passing over information that they could check out was correct, but then got frightened and decided to pull out.'

He paused to applaud a smart stop in the gully area.

'The *Star* said that from his BOSS contacts he knew they were after the white leader of the liberal wing at Wits, a young man he had known as a junior at school. So he passed some strongly misleading information, grabbed his friend and drove off in a stolen Mercedes to the Namibian border while BOSS were looking for him in Port Elizabeth. According to the story, and neither BOSS nor Keith did anything to counter it, he had out-driven the South African police cars, dodged helicopters and escaped two army ambushes before making it across the Caprivi Strip into Zambia with both his skin and that of his friend intact.

'His friend stayed in Zambia and joined the ANC, but Keith used his story and the British passport to hitch a ride with BOAC, as it was then, back to London at taxpayers' expense. There was a bit of a buzz in the Press, a picture or two of the young hero being greeted by the Anti-Apartheid movement, the ANC and a couple of Labour MPs. He didn't have a job, of course, but he looked up contacts from his Rhodesian days and soon became a scriptwriter with one of the TV agencies. I was put on to him because someone at the FO – the Foreign and Commonwealth Office it was known as then – remembered him from Rhodesia and felt that his bright new liberal image did not fit the man she'd known in Salisbury. It was about the time that suspicions were growing about BOSS activities in this country – d'you recall the allegations in the Thorpe affair? – so MI5 did a bit of digging and found there were some gaping holes in his story.'

Ashcroft paused in his narrative to walk slowly round the room and study the television monitors as if collecting his thoughts. For the time being he seemed oblivious to the match going on outside.

'We still had some contact with the South African police – the regulars, not BOSS, of course – at the time, and the word came back that the whole thing was a put-up stunt by Keith to get himself out of the country before his creditors caught up with him. Apparently on a salary of a couple of thousand a year he'd managed to run up debts of £25,000 or more. The Mercedes was part of it – it hadn't been actually stolen, but bought on tick and he couldn't keep up the payments. The SA police didn't want him back – the debts were civil and we were welcome to him. They had nothing against him criminally, apart from a couple of unpaid speeding fines.

'There didn't seem much we could do about him. His passport was genuine enough, and unless he misbehaved himself here he was none of our business. However, someone high up must have had more suspicions, because I was taken off duty and temporarily seconded to SB to keep an eye on him. It was a funny sort of a job. They call it surveillance in the spy novels. You do it either from the inside or outside – get to know the bloke like a brother or keep tabs on him without his knowledge. My orders were to do the latter, so I never spoke to him.

'I got to know him pretty well, though, and the one thing William Keith was not was a liberal. He mixed a lot with the London liberal set, buying drinks and so on, and sleeping with any of the girls who would have him, and later on, when he got a job as motor-cycle correspondent of one of the national papers, he travelled a great deal on the Continent, particularly Italy and Germany. He was tall, with an arrogant manner, and always dressed very expensively. He affected a pipe but was virtually a chain-smoker of cigarettes. There was some suspicion he used drugs, but that was before they became fashionable. He certainly drank like a fish, and seemed to have far more money to throw

94

about than most young single men of his class, even with the expenses he pulled down from his paper. He rented a furnished ground-floor maisonette in South Kensington and bought himself an MG sports saloon.'

'All right for some,' murmured Light. Ashcroft did not hear him.

'He was very conscious of security. He showed at least two of his friends a Browning 9mm pistol, and claimed to have been of marksman class at university. He said he was on continual alert lest BOSS "came for him", with heavy hints as to what that meant. And he bought himself a guard dog – a huge German shepherd, Alsatian to me – and kept it half-starved in his flat. No one in the block dared go near it. The milkman even refused to deliver to the outside of the door, lest the dog break through. It was quite a fearsome animal.'

'Where is he buried?' Light asked, jocularly. Ashcroft affected not to notice.

'In the last week I watched him Keith was drunk every night. On the last night I followed him to his door. It was up one of those half-flights of steps in Stanhope Gardens – pretty exclusive area – with a sunken basement, so the front window was about ten feet above the paved basement entrance. He was struggling with his latchkey and the dog was barking inside the door when I left him. Putting a drunk to bed was no part of my brief.

'The next morning when he didn't turn up at the newspaper his desk rang the flat a couple of times but got no reply. They didn't bother – a reputation for drinking is nothing new in Fleet Street – but in the afternoon the News Editor sent a cub reporter round with the message that if Keith didn't turn up for work he was fired. The lad found Keith's body on the stone flags outside the basement. He called the police and the local man found the dog half mad from starvation inside. They had to get the RSPCA to sedate it and take it away. I was brought in, of course, but there was little I could add to the sum of human knowledge. The coroner's verdict was misadventure. He calculated that Keith had been too tight to manage his latchkey, and from some vague marks found on the window ledge had tried to climb in through the window, had slipped and fallen to the ground, knocking himself unconscious and dying of hypothermia. It was in the middle of a freezing spell in February that year. The coroner added some remarks about the dangers of drink to young ambitious men and left it at that. It was a bit of a black mark for me, in that the man I was minding died, but I had long decided that the SB wasn't for me and was only too glad to get back to the safe old CID. My superiors were equally divided in their theories. One side thought that Keith had been double-crossing BOSS and been liquidated; others believed that either the ANC or SWAPO, the Namibian lot, had got fed up with his shopping their best contacts; and still more believed that a European bunch like the Red Brigades had disliked this brash young man making a nuisance of himself on their territory.'

Ashcroft sighed.

'What do I think? I never believed the Africans did it. They weren't sophisticated enough in their methods, then. Now would be a different matter. The European theory was always a bit far-fetched to my mind, but then in those days so was the BOSS theory. White men wouldn't do a thing like that, would they? Certainly not colonials. Our kith and kin. It wasn't suicide – there was no motive, no note, and Keith would never have left the dog to starve. It was the one thing Keith showed any modicum of affection for, apart from himself. No, accident was the convenient way out for everyone.' He looked at Light. 'To answer your question, Amber, the dog was incinerated at Battersea and Keith's body was flown by the South African authorities back to Durban where it, too, was cremated with military honours. Not full military honours, you understand. Just military honours. No one ever asked why. He wasn't even in the army.'

'And he held a British passport,' said Light.

Ashcroft nodded approvingly. 'We didn't inquire any further. The case was closed. But I wondered then, and I still do. I still feel that a man was murdered on my patch and the murderer got away with it.' He looked up at the cherrypicker but said nothing. Behind them the clear voice of WPC Todd spoke two words:

'That's odd.'

Ashcroft woke from his reverie.

'What's odd?' he demanded.

'The picture. It's the wrong one. Normally when they're bowling from that end – the Nursery End – the camera follows the bowler in and closes up on the batsman while he's playing the shot. Then he pulls out to follow the ball into the field.

96

It's the one they do the replays on when there's an lbw appeal or a caught behind. It must have broken down.'

Ashcroft did not move in his chair, but his voice took control.

'Thank you, Todd. Thomas, go and get Forrester, the BBC Outside Broadcast man, here immediately. Tell him to bring down that chairlift or whatever they call it in five minutes precisely. That's an order. If he refuses, arrest him. The BBC will have to carry on without it for the rest of the day. Light, take those two thugs on the door and be on the ground when the cherry-picker comes down. I'll get a doctor there as soon as I can.' He leaned across the table and spoke urgently into the microphone connecting him to the incident room at Scotland Yard. 'Smithson! A dozen men each to the flats overlooking Lord's in St John's Wood Road. They'll be looking for a man or a woman with a rifle or something like it. He or she will be gone, of course, but we've got to do it. Go through every flat with a toothcomb and report anything, anyone out of the ordinary. And ask any prowlers to pick up any suspicious characters in the neighbourhood. And I want a doctor here, by the sightscreen, as soon as possible. A man's been seriously hurt, if not killed. All right, if Heatherington's here, bleep him. Thank you.'

Thomas and Light had left the room with the obedience of long training before Ashcroft finished speaking. WPC Todd, flushed with the knowledge that she, and not one of the men, had triggered off this burst of activity, but only half guessing the importance of her inspired piece of observation, saw that Ashcroft had swung his chair round again and was gazing out at the field of play. Coetzee glanced a lazy ball fine to the edge of the Nursery End sightscreen, but Ashcroft seemed not to notice. WPC Todd ventured a question.

'Excuse me, sir, but do you think the man in the cherrypicker is badly hurt?'

Ashcroft turned his whole body to look at her. As far as she could see his face had not changed; nor had his voice. But she remembered his eyes: cold, grey, policeman's eyes. And his words. She remembered them. 'No, Todd. I think he's dead. And it couldn't happen to a nicer fellow.'

*   *   *

A minute later the lanky figure of Alec Forrester, known through-out the BBC as 'The Imperturbable', leaned his haunches casually against the polished light oak of the TCCB Committee Room's table and inquired: 'What's the hassle, Superintendent? This little man got quite aerated.' He indicated Thomas, perspiring beside him. 'Anything I can do, of course, but I'd be obliged if you would remember that the great British public is outside there watching this in some millions, not to say a considerable proportion of the Australasian sub-continent, and they're likely to ask a few questions if they don't see their favourite shots on the box. So, I may add, are my masters, who've quite a bit of clout with your masters up at Westminster, whatever the Press may say. You can't be throwing all this weight around for nothing. What's up?'

Ashcroft passed him the binoculars. Forrester peered through them at the cherrypicker. He brought the camera into focus and saw collapsed over it, almost cradling it in his arms, the figure of Phillips, motionless with the cowl of his anorak pulled down over is head. Forrester lost some of his laid-back demeanour.

'I'm sorry to disturb your excellent arrangements, Mr Forrester, but I expect confirmation within the next few minutes that your cameraman is dead, probably murdered. That is all you need to know at this moment, and I would be grateful if the rest of Lord's remains in ignorance of the fact at least until after the end of play. You understand I cannot order you to stay silent, although I could hold you here for questioning for an hour or two if I wished.'

Forrester grinned tautly. 'You wouldn't be half so amiable if you were going to arrest me,' he said. 'But I'll stay mum. I'm not a newsman, I'm an OB director with no conscience. Try me.'

'When did Phillips fail to respond to your commands?'

'5.47 precisely. The PAs keep an exact log. We have to work to a second's tolerance on everything – sometimes even closer than that. If there's even a half-second overlap our expert viewers scream 'amateur' at us. To say nothing of the presenters. They think you've cut their balls off if you so much as touch a precious syllable.'

'What happened?'

'Oh, it was the change of overs, from the Pavilion to the Nursery End. I was doing some tricky crowd stuff with cameras 4 and 5 – they're the ground-level ones on the boundary – because everyone was getting bored as hell with the cricket, and I'd put camera 3 – Phillips – onto wide-angle hold and told him to lean back and have a drag for a couple of minutes. You get strangulated eyeballs looking at those tiny screens for long. I like to give them a rest periodically, though I must say Phillips is one of the toughest cameramen around. Anyway, when they started to form up I gave the routine instruction to David to stand by for the over. Not that it was necessary, he wouldn't miss a trick. But this time he did. Nothing happened. No answer over the talkback, no nice change of shot, fade to bowler's back, nothing. I thought he must have been taken ill, had a stroke or something. Or something had gone wrong with his camera controls. So I switched to camera 4 for the run-in from the side and then fudged it with 1 and 2 for the rest of the over. But by then the Inspector here was arresting me, or whatever. So I handed over to Jake and here I am. I say, I hope you're wrong about Phillips. He's one of the best we've got.'

'But you don't like him?'

'Like? What's like got to do with it? He's a bloody good cameraman. They don't grow on trees.'

'What more do you know about him?'

'Not much. You can get it all from Personnel. He is, or was married. There's some form of trouble there. There quite often is with these travelling cameramen. You were asking about that Australian business. With Viner's wife. When I asked him, he said he didn't know anything about it, but Jake, my number 2, reckons it was Phillips himself. I don't think he's got many friends. He's a hard bastard. Likes going to war, wearing flak jackets and all that crap. I think he's a member of a rifle club, or something. I've seen him loading his car with a rifle case once or twice. Never thought anything of it. Quite a lot of the lads have expensive hobbies. They can afford them these days, especially on the road. Ah, down it comes.'

They watched as the long angled arm of the cherrypicker folded in on itself, bringing down its railed-in platform, the still figure slumped over the camera. Through the glasses Ashcroft saw Light's lithe figure leap over the railings, pause, and turn to wave an order at the driver in the cherrypicker's cab. The little platform rose again above the heads of the staring crowds. Light's shocked voice came loud and clear over the hand-held radio.

'Sorry, Mr Ashcroft. You'll have to clear the ground. It was a 45 Magnum. I've seen them in Ulster. There's no back to his head and the platform's swimming in blood. I'm back up here to get away from the crowd.'

England v Australia (Second Day)

Australia (First Innings)

Overnight: 255/6

C.B. Comberton	b Spencer	48
B.F. Rose	not out	36
M. Martin	c Alexander b Spencer	9
G. Jones	c Woodman b Mandell	0
N. Walters	c Alexander b Mandell	16
	Extras	22
	Total	310

Fall of wickets: 7/259, 8/270, 9/271, 10/310

Bowling	O	M	R	W
V.J. Carter	25	8	59	5
D.A. Spencer	28	7	81	2
C.J.A. Bowyer-Smith	22	10	44	0
A.B. Prettyman	15	3	51	0
P.Q. Mandell	15.3	3	53	2

England (First Innings)

A.B. Prettyman	not out	51
F.A. Williamson	c Rose b Walters	0
P. Graham	c Comberton b Walters	4
G. Broadbent	b Smart	13
B. Coetzee	not out	49
	Extras	14
	Total (for 3 wickets)	127

Fall of wickets 1/1, 2/10, 3/27

Bowling	O	M	R	W
N. Walters	14	5	18	2
M. Martin	8	1	36	0
G. Jones	9	2	37	0
S.S. Smart	7	0	22	1

Chapter 4

The Second Evening

By gum, thought Light as he directed the Rover along the A40, squinting into the evening sunlight, Old Bill may look like Rip Van Winkle but he can get a move on when he puts his mind to it. Within five minutes of his frantic radio message, play had been called off for the day, the gawping crowds in the east stands cleared and the remainder of the ground was emptying rapidly. A cordon of uniformed constables formed a ring round the cherry-picker's platform, now on the ground with its flooring soaked in congealing blood. The body of the murdered cameraman had been examined in situ by Dr Heatherington and Detective Chief Superintendent Ashcroft, expertly wrapped in a plastic sheet and removed by a pair of inquisitive ambulancemen. Within half an hour the BBC personnel department had copied its file on David Michael Phillips, TV cameraman deceased, and telexed its contents to the incident room at Lord's. A copy lay in a brown cardboard folder on the passenger seat next to Light.

A woman PC had been despatched from Chalfont St Giles to Number Four, Shire Heights, Phillips' address, which apparently still housed Mrs Sharon Phillips despite the couple's having been formally separated since the previous Christmas. 'It's an odd arrangement,' the crusty old desk sergeant at Chalfont said over the telephone. 'But then she's an odd woman. Tough as they come. He's hardly ever there. Some television job. It's a bit isolated up there on the Heights, so we keep an eye on the properties. Number Four's more like a fortress than a house. All electric gadgets, or so Millie Flower said. She did the cleaning twice a week up there, but she said she couldn't stand Mrs Phillips. Cold as mutton, she said, and that sarcastic. They've got some sort of au pair there now.' The desk sergeant had an encyclopaedic knowledge of his patch and liked to demonstrate it to smart-arses from the smoke.

He had also given minutely accurate directions to the Phillips property and, following them carefully, Light turned off the A40 some distance before Chalfont St Giles itself into a narrow lane flanked by drifts of late-flowering May interspersed with uncut cliffs of bramble and dog roses. The air was warm and balmy, and Light rolled down his window to allow the scent of summer to drift into the car. He pulled over into what he called a lay-by but was in fact a passing-by place for the motor car constructed in 1906, braked gently to a halt and opened the Phillips folder. The information was sparse.

'Phillips, David. Born 1949 in Gwelo, Southern Rhodesia of English emigrant parents, who bought a tobacco farm in Hartley, Southern Rhodesia, in 1958. Educated at Prince Edward School, Salisbury, Southern Rhodesia. Parents both killed in bush war, 1971, while Phillips was in Rhodesian army. After independence he claimed British citizenship and came to London. Joined Samuelsons as electrician/maintenance man. Left after two years with good record to join ITN as soundman/apprentice cameraman. Joined BBC 1977 as cameraman after good work for ITN crews in Israel and Vietnam. Excellent cameraman with penchant for war situations. Herograms for work in Angola, Lebanon and El Salvador. First reserve cameraman for Falklands, but took to sport instead. Excellent at filming cricket, football, rugby. Some reporters think highly of him; others have mixed feelings, particularly Slocombe after the Australia trip, when he was disciplined for making a pass at Mrs Viner, wife of the Australian captain. Slocombe wanted him sent home, but there was no one else to replace him at the time. Married to Sharon Sweet (real name unknown) minor TV soap actress with some blue video experience. Recently thought to be separated but still living in same house. Salary: £30,000 approx, plus another £20,000 minimum on expenses. Hobbies: Shooting (member of the Bucks Shottists), blue movies, sport and, recently, bird photography (the feathered kind). Address: Number Four, Shire Heights, Chalfont St Giles, Buckinghamshire.'

Light returned the sheets to the folder and drove on, watching the road carefully. Even so, he nearly missed the sharp turn into a rutted track dignified by a small overgrown sign, 'The Heights', and winding steeply up through a dense nutwood interspersed with other trees, of which Light could only recognise oak. Number Four seemed to be the last house a long way up the track, standing alone in a sparse clearing in the wood with a small sea of tarmacadam taking the place of a garden. Such seclusion cost money, Light thought. So did the house itself. It presented a long blank wall to the visitor, with a high row of narrow windows tucked tight under low eaves, ranch-style. There were no chimneys, but four large oblong solar panels took up most of the roof space. At one end, the bland blank doors of a double garage gave no hint of occupancy, nor even any sign of a lock; the flat heavy oak front door was unrelieved by a porch and its only ornamentation was the pearl-like button of a spy-hole and a flush bell-push. Light pushed it and heard nothing, but shortly afterwards the door opened, seemingly of its own volition. A fresh-faced girl in police uniform greeted him politely.

'Detective Sergeant Light? WPC Clarke. With an E.' She held out a hand.

Light, slightly amused, shook it.

'No, Sergeant. Your ID, please.'

Light fumbled for his card, mildly angry with himself for placing himself at a disadvantage. He did not like women PCs, particularly efficient ones.

'How has Mrs Phillips taken it?' he asked brusquely.

'If you mean how has she taken the death of her husband, it seems very well. She does not seem to mind whether he is dead or alive.' Despite her efficiency, WPC Clarke could not help sounding shocked at such callousness. Light thought she looked about 18. She added: 'She's very angry.'

'Do you know why?'

'She says it's because of my presence here. She keeps ordering me out of the house and threatening me when I tell her my orders are to stay with her until you arrive.'

'Threatening you?'

'Oh, don't worry, sir. It was nothing I couldn't take care of.'

'Tell me.'

'First she threatened to report me directly to Sir Joshua Clarke, the Chief Constable. She said he is a personal friend. I told her he was my father and suggested she rang Sergeant Dobell on the desk instead. She couldn't get through. Then she threatened to turn her dog loose on me, but I said that wouldn't be any use as I'd just completed six weeks training at the Police Dog School. So she rang her lawyer to demand he come over, poured herself a stiff drink and is sitting in there fuming. I just thought I'd warn you.'

'Thank you, Miss Clarke,' said Light gravely. But when he saw Mrs Sharon Phillips he was inclined to take the situation somewhat more seriously. Once, she had obviously been a very good-looking woman. Now, in her late thirties, she was still striking, sitting upright in a black leather armchair with her legs crossed and holding an empty cut-glass tumbler. Her eyes blazed at him, ignoring his outstretched ID card.

'Now you're here, Sergeant, you can get the hell out of here and take that snotty little bitch with you. You have no right to imprison me in my own home. I have nothing to say to you. My lawyer will be here shortly and he will answer any questions you have.'

Light hitched his haunches on the edge of a plate-glass and steel table and looked down at her.

'Little Dolly Daydream,' he said mildly.

She leaned forward out of the chair, half-lifting the glass, her face contorted.

'You bastard.' She could hardly get the words out.

'Little Dolly Daydream. Frith Street, as I recall. Mary the Milkmaid. Dean Street. Sal the Soho Sucker. Alias Sharon Smith. Five years, you got. They threw the book at you. Prostitution, soliciting, under-age, bestiality, conspiracy, robbery, the lot. No wonder you're so touchy when the law arrives.'

'You bastard. You've got nothing on me. I did my time.'

'Oh yes, you did. But now, lawyer or not, you could be straight down the nick again on a charge of threatening behaviour, obstructing the police, and if you throw that glass, assault. Why don't you just be sensible and answer a few questions? After all, it's not every day you lose a husband. You might show some remorse, at least, or try to.'

'You bastard,' she said again, but to WPC Clarke's surprise her rage seemed to have passed. She got up and refilled her glass with whisky, adding a splash of soda. 'He wasn't my husband,' she said over her shoulder.

'No? But you were living together here as man and wife. Why the play-acting?'

'I dunno. It was all Dave's idea. When I came out he was at the gate. He said he had always remembered my acts, he'd seen every one of them. I didn't remember him, but he said he always used to hang about at the back. You couldn't see a thing in those flea-pits.'

'It's all a bit difficult to believe, Sharon.'

'I know it is, but it's true. He said he wanted me to live here, as a housekeeper he said, but I'd be known as Mrs Phillips. He didn't want sex, he said, but sometimes he'd be having a party, and he'd like to take a few pictures for a blue movie he was making. He said he'd pay me well.'

'How much?'

'Two hundred a week and all found. Extra for the filming. I had to act natural, like I was Mrs Phillips, in the village. He said no one would know me from the past. It was a totally different environment. Smart places like Chalfont would never think of anyone coming from Soho, particularly if they had money.'

'How long has this been going on?'

'Best part of two years now. It's over, of course. I knew it when I saw him being taken off that platform on the telly at the end of the cricket. You couldn't see much, of course, but they said it was a cameraman called Phillips.' She turned to WPC Clarke. 'Then you turned up. And when you said the fuzz was coming down from London I knew for certain. Now I'll be all over the papers again and I won't get a penny.'

'Come off it, Sharon. Your story will be worth a fortune to the grotties. And those pictures. Surely he took stills as well as video.'

She was not listening.

'And he promised to put the house in my name. He said it was worth a half of a million. That was why he told everyone at the Beeb we were separated and getting a divorce. It was supposed to be part of the settlement.'

'Did you have any picture parties?'

'Only two. One last year, one this. They weren't big at all. Just three men. Two girls and me. Two of the men were the same both times. Middle-aged and real crude. The third man was different each time. But big, and young, both of them. We all got drunk and the men had a sniff or two, and Dave suggested I gave them a show with the youngster. The two old men began working on their girls while I gave Dave enough skin shots with the boy to launch a year's centre-page spreads.'

'Where was the camera?'

She pointed round the room.

'There. And there. And there. Dave sat at the table and worked three little remote control buttons. They never noticed.'

'How much did he pay you for the performance?'

'Another thousand. Both times.'

'What did he use the videos for?'

'I never knew. Blackmail, probably. He never told me.'

'Did he enjoy the performance?'

'Enjoy? Dave Phillips never enjoyed anything. He was the coldest bastard under the sun. Except power. He liked to control things, like he did those TV cameras. Mostly he gave me the creeps. But he was away a lot, for the BBC. So I didn't have to put up with him for long. And when he was here he used to spend most of the time in the woods, taking pictures of the birds.'

'I noticed that in his notes. It doesn't sound like him.'

'No, it wasn't. But he said it was a challenge. He'd got a commission from some freelance company to shoot English birds in close-up. He built a hide up in the woods. He took me up there once to show me where it was, to warn me to keep away when he was up there, in case I came barging along with the dog and disturbed the birds in the middle of an important shot. He was like he was about most things. Fierce. And yet cold.'

She shivered.

'Did you sleep together?'

'No, nothing like that. It was strictly business. He's got his own room, and his bathroom, and his workshop, and most of the time he kept them locked. I've got my own rooms.'

'Show us.'

'But I haven't got a key. Millie used to have one, when she came up once a week to clean, but since she's gone Trudi's done them. That's the au pair. She's off tonight. But she doesn't have a key anyway. Dave lets her in when he's here to tidy up. I once asked him what should I do if there was a fire, and he said to let the bloody place burn down, he could do with the insurance.'

'Was he short of the readies, then?'

108

'What, Dave? Not bloody likely. He was rolling in it. The BBC must pay like there was no tomorrow. Look at this lot.'

She gestured round the room. Black leather, chrome and stainless steel furniture, a thick white pile carpet with black sheepskin scatter rugs, a fully stocked bar and a 26-inch television set, video machine and CD player all in a black mahogany console testified to an expensive taste, if not, Light thought, everyone's. He recognised the glass she was still holding. He'd been admiring a set of them in Selfridge's windows, six priced at £240. He was glad she hadn't thrown it at him. He produced Phillips' key ring from his pocket.

'It doesn't matter. I've come equipped. Let's go.'

But before they could move there was a ring at the door. The woman pressed a button and the television screen sprang to life, showing the distorted head and shoulders of a youngish man in a grey suit. She relaxed visibly.

'It's Leslie. Leslie Garner. My lawyer.' She smiled ingratiatingly at WPC Clarke. 'Let him in for me, there's a love. Leslie likes them young.' She turned to Light. 'He can go round with you. He was Dave's lawyer too. He drew up our contract. He can tell you all about it.'

Leslie Garner could tell them all about it. He was, judged Light, in his early thirties, expensively dressed by Savile Row in a manner that proclaimed the jet set, and he adopted a proprietorial attitude at once.

'Sharon, my dear, what can I say? It's so dreadful for you.' He hastened across the room and took her arm. 'I hope the police haven't been bullying you. I have ways of dealing with things like that.' He glared theatrically across the room at Light. 'I hope you haven't been telling him anything you shouldn't.'

Sharon seemed alarmed. Light thought she looked frightened.

'Oh, no Leslie,' she said hastily. 'I wouldn't, you know that. Just about Dave and me, and our agreement. You know, the one you drew up.'

Light said: 'Miss Smith told me that you would be able to clarify the agreement between her and Mr Phillips, Mr Garner. As I understand it, she was to live here as his wife, but in fact act as housekeeper to him for a salary of £200 a week, and he would place this house in her name.'

109

Garner looked quickly down at Sharon.

'That's right. What about it?'

'It seems to be both a curious arrangement and a curiously generous one.'

'That was his business.'

'Did you advise him?'

'Mr Phillips was not the sort of man to take advice. Nor was I his conscience. He paid me well enough for my legal services.'

'What were they, apart from drawing up this agreement?'

'So far, nothing much. I've only known him for a couple of years. I acted for him in the purchase of this house and vetted his BBC contract. He hinted that there would be much more lucrative work in the near future.'

'What sort of work?'

'He didn't say, but I gathered it was in the field of contracts.'

'Do you know anything about cricket, Mr Garner?'

'Not a thing. I thought leg glances went out with miniskirts.'

Sharon pulled his arm urgently.

'It is all right. Everything's all right, isn't it? About the agreement. The house is mine now, isn't it?'

Garner smiled down at her, moving his hand from her arm and placing it around her shoulders. 'Of course it is, my dear.' He gave her a little hug. 'As the putative Mrs Phillips, you have nothing to worry about. Unless you took a gun to Lord's today and blew his head off, in which case the law here might have something to say about it.'

Light said nothing. Miss Smith had shown less reaction to the callous suggestion than to the idea that she might have said too much. He got to his feet.

'Unless you have anything more constructive to contribute to this case, Mr Garner, I suggest you go home.'

'No! No! Leslie, please stay. I . . . I need your help.' Sharon's voice was breathless. Garner showed no signs of moving. He planted his feet more squarely and his arm slipped from Sharon's shoulders to her waist.

'Now don't you worry one little bit,' he said, as if he was reassuring a child. 'The sergeant here was only joking. Weren't you, Sergeant?'

'No, sir, I wasn't joking. But if Miss Smith wants you here as her legal adviser, I won't object. I was just about to look around the house. Perhaps you'd like to come with me, Mr Garner. WPC Clarke can stay with Miss Smith if she would prefer to remain here.'

The house was surprisingly large for a single-storey residence, built in the form of a curved capital E. Garner seemed to know his way around. Three main rooms opening on to the carpeted hallway and the entrance hall made up the backbone of the E, with a large modern kitchen and the au pair's bedroom taking up the central bar. At each end suites of three rooms and a bathroom backed off the hallway, making the curious living arrangements of the Phillips household at least feasible. Light noted that of the rooms occupied by Sharon Smith only two – the bedroom and the bathroom – showed signs of use, with the bedclothes pulled back, underclothes scattered here and there, a cupboard door half-open showing dresses and coats untidily on hangers. Another cupboard was locked, with no key visible, but Light found a small key on Phillips' ring which fitted. He swung the door open and stood back, surveying an array of leather and rubber clothing, a harness-like arrangement of leather straps, a pair of handcuffs, a schoolgirl's green uniform and a boater. Leaning against the wall were three riding crops and a long vicious-looking whip, apparently made of a continuous piece of leather.

Light looked at his companion. Mr Garner had lost his air of sophisticated superiority and was staring with open eyes at the collection.

'Tools of the trade,' Light said. 'There'll be more in the drawers. Does it shock you?'

'No. I've read about such things, of course. But Sharon? She couldn't . . .' He gulped and licked his lips.

Light said: 'Oh yes she could. And did. I've known your Mrs Phillips for ten years, Mr Garner, since I was on the vice squad in Soho. There wasn't anything she wouldn't do. And I mean anything. Whatever Phillips got her down here for, it wasn't to play housey-housey. Will this so-called agreement really stand up in court?'

Garner gulped again. 'I can't, I can't believe it. But yes, Sergeant, it is a legal document, and genuine. The house and all its contents are hers.' He seemed to be recovering fast. 'Poor girl. I think I'd better go to her.'

111

'You can do that when we've looked over the rest of the house, Mr Garner. She's all right with WPC Clarke. You stay with me. I need a witness that I haven't nicked any of the silver.'

But the rest of the house seemed as though it would yield nothing for Light's interest, until they came to Phillips' own rooms. Like the remainder of the house, they were expensively decorated and furnished in the stark modern Scandinavian style with a preponderance of glass and chrome, but they revealed very little of Phillips' personality.

His few clothes were good, but workmanlike. Two well-worn safari suits testified to his time in warmer climes; two camouflage anoraks spoke of experience with the American or Israeli forces; and a kapok-lined all-over flying suit matched the sets of thermal underwear which could do duty in the Antarctic or even, Light reflected, on the goal-line at Wembley in the snow.

The rooms had the air of being occupied by an experienced traveller, ready to move at less than a moment's notice. There was a desk in the living-room, but that yielded nothing but a fairly new passport, with Phillips' occupation described only as 'director', the media man's way of avoiding the potentially embarrassing questions 'journalist' or 'television cameraman' might evoke in many a suspicious immigration officer.

A small stack of magazines proved to contain nothing more incriminating than *Electronics*, *The Metalworker*, and *Guns and Ammo Annual* which carried an article entitled 'The Return of the Crossbow', and a six-year-old copy of *Knave*. The centre-spread of the latter comprised a totally revealing photograph in full colour of a much younger Sharon Smith, or 'Susie Bedworth', as she had apparently been called in those days. There was also, tucked into a small pocket of the desk so well-hidden it might almost have been termed a secret drawer, a flat black plastic oblong about the size of a small packet of chocolate with no apparent function or means of opening.

'That's an electronic key,' Garner said by his side. 'It opens the workshop door. I've seen Dave use it before. You just point it at the door.' Light did as suggested, and the door swung open with a subdued clicking sound.

'Clever people, these Chinese,' he murmured fatuously to

himself. But when his eyes swept quickly round the room he could not suppress a long low whistle.

'Impressive, isn't it?' Garner's voice at his side was curiously triumphant. 'Dave was a real craftsman. He could do anything with his hands.'

Certainly the workshop was well equipped. Along one wall ran a steel workbench, with a small arsenal of metal-working tools ranged in racks above it. A powerful lathe occupied one end of the bench and there was a full set of electric welding and cutting equipment. Light thought Garner's words were accurate. This was a craftsman's set-up.

Four small but obviously powerful crossbows stood in one corner, seemingly discarded, while the broken-down pieces of a fifth had been thrust out of the way under the bench. But the object held delicately in the velvet-lined half-cups of a vice monopolised Light's attention. It was a steel tube, about 30 inches in length and just under two inches in diameter. One end was open, and Light could see the rifling plainly on the inside. The other end of the tube was welded into an oblong steel box, plain except for a small steel button protruding from the rear end and a small lever from the right-hand side. Light touched the button gingerly. It moved, but nothing happened. He tried the small lever, but he was only able to move it a fraction of an inch with his fingers. He found a steel ball-point pen on the bench, unscrewed the barrel and fitted it over the lever. With the greater leverage, he found he could use the barrel as a pump-handle, working it back and forth until a click told him he could go no further. He pressed the button again, and the compressed air spat explosively down the tube. So this was how Jack Viner had been killed. This was the home-made air rifle so well described by Superintendent Armitage. But how was it loaded? There was no breech. It must be a muzzle-loader, like the old-fashioned cannon.

Oblivious of Garner who was watching him in fascination, Light cast about him for fresh ideas. A plastic box on the bench held half a dozen ball-bearings. He tried one in the barrel, but although it almost fitted, it was too small. It rolled of its own volition down the barrel. No good. What had Armitage said? 'A soft plastic or leather sabot.' In the bottom of the box were six three-inch squares of chamois leather. Wrapping one round a ball-bearing he put it in the mouth of the barrel. It fitted so snugly he could not force it down, but when he pumped the little handle the suction drew the bearing and its sabot into the barrel. He did not try to load the barrel to full pressure, but halted after two pumps on the handle. Holding a cushion over the end of the barrel he pressed the firing button again and the ball-bearing flew out, striking the cushion with considerable force. The sabot fell to the floor.

He knew now how it was fired. But how was it held? It had no stock. How was it aimed? It had no sight, not even a simple open sight, let alone the necessary telescopic one. Surely it was too crude a weapon to be used as Light knew it must have been? And would not the cameraman have placed himself at obvious risk, even though every single person at Lord's could be guaranteed to be watching the first over of the Test match, and not the antics of the television cameraman 30ft above their heads? But there might always be an inquisitive small boy, with his eyes in the air. And what about the BBC TV men themselves? Surely the director, PA or someone would notice if Phillips was not at his camera, zooming in to coordinate with the bowler's run-up to the wicket? In any case, he *had* been at his camera. Everyone had commented on the quality of his camera work.

Light hit himself gently on the side of the head. Zooming in. That was it. Perhaps, somehow, Phillips had used the videocamera as the sight. Its 2,000/1 zoom lens was as accurate as any telescope. And Phillips was an expert. He must have fitted the air rifle to the camera with some form of clamp, and practised somewhere until he could guarantee to hit the precise target at which he was aiming.

Light examined the barrel minutely. He found a fine line scratched about halfway along it, but that was all. There was nothing else in the workshop to give any clues, except two short sawn-off pieces of aluminium rod. He would have to leave it at that until he could examine Phillips' camera car and equipment. Perhaps the mystery could be solved then.

Elated by his discoveries, Light carefully wrapped the home-made air rifle in a blanket and found a plastic bag for the box of ball-bearings. There was nothing more he could do here.

He looked at his watch. Eight-thirty. He hadn't eaten all day, except for a sandwich. Perhaps WPC Clarke would know of a decent restaurant in Chalfont. His side of the investigation was nearly over. Now it was up to Old Bill to decide where they went from here. Bloody awkward, having your murderer murdered just as you were about to arrest him.

'Sergeant?' Garner's high voice broke into his reverie. The lawyer was leaning against the end of the workbench, looking slightly sick. 'Is that – weapon – lethal?'

'Yes it is, Mr Garner, but you needn't let it concern you, unless you helped Phillips make it.' He felt he owed the man one for his callousness towards Sharon Smith. Garner began a hasty denial of the imputation, but Light did not listen. Taking his trophies, he led the way from the workroom, letting the door close and lock behind them.

'Forensic will have to go over this with a toothcomb, so I'm taking this gadget,' he said, pocketing the electronic key. 'I'm going to lock these other rooms too, and I'm phoning for a constable to keep watch until they arrive. Do you have any objections as Mrs Phillips' – Miss Smith's lawyer?'

'No, of course not. None at all. And thank you, Sergeant. I've found it all most interesting.' Strangely, he seemed to be sincere. 'I have never watched an investigation in the flesh before.'

'Well, I don't have to tell you not to talk in the bar – either sort – until the case is over, Mr Garner. I don't have to remind you that you're a material witness.'

'Indeed. But now I must concern myself with Miss Smith's legal interests. I am acting for her, you know.'

'I know, Mr Garner. I wish you luck with them.'

'What do you mean?'

'Nothing,' said Light, suddenly weary. He opened the door of the living-room to see Sharon Smith and WPC Clarke sitting in the chairs where he had left them. It reminded him that only ten minutes had passed. He told them what was happening, and left Garner to make what explanations he felt necessary to his client. The lawyer's motives might be obvious, but Light nearly found it possible to regret what was going to happen to him.

'Come along, Miss Clarke,' he said. 'Time we were on our way. We can let ourselves out.'

They had reached the front door when the WPC stopped him.

'Sergeant,' she said. He realised it was the first word she had uttered in his hearing since they entered the house. 'Sergeant. Excuse me, but there is something that is worrying me.'

She was slightly flushed. Light thought she looked about 17, and determined. It made him gruff.

'Well?' He hadn't meant it to come out as a bark. She went on as though she hadn't heard him.

'It's just that Mr Phillips' hobby was supposed to be filming and photographing birds. But there wasn't a single picture of a bird in that house. I looked while you were in the workshop. Did you see any?'

'No, but what does it matter? She knew it was his hobby, the Beeb knew. He even had a hide up in the woods. What the hell d'you think he might have been doing up there? Come on, let's go,' he said impatiently.

'Well, if you don't think it matters, sir.'

Light stopped with his hand on the door lock.

'Jesus!' he said angrily. Then: 'Jesus!' again in a totally different tone. He strode swiftly back to the living-room, ignoring the fact that Garner and Sharon Phillips were sharing the same settee, with very little space between them.

'Sharon,' he said. 'Where is this hide in the woods? I'm just going to have a look at it.'

'Out of the gate, turn left along the track and take the left fork. You come to a firebreak and it's along on the right about 50 yards. Up a tree. You'll see the ladder. Do you want me to show you?' She sounded reluctant.

'No thank you, we'll find it. Good evening,' he said impartially, and left them.

The sun was going down, but it was still a warm evening with plenty of light as they walked up the path. WPC Clarke took off her uniform hat and shook her head to make the short black curls tumble to her collar. Light thought she looked about 15. He imagined other walks through the woods, which had nothing to do with a murder inquiry.

'Constable Clarke,' he said stiffly.

'Yes, sir?' She sounded perfectly matter-of-fact.

'I apologise for what I said just now. You were quite right.'

116

'It's nothing, sir.'

They did not speak again until they found the fork in the track, and the firebreak.

'There's the ladder,' she said. 'Come on.'

She broke into a run in front of him, holding her hat in her hand. He followed more sedately, and found her standing at the foot of the ladder ruefully examining her legs.

'Damn,' she said cheerfully. 'Another pair gone. All in a good cause. Come on.'

She set foot on the ladder.

'Aren't you coming?'

'You go on up and tell me what you find. I don't think there'll be much up there to see, but I've an idea I want to put to the test.'

'Hmm,' WPC Clarke looked at him speculatively as if about to say something, but decided against it and began to climb briskly up the ladder. Light found himself watching the black-stockinged legs until he reminded himself sharply that he was on duty. When he looked up again she was out of sight among the branches. He heard a scuffling and called out, 'Are you all right, Constable?'

A disembodied voice answered, between breaths.

'Yes, OK. But the last bit's tricky . . . the ladder stops short of the platform and I've got to climb up the tree . . . I'll have to put in for a new uniform as well . . . here we go.'

'Be careful,' he called. She did not answer, but after a minute or two her voice came seemingly from much higher.

'It's all right Sergeant, I'm here. It's not difficult. Do you want to come up?' Light felt the voice carried a faintly mocking tone. He shouted back, 'No, tell me what you can see.'

'It's just a bare platform of planks about six feet square. It's pretty solid. Nailed onto poles between the branches and the trunk. About 30 feet up. Fairly level. No sides or roof. Not like any hide I've seen. There are two, no three holes about an inch wide drilled in the platform, in a triangle. About three feet apart. That's all. I can't see much for the leaves, except in one direction where there's a gap in the branches.'

'What can you see there?'

'I'm looking down to the other side of the windbreak. About a hundred yards or so. Nothing else but trees.'

'Hang on. I'm going over there and I want you to call if I'm going in the right direction for your line of sight.'

'All right.'

Light headed out across the freshly growing bracken of the firebreak, counting his strides. He had not progressed more than 30 paces when her voice called out: 'I can see you now. Head a bit right . . . That's it. Go straight now.'

The ground underfoot was rough with occasional brambles, and Light could not see where to put his feet, but he kept an even pace as best he could. He calculated that he had gone about 140 paces diagonally across the firebreak before he came to the trees on the other side. He turned and looked back, cupping his mouth in his hands.

'Can you still see me?'

'Yes.' The answer floated high and clear on the evening air.

'Come down here, Constable!' He made beckoning signs with both arms and saw her hand waving in response. He turned to inspect the wood. He realised now what he had missed before – that on this side of the firebreak the wood was no longer indigenous. Twenty years ago or more a plantation of spruce had been laid out, and fairly well maintained. Now the trunks marched in straight lines about five yards apart under their dark covering of pine needles. Each was about 18 inches in diameter. He began to examine each trunk carefully. A dishevelled WPC Clarke joined him.

'What are you looking for, Sergeant? Can I help?'

Light turned from the tree he was inspecting with minute attention.

'Thank you, Constable. I don't think so. I think I've found what I was looking for. See for yourself.'

She came forward curiously. The bark of the spruce was pockmarked with small holes about 1½ inches in diameter, and here and there the bark had been chipped off. Around the edges of the holes were tiny flakes of some grey material. Light poked a forefinger into one of the holes.

'Feel down there,' he said. WPC Clarke inserted a cautious finger, and felt something smooth and rounded. 'It feels like a stone. Or a marble,' she said, puzzled.

'It's a ball-bearing' said Light with grim satisfaction. 'This is where he practised.' He pointed to the flakes of grey round the holes. 'I think he came up here with his camera and his home-made air rifle, and practised. He pinned a target up against the tree, climbed up to his platform, and fired away until he perfected his aim. He was a marksman, after all. We must get Forensic down here as well.'

He was gratified with her response. WPC Clarke, whose only knowledge of the case so far was that Mr Phillips had been grue-somely murdered at Lord's, had no idea what he was talking about, but the triumph in his voice was unmistakable, and she had no wish to spoil the moment. She looked at him with wide grey eyes and asked him to explain, which he did as they walked back to their cars in the gathering dusk.

He spoke on the radio and learnt that the forensic team had just finished at Lord's and would be with him shortly, and Detective Chief Superintendent Ashcroft suggested he found somewhere to eat. It looked like a long night. Light had done well but he, Ashcroft, had had no luck. He had gone with Cousins to the Churchill Hotel to find that Mr Du Plooy and his friend had checked out that morning, leaving no forwarding address. Mr Ashcroft would be at Heathrow's Terminal Three for breakfast at 7.30 am. He would see Light there.

Light signed off resignedly. It did look like a long night. WPC Clarke had contacted her station, and said she expected her relief at any moment. She had brushed most of the lichen from climbing the tree off her uniform, but there was a slight rip in her skirt, her shoes were scuffed and a strong ladder ran up from her right knee. She had her hat on again, but her hair curled rebelliously under its severe brim. Light thought she looked about 14. He grinned at her.

'St Trinians?' he said.

WPC Clarke flushed slightly, but grinned back at him.

'One doesn't expect to go climbing trees in regulation dress,' she said with dignity. 'But I must admit I enjoyed it. If you've got to spend the night here, there isn't much in the village. You'd do better to drive up to Aylesbury. I'll get Sergeant Dobell to book you in and ask them to save you some supper, if you like.'

'That would be very kind of you.'

While she was on the radio again two more police cars drove up the track and parked alongside them. Inspector Harris and his forensic team from the Yard alighted from one and began decanting their cameras and boxes of equipment. The other contained a fresh-faced PC from the village, who greeted them cheerfully.

'Evening, Sergeant. Found your lot looking lost down the road, so I brought them up. Hullo, Jilly. What have you been up to? No, don't tell me. Off you go. It's past your bedtime.'

WPC Clarke looked mutinous. Light had no wish to get involved with a domestic spat, so he said: 'Good evening, Constable. What took you so long? Constable Clarke has been helping me. Thank you very much, Miss Clarke. You've been of great assistance indeed. I shall be putting that in my report.'

'Thank you, Sergeant,' she said. 'It was a good thing you remembered the hide, wasn't it? I'm glad you found what you wanted. D'you know, when you told me to climb that ladder, I thought you were going to say you had no head for heights. Goodnight, Sergeant.'

'Goodnight, Constable.'

As he led the way into the house he felt grateful that he had not invited her to dine with him that night. Detective Sergeant Light of the Met could not be sure what her response might have been.

At about the same time, 30,000ft over the Indian Ocean, Mrs Julie Viner switched on her overhead light and opened her briefcase. She felt desperately weary, but she could not sleep. She rang for the Concorde steward and ordered two Paracetamol and a cup of black coffee. She wanted to check that everything was in order in her mind, as well as in the voluminous files, before she saw Scotland Yard in the morning. She owed it to Jack. Poor Jack. She owed everything to Jack, her children, even her life. Now Jack was gone and she had to take up the battle. Once, in a depressed mood, he had said to her: 'If anything happens to me, it'll be up to you, Julie.' And she had laughed him off, saying that nothing could happen to the captain of the Australian cricket team. But now he was dead, and although the papers said he'd been killed by a bouncer, she knew it wasn't true. The British police would tell her, and perhaps they would believe what she had to tell them. She turned to the briefcase.

Chapter 5

The Third Day

The snack bar at Terminal Three at Heathrow was one very good reason why Terminal Four had to be built, Light thought as he scanned the rows of round plastic tables. Cramped at the end of the narrow crowded ground-floor concourse opposite the bookstall and the entrance to the public conveniences, it offered no view except the huddled pushing backs of spectators waiting impatiently to welcome their relations from the far-flung corners of the earth. The ventilation seemed inadequate to deal with the stale smell of cigarette smoke, the seating designed to fit a race of pygmies. Yet there was the familiar figure of Detective Chief Superintendent Ashcroft of the CID contentedly tucking into bacon and eggs and signalling Light to join him.

'Morning, Amber. Busy night?'

'Not too bad, sir.' Light had finally crawled into bed in the Aylesbury Duckling at three o'clock in the morning, having washed down a round of dry ham sandwiches with a bottle of semi-warm lager, to be awakened at 6 am by a bright young man who identified himself as Assistant Floor Manager Perkins and presented Light with a bill for bed and breakfast of £50, plus £5 for sandwiches and beer and room service, plus VAT, and the information that breakfast was not served until 7.30 am. At least the shower was piping hot, and Light had driven shaved, clean and hungry to Heathrow. Ashcroft sipped his coffee patiently while Light satisfied his more urgent appetite. Then, 'I gather things went well, Amber.'

'Very well, sir. We can prove Phillips killed Viner, and how he did it. Inspector Harris found one of those tubular document cases in his BBC Volvo, with BBC markings on it and the gun barrel inside it. And a light aluminium clamp with padded feet in the bottom of the camera case. It looked like another piece of genuine equipment. We fitted it up, sir, at two o'clock this morning, and the clamp fits exactly to the markings on the air rifle and on the camera. Harris said it would be easy for Phillips to fix up an accurate sight on the camera lens – the old reflex manual cameras had a pinpoint focus for clarity, and Phillips had been trained by Samuelsons, the electrical equipment people, and they don't come any better than that. They took torches to the woods and dug out two of the ball-bearings from the fir tree, and they're identical to the one that killed Viner. Harris reckons they come from one of the old Sheffield firms who supply Rolls-Royce and people like that, and he's checking this morning. We found some cardboard targets in the house. And the holes in the platform that Constable Clarke described fit exactly the feet of Phillips' camera tripod. They're the old-fashioned spiked sort. I think that wraps it up, sir.'

'Not quite yet, Light. Remember the Bible. And the Lord said: Faith, Hope and Charity; and the greatest of these is Charity. We've the murderer, the method, but not the all-important motive. We've solved the simple problem. Now we have to find whoever murdered our murderer. Which is why we're here now and not a soft and sympathetic delegation from the world of cricket. Mrs Julie Viner is coming to see us, not Lord Holmbush, and certainly not your Mr Cousins, to whom I have taken a palpable dislike. Come along, if you've finished. Concorde is about to deliver us an avenging angel.'

There was very little delay. British Airways treat Concorde passengers as though they are gold-dust, which probably reflects the premium paid on each seat. Ashcroft and Light waited in a small glassed-in booth behind the row of immigration officials the international traveller encounters after he has collected his luggage and before he goes through Customs. They saw the nearest immigration officer check the passport of a tall slim woman in black, smile at her, and indicate she should wait. She nodded and stood aside, and at the same time a red light flashed in their booth.

'Have you ever reflected, Amber, that so much of our efficiency depends on the quite arbitrary infringement of personal rights?' Ashcroft murmured, but before he could answer they had reached Mrs Viner. Light caught his breath. She was, quite simply, the most beautiful woman he had ever seen. Beneath her elegant black hat her jet-black hair fitted her head and neck like a bathing-cap, in a style which harked back to his grandfather's day, but which on her looked as modern as spacecraft. The dark shadows of tiredness failed to conceal the liquid black blaze of her eyes or the perfection of her skin, the symmetry of her face or the line of her throat; just as the high-necked black dress failed to conceal the figure that moved so lithely underneath it. There was an impression of electricity, tightly under control. Light thought Ashcroft's mundane greeting quite inadequate for the occasion. He would have preferred a trumpet voluntary.

'Good morning, Mrs Viner. We are from Scotland Yard. I am Detective Chief Superindendent Ashcroft and this is Detective Sergeant Light. We are very sorry to meet you in these circumstances, but I am sure you understand that we have to question you and at the same time are most anxious to receive the information you have said you are ready to offer us.'

'Thank you, Chief Superintendent.' She shook them both by the hand and Light had the impression of drowning in a pool of black pearls as their eyes met. But there was nothing soft in her words when they had settled into the car, Light driving with Julie Viner beside him in the front passenger seat, Ashcroft in the rear. He could just see her profile in the periphery of his vision.

'Have you got the bastard?' The word stood out harshly in her soft Australian accent.

Light was glad that Ashcroft answered. His own tongue seemed to be glued to the roof of his mouth.

'Yes, Mrs Viner, we know who killed your husband. Sergeant Light here proved that last night. But unfortunately someone else got there before we did. The murderer was killed himself late yesterday afternoon.'

She did not seem interested.

'Who is he? Who is the bastard?'

'The man who killed your husband? A television cameraman called Phillips. David Phillips. I believe you met him once?'

She laughed shortly, a machine-gun burst.

'Him? That shit? I told Jack he should have finished him.'

'What happened? We know there was an incident at a party on the last cricket tour.'

'Incident? Incident?' She was scornful. 'The bastard got me in a corner and made a heavy pass at me. That was nothing. I can cope with that. Most white men like to have a go at an Abo. Am I shocking you? It's true. But I didn't want to have a scene at Jack's party, because there were Press about, and in any case I thought this guy was one of the cricketers. That would have been asking for a real scandal. So I let him down lightly, and went out to get some fresh air. But he took that as a come-on and followed me. He was drunk, of course, but quite cold. Remorseless. He backed me round the pool to behind the changing rooms, telling me exactly what he was going to do to me, and what I was going to do to him. He seemed to delight in calling me a black whore.'

'You were frightened.' It was a statement rather than a question.

'Scared out of my mind. He was much stronger than I was. He swung me round and got an arm round my neck, half-throttling me so I couldn't call out. He lifted the back of my dress and was just starting to . . . when Jack hit him across the back of the neck and pulled him away. He never stood a chance. Jack hit him three, four times across the face and then kicked him as hard as he could in the . . . between the legs. This Phillips just lay there bleeding and moaning and clutching at himself. I said: "Finish him, Jack" and Jack picked him up and threw him in the pool. He tried to shout and struggle, but Jack knelt down and held his head under the water.'

The animation went out of her voice.

'And then everyone came rushing out and pulled Jack off. They treated it as a drunken brawl and as most of them were tight by this time everybody agreed to hush it up. Most of them thought it was a bit of a joke, anyway. But someone passed the word to the BBC that this man Phillips was not to be trusted on tour.'

She turned and looked Ashcroft fully in the eyes.

'You say someone killed him? I'm glad. If you had caught him you'd have sent him to jail for a few years and pampered him, and then let him go. If I'd got there first I would have killed him myself, but slowly, ever so slowly. He was evil. So evil. Do you believe me?'

'Yes Mrs Viner, I do. But I am not concerned with morality, only the law. In my eyes the person who killed your husband's murderer is equally guilty and it is equally important that he is brought to justice. It seems a patent fact that the two murders are linked, and I believe you may be able to help me establish that link. Do you think you can?'

'I don't know,' she said dully, all passion spent. 'When I heard Jack had been killed I thought – when I could think – I knew why.

That's why I'm here. But now you've told me who did it I don't know. It might have been revenge for what Jack did to him, or hatred, or anything. I must think.'

She lay back in the seat and rested her head, her eyes closed. Ashcroft said nothing, and presently she spoke to Light.

'Take me to Claridges, please, Sergeant. I won't run away, I promise you, but I must have time to think.'

They drove on in silence through the thickening London rush hour. She refused their offers of assistance and strode through the modest doors of London's most expensive establishment for those who can afford solitary luxury, with a mere nod to the doorman who took her suitcase. Light did not know why, but he thought she had the air of a tiger on the prowl. He whistled.

'I don't know what you mean by that, Amber, but if it's what I think it means, I forgive you. Mrs Viner is a remarkable woman. Go and see her this afternoon. She's making up her mind whether to unburden her problem on me, the father figure, or you, the man who is going to avenge her. I don't mind which, but if you see her by herself you might help her come to a decision. Do you find her attractive?'

'Well, er, she's a good-looking woman, sir,' said Light, taken aback. 'But I don't think I've ever let that get in the way of an investigation before.'

'Then keep it that way.' Light had the impression that Ashcroft was going to say something else.

'I'm never likely to be anyone's knight in shining armour,' he said lightly. 'I'm too old, don't you think, sir?'

'Nothing would surprise me more, Amber, but you never can tell. There were times when we were driving in from the airport that I had the impression your attention might not have been strictly on the road.'

Light flushed despite himself. He changed the subject.

'How do you think she can help us, sir?'

'I think that is what you will find out when you see her this afternoon. Let us get along to Lord's. I want to see half an hour's play, at least. Then I'm off to Chelmsford. I'm going to talk to Mrs Carter – Vincent's mother. And I want you to talk to Alexander, the England wicketkeeper. He's batting when the next wicket falls, so wait until he's out. It shouldn't be too long. He's not the batsman he used to be, and Imrie's too old a hand not to know how to get him out.'

'How on earth do you know that, sir? You should be out there skippering England. In any case, you said only yesterday that you could never predict what would happen in cricket.'

Ashcroft said mildly: 'That's quite right. But I have a certain pricking of my thumbs, Amber, that things are beginning to move. There's a nip in the air today. England may well have their backs up against it by the end of the morning. If I were a betting man, Amber, I'd lay you five to one in new pound coins that England are all out by lunchtime.' His voice changed abruptly. 'Watch the road, Sergeant!'

Light braked sharply, swerved and missed a wandering cyclist by six inches.

'Sorry, sir,' he said. 'But did I hear you offer me a bet?'

'No, Amber, I'm not a betting man, as you very well know. But if you go down to the betting shop at the Nursery End before play starts, you might well place a pound for yourself on the unlikely event of my being right, and I think you'll get better odds than five to one. You might also learn something of cricketers' gambling habits at first hand while you're there.'

'If I lose can I claim, sir?'

'On expenses? No. But if you win, we will share a good bottle of claret when this case is over. At your expense.'

'Oh, well,' said Light resignedly, and flicked the indicator switch preparatory to turning into St John's Wood Road.

Lord's Cricket Ground on a sunny Saturday morning of an evenly poised June Test match against an Australian XI has a special excitement all of its own. The anachronisms, the architectural paradox of Victorian Gothic and late Twentieth-Century concrete; the amazing spring green of the playing surface itself, mown in militarily exact bands of light and dark; the early jostling for plastic cushions, scorecards and plastic pints of beer; the cheerful banter and the hectoring stewards; the arrogant male-only-ness of the pavilion, with its pomposity of moustaches and ripe red countenances; all these meld in the sunlight into an atmosphere of anticipation any cricket-lover could almost reach out and touch.

Today there was an extra tension in the crowd, superimposed by the devastating second death of this Test match, and fuelled by the most lurid speculation the tabloids could muster in six-inch-tall headlines.

Ashcroft glanced at them. 'TEST KILL No 2!' was the *Sun*'s. 'WHO IS NEXT?' screamed the *Daily Express*. 'STOP THIS MASSACRE!' ranted the *Star*, rather short on ideas, for it was identical to the headline used three times during the last Test series against the West Indies. But the more thoughtful newspapers, too, were beginning to display an impatience with both the cricket authorities and the police. Several articles speculated on some form of link between the two killings, and one more enterprising reporter had put together a theory that Moscow had engineered the murders to discredit the Western world's most prestigious sporting event. He had apparently been told by a 'high Western diplomatic source who did not wish to be identified' that the last Communist Party conference in the Kremlin had decided in secret conclave to launch an all-out attack on Britain's traditional institutions. 'Destabilisation begins from the top', the hierarchy had been told, according to the article, which opined that only typical Soviet inefficiency had saved the Queen from being the victim of the second murder, leaving the unfortunate Phillips to receive the assassin's bullet.

With a sigh, Ashcroft told Inspector Thomas to schedule a Press conference for 12 noon, in time for the one o'clock news bulletins and for the main afternoon editions of the evening papers. Fifteen minutes only for a short statement and questions, and no special interviews for television or radio; it was too early in the investigation.

Then he told Thomas he was not to be disturbed and settled down to watch an hour's cricket, just as the Australian team trotted briskly out from the pavilion behind their acting captain, Imrie, throwing a ball about between them with an air of collective purpose that boded ill for the England batsmen. Ashcroft wondered if Light had placed the suggested bet.

Imrie, indeed, was coming into his own as a captain in the crisis. He was a quiet competent man who had been content for five years to play for his country under Jack Viner, the natural leader. Viner had inspired an Australian revival after the depredations of the

127

Packer revolution and the lure of gold on the Rand had threatened to destroy the foundations of cricket in his country. Imrie admired his drive and his outspoken courage, without ever trying to emulate them; but the wiser heads on the Australian Cricket Board knew that much of Viner's success was due to Imrie's patient support and his often deep analysis of the game. Viner's death had saddened him deeply, and the shocking subsequent knowledge that his captain had been murdered sparked a smouldering fury that developed into a determination to complete the job Jack Viner had begun. Immediately, that was to beat England and restore the mythical Ashes to their rightful owners. Other things might come later. That would be enough for now.

He had tried to impart something of what he felt at the morning's team talk and during their customary hour at the nets before the game. Like Viner, he had little regard for the manager, Cousins, who had been forbidden by the late skipper to have anything to do with the cricketing side of the tour and was used by the whole team as a booking agent and baggage man.

'You answer to me from here on. No one else,' he told them. 'I'll answer to the Board. You don't talk to the Press – by God you don't – and you'll talk to the cops only if I'm there with you. Anyone who forgets this will be on the next plane home. If you think you've got anything to say, say it to me first and I'll decide. Jack was an Aussie skipper, and we don't want the Poms muscling in on an Aussie problem. Now come along with me. I want to show you something.'

He led them onto the little balcony looking out over the ground. It was just after nine o'clock and the Lord's groundsmen were beginning to remove the covers. Although the sun was shining in a clear blue sky, there was still a morning ground haze that threw their shadows as blurred figures along the grass.

'That's a good wicket down there,' Imrie said. 'But it was a bit of a chill night, and the pitch will have been sweating all night. It should give us something early on.'

There was a murmur of assent from the fast bowlers. The third seamer, Viljoen, who had not yet bowled in the match, said: 'Should get some movement, you mean, skip?'

'Yeah, and some bounce too. So I'll tell you what we are going to do. The Poms will be having the same ideas. Badger's not daft, and

128

Roly Anderson's seen more cricket than any of us have had hot dinners. They'll be expecting us to try to bounce the hell out of them from both ends for at least the first hour. That's what they'd do, and if it didn't work they'd have the spinners on at one o'clock, ten minutes before lunchtime.

'So we won't do that. You'll open, Neale, from the Nursery End. They'll expect that. And go flat out from first ball. No looseners – you'll do those in the nets just now. You'll only have two overs, whether you take wickets or not. Then you'll come off and Gary, you'll have one over, maybe two. Then you, Both. I'll switch you around until they won't know if they're coming or going. Meantime Sissie here will bowl the whole time from this end, or if he gets tanked you'll have a go, Toffee. Or you, Shiner.

'One thing, and this goes for all of you. You all know your positions in the field for every bowler. We've rehearsed them enough times. We'll all RUN between overs to keep the pressure on. No pauses. No field placing. EVERY ball back smack into Fingers' gloves as fast as you can, unless there's a run-out chance at the other end. Shiner, you're in short both ends. If you want a box and shinpads, put 'em on before we go out. No buggering about with a helmet. If you don't like it, drop back a yard or two. And everyone, have your piss or whatever before we get out there. Nobody goes off. Nobody calls for a sweater. Or takes one off. Just sweat. I don't want any delay. The Poms were bowling at 14 overs an hour, and they think it's an improvement. We'll show them improvement. I want 20 an hour, at least until lunchtime.'

'Bloody great.' Foster, the young whizz-kid from New South Wales, could not contain himself. 'They won't know what's hit 'em.'

Comberton rubbed his groin. 'Flaming Ida. Nor will I,' he said ruefully. They all laughed. No one questioned the plan. And when they trooped off to the nets there was a spring in their step that hadn't been there since Viner was struck down. There was even some laughing and joking, noted by the correspondent of one of the stuffier daily newspapers with some disapproval as being unseemly in the circumstances. But when they ran urgently onto the field to take their places for the opening over, the customary ripple of applause from the attentive stands swelled into an anticipatory roar. Prettyman and Coetzee, the overnight batsmen with a stand of 96 behind them, walked out to take their guards at the wicket in an atmosphere already alive with anticipation. Neale Walters was poised at his mark and began to run in at top speed the moment the umpire called 'Play'.

Prettyman, declining to be taken by surprise, backed away from the crease holding up his left hand in the policeman's 'stop' signal, checking Walters in his stride and causing him to decelerate lamely past the bowling crease. It was the experienced batsman's counter to the bowler's first-strike ploy, and Prettyman grinned as he carefully took guard again and settled for Walters' next ball. Honours even, he thought. Now this one is going to be a bouncer. Even a beamer. Watch it, he's quite fast.

Much the same thought was in Walters' mind as he stumped back to his mark, turned and began his run-up, very fast. He intended to whistle the ball close past Prettyman's ear to let him know who was boss right from the start. After all, he'd only got two overs.

A fast bowler does not have much time to think, even with the 25 to 30 yard run-up some of them use, but it is not true to claim, as some spectators and writers do, that thought is not part of any fast bowler's make-up. His problems are rhythm, balance, acceleration, body position, arm action and above all position of the front foot. It can land on, but not past, the popping crease, and within the return crease, or the dreaded cry of 'No Ball!' from the umpire will mean not only a run against the bowler's average, and a run to the other side, but a great deal of explosive effort expended to no purpose. The only thing that upsets a fast bowler more than to be no-balled is to be hit back over his head for six in the first over of the day.

Walters, however, had the imp of mischief in him that affects some cricketers from time to time. In the tradition of Keith Miller, Denis Compton, Derek Randall and a number of others, Walters liked to do the unexpected, and it flashed across his mind in the few seconds as he ran flat out for the bowling crease that a fast bumper was exactly what Prettyman was expecting. With no time to analyse the impulse, he checked his arm at the last minute and, instead, delivered a high, floating full toss, just asking to be smitten over the stands.

All Prettyman's disciplined experience was no protection from the latent wish of every batsman to hit a six off a 'sucker' ball. Instead of waiting and despatching it to any part of the ground he chose for a certain four, he leapt down the pitch, swung mightily too close to and across the ball, and missed completely. As he did so, he knew he had made a fool of himself, and the click of the wicket going down behind him coupled with the roar of the crowd merely confirmed this. He completed his swing and kept walking for the pavilion, some not unsympathetic applause compounding his fury with every step of the long walk. Spencer, the next batsman, contented himself with a raised eyebrow as they crossed at the gate. From the look on Prettyman's face, even a friendly remark might have provoked sudden violence.

Worse, from England's point of view, was to follow. Spencer played out the rest of Walters' over with an air of confidence, if with some luck, and then the other overnight batsman, Boris Coetzee, faced Smart. This was unexpected, as Imrie had foreseen, and caused Coetzee to have a long suspicious look at the pitch after he had taken guard, prodding it a few times with the end of his bat. It was very unusual to open the day with a spinner, anywhere, but especially at Lord's. Coetzee wondered what hidden devils Imrie had discovered, forgetting that the previous evening he had had little difficulty in coping with Smart and the other Australian bowlers, and no trouble at all with the pitch. Imrie, noting his caution, increased the psychological pressure by moving himself from mid-off, where he liked to field, to silly point, two yards from the bat. He was taking a bit of a chance because Cissie Smart was not the most accurate of off-spinners. So Coetzee was batting with four close catchers and the wicketkeeper surrounding him – a slip, silly point, forward and backward short-legs.

Whatever his shortcomings as a batsman, Coetzee did not lack courage, and his method of coping with this threatening field placing was to hit his way through it. It was a method that had stood him in good stead in the past. Unfortunately for him Smart struck a length with his first ball; and it was not until the fifth ball of the over that he received one that looked of a length to hit. Seizing his chance, Coetzee went down on one knee to sweep, but the bowler had flighted the ball with some cunning, holding it back so that it dropped slightly shorter than expected. The ball spun off the top edge of the bat, cracking Coetzee sharply on the side of the head and popping up gently into Imrie's hands. Coetzee, dazed, sore and furious with himself, followed Prettyman to the pavilion, two

131

wickets having fallen with the score at the overnight total of 127.

Alexander, a small man with a nut-brown, prematurely wizened face made his way jauntily to the wicket. He was never nervous, however strong the pressure, and confidently expected to see off this crap attack, as he called it. He watched Spencer get his head down for Walters' next over, scoring a two to very fine leg off a snick, but otherwise negotiating it safely. Imrie took the opportunity while the batsmen's attention was occupied with the runs to have a quick word with Smart.

'Give Great a couple on the middle stump and he'll whack them. I'll get Knife to edge back quietly to the extra cover boundary. Put the third a bit shorter and straight outside the off stump and it's a pound to a pinch of snuff the bugger will hole out.'

'Right on, skip.'

The first ball, on the middle stump, Alexander pulled over the ropes into the Tavern, doing severe damage to a plastic pint held by one of his young fans who unfortunately was singing, not watching, at the time; the second bounced on the concrete parapet of Lord Holmbush's private box and shattered one of the plate-glass sliding doors, incidentally doing some harm to Smart's bowling average. Alexander advanced on the third, wide outside the off stump and slashed, rather than drove. He hit it well but not quite in the middle, a shank in golfing terms, and the ball described a curved arc precisely into the waiting hands of Martin at deep extra cover, who caught it nervelessly two-handed at his right shoulder in the Australian manner.

Smart accepted the team's congratulations and the crowd's applause with becoming modesty. He shook Imrie by the hand while the captain tried to maintain a dourly unmoved countenance, but was unable completely to disguise a quiet smile.

'Bloody great, skip, bloody great.'

'We've got the bastards on the run, fair dinkum.'

'Great catch, Knife.'

'Like shelling peas. How d'you know it was going to be the third ball, skip?'

'Never you mind, Knife. Just a bit of luck.'

'Bloody Wrecker's luck.'

And so a legend was born, and consolidated as England's last four wickets fell with almost automatic regularity for the addition of 54 more runs. It seemed that Imrie could do no wrong, as Smart, bowling like a man inspired, ran through the tail. Only Percy Mandell, scoring 17 in a last-wicket stand of 21 while keeping Carter from the bowling, held up the Australian attack, and England were all out on the stroke of lunch for a total of 187, a deficit of 123. It was generally agreed that on a perfect batting pitch this had been a 'pitiful' display of batting, with Prettyman and Coetzee, Fridays's heroes, turned instantly into Saturday's villains. As for Bart Imrie, it confirmed him in the eyes of the Australian selectors and public as the saviour of their cricket, at least for the time being. 'Wrecker's luck' was to see Australia through a number of tight corners in the next few years.

Light missed most of the excitement, although the more raucous outbursts of the spectators penetrated the bookmakers' marquee with some regularity, and a large television screen kept a constant string of customers informed of the events on the field while they were placing their bets. Other monitors displayed the odds at half a dozen horse race meetings. The fresh-faced manager in charge told Light that in the evening they changed to the greyhound races, on which betting was usually much heavier than on the horses.

'Do the cricketers bet heavily?' Light asked casually.

'Not really,' said the manager. 'Not in our terms. Heavily would mean in thousands, but it's not often we get a bet of more than £25 from any of them during the day. But it's odd that you should ask. I took £500 on Thursday morning before the start of play from young Vince Carter. It was an odd bet. Nothing nasty, like. Ever since that Aussie business some years back we've been warned off taking bets from players against themselves, or against their side. It's not good for our image. We wouldn't want to be kicked off this site, though I doubt it would happen. We pay enough for the privilege.'

'Carter said he bet on a horse. He didn't say which one.'

'No, Carter bet on himself. He took me aside and asked me what the odds would be against him getting Jack Viner out in the first over, and I gave him five to one. He whacked out this bunch of fivers, still in its bank wrapper, and said, 'Right, you're on.' He was a bit nervous. I think it was the first bet he ever placed himself, and he didn't want anybody to know about it. Doc Wright, the physio, came in while I was writing out his slip, and looked rather surprised to find him there. Carter laughed a bit shame-faced, I thought, and

133

said: 'Just had second thoughts, Doc.' Wright thought he was trying to do him out of a commission. He usually lays the bets for the lads. It's not good for their image to be seen in here too often. It's usually in fives, tens and twenties – small stuff like that.'

'What do they pay him?'

'He told me about five per cent on a winning bet.'

'Do you pay him a commission as well?'

'Er, well not exactly, but we see he's all right at Christmas.'

Light switched back to Carter. 'So Carter won, then. Two and a half grand. That's not peanuts.'

'No, but it's all good for the image. The money doesn't matter.'

'I don't see how it benefits you to lose £2,500.'

'It'll get out. It always does, and we'll get a mention in the papers, and on telly and radio with any luck. Worth twenty times that.'

Light thanked him for the information, and stood aside thoughtfully while he dealt with a fresh batch of customers. He heard wagers placed on a wide variety of sporting events. One optimist placed £35 at 100 to one on the next five Christmases being white. The manager rolled an eye at him and turned to his next customer. Phil Alexander, the wicketkeeper, presented a slip and received a small pile of £5 notes in return. He tucked them in his back pocket and turned away. Light intercepted him.

'Mind if I walk back to the pavilion with you? I'd like a word with you away from the crowd.'

'Press?'

'No, police.'

'Oh, well, if you must.' He paused to sign a couple of autograph books. 'No sonny, no bits of paper. What's it about? Silly question. But it's nothing to do with me. All right, come along.'

They pushed their way through the crowds milling under the south stands back to the pavilion.

'Rather your place than mine.' Alexander seemed unimpressed by the prospect of being questioned.

'Why so?'

'Doesn't do your reputation any good, talking to the bleedin' fuzz. Still, I suppose you've got your job to do, cock.' Alexander was home-grown Cockney, tough, jaunty and self-reliant as a London sparrow. As a wicketkeeper he was known for his speed with his hands. He was very much an old-fashioned keeper, noted for his ability to stand up even to the fastest of bowling when he deemed it necessary. His number of stumpings compared to catches was better than one in three, which testified to his ability and his courage. He was contemptuous of 'long-stops with gloves on' – the modern brand of wicketkeeper who did his job from a safe distance behind the stumps, even when facing medium-paced trundlers. Light knew nothing of his cricket, but he recognised the man. He went straight to the point.

'What do you know about young Carter?'

'Why? Wot's 'e done?' Alexander was instantly defensive of a colleague.

'He bowled the ball when Viner was killed.' Light phrased his words carefully. 'We understand that you were among several people who urged him to bowl a bouncer on that particular ball. You were one, Spencer another, and the captain, Broadbent, was a third.'

'That's right. We wanted Vince to shake them up early on. There's nothing in the laws to prevent it.' Light noticed he used the word 'laws'. Only the cricketer and the cricket buffs know instinctively that the game is controlled not by the rules, but by the Laws of Cricket.

'But there's a bit more to it, isn't there? Suppose you had a bet on, at five to one or better, that a bouncer would be bowled on that particular ball? Or rather that one particular ball would take a wicket?'

'Suppose I did? So what? You don't think the skipper would stand for a thing like that? He told Vince to bounce Wino a bit. No one knew the bloody ball would kill him.'

'No, Mr Alexander. But someone DID know that Jack Viner was to die on that ball. Broadbent didn't bet on that ball. He's not a betting man, and as you say wouldn't stand for anything like that. But you and Spencer could – and did. How much did you win?'

'Find out.' Alexander was sulky, but not particularly perturbed.

'We will, if it's necessary,' said Light cheerfully. 'But at least one other member of the team benefited as well.'

'Clever bugger.'

'Not quite so-clever, when you realise that it was Carter himself.'

'What, betting on a bumper he was going to bowl? You must be

135

joking. No bookie would take a bloody bet like that. He'd be off his trolley.'

'Not quite like that. Carter put £500 on getting Viner out in that over. He was given five to one. He won £2,500.'

'Jesus Christ!' Alexander's astonishment looked genuine. 'The sneaky little bugger. I thought he was up to something.' A thought struck him. 'But where did he get five hundred quid to bet anyway? He hasn't got that sort of money. If he had, he wouldn't be a bloody cricketer. Christ, you only get about a thousand if you win the NatWest trophy, and that's if you're lucky. His ma's a widow. His pa was a copper. And they don't make that sort of loot unless they're on the fraud squad.'

Light ignored the familiar jibe. 'That's where I think you can help us. We have an idea that you introduced Carter to two South Africans. Du Plooy and Hennie, we think their names are.'

'Oh, you mean Gog and Magog. They're always sniffing around the circuit. They're always good for a few drinks. You just kid them along that you're interested in one of their stupid bloody cricket tours and they'll buy rounds all evening. Let's think. They were here last June, after we played Essex at Lord's. That's right. In the Tavern, outside the gates. We usually get in there for a pint or two after the game. Vince was drinking with the Middlesex boys and they were there. That's right. They took him off into a corner and fed him their usual line of bullshit. I had a word with him afterwards because he's a bit young, but he said he'd told them he wasn't interested. But they're as thick as two short planks. It's just the bloody silly sort of thing they'd do. Try to fix a bloody cricket match. The . . .'

'Would they try to fix a murder, Mr Alexander? Would you?'

'Here, I don't like the way this is going. Of course I wouldn't.'

'How much did you win, Mr Alexander?'

'Oh, well, you may as well know. A hundred. A tenner at ten to one. Monkey – that's Spencer – did the same.'

'Why Monkey?'

Alexander was happier with the sudden switch in questioning.

'That's easy. Spencer is known as the poor man's Botham. Both used to be known as Guy – the gorilla, you know. He doesn't like it, but these things stick. We've all got nicknames. 'Mine's Great, after

136

Alexander the . . . get it? Coetzee is Cagey, because his Christian name is Boris and that sounds Russian.'

'But?'

'KGB. Cagey Boris.'

Light would have been content to delve further into the mysteries of nicknames, but instead he escorted Alexander back to the dressing-room with a warning not to discuss the matter with Carter and collared Spencer in his place. But he got very little further with his investigation, beyond the fact that Spencer was even more contemptuous of the South African pair than Alexander had been.

'How long have they been around the cricket circuit?'

'Oh, it must be four or five years now. One of the guys said he thought he'd seen Du Plooy – that's the bigger one – as long as seven or eight years ago, but I can't be sure. They're pretty harmless, so long as you don't cross them. But they're only bullies. It seems to be in the Afrikaner character.'

'Would you go to South Africa?'

'Not on your Nellie. They tried me once, but I've got a good contract in Sydney for the next three years, if I get kicked out of this lot. Which is quite likely, if I go on playing like a bloody wally.'

'What did you get today?'

'Sixteen. Then I tried to cut that bloody Sissie and nicked it. Never cut before lunch, my father used to say. The last time I saw him he said that, and I told him he'd never played for England. Serves me right. He was watching on the box, and called before I could get into the showers. Gave me a right rollocking. So did Badger. Oh well, win some, lose some.'

'Jack Viner lost his life, Mr Spencer.'

'Yes, poor bugger. But at least he died doing what he lived for. My dad's dying of leukaemia. He's only got a few days to go.'

Mrs Carter invited Ashcroft into the room she still called the front parlour. He was glad the Rover was an anonymous black and was not decorated with flashing blue lights and luminous orange stripes. A visit by an official police car in this highly respectable estate would be a nine days wonder, a source of endless gossip. He noticed at least three lace curtains moving as he opened the little

137

wicket gate and made his way up the crazy-paving path.

She had the tea ready, but there was a decanter of whisky on the sideboard in case he felt like something stronger. The room was spotless, and smelt of furniture polish. A vase of early roses sat primly on a doyley in the centre of the square oak table. Before Ashcroft sat down in the armchair she indicated beside the fireplace, already laid for next winter, he leant over to smell them.

'Do you grow them, Mrs Carter?'

She smiled, a trifle sadly.

'Well, I try to look after them since my husband passed on. He was so fond of them. He grew them all his life. They were his pride and joy. And Vincent, of course.'

'He was in the Force, wasn't he? Your husband?'

'Yes, he was Sergeant at Writtle for 20 years. But he got pneumonia that dreadful winter, and he never recovered.'

'Mrs Carter, I've come to talk to you about your son.'

'Yes, I know, and I'm so grateful. Dad wanted him to go into cricket, but if he'd known what was going to happen he'd never have allowed it.'

'Oh, I hardly think you can blame yourself for what happened at Lord's. In any case, I can assure you that the ball your son bowled did not kill Viner. He died from another blow. That's why I'm here. There are one or two things I want to ask you.'

'Oh dear, I suppose that's something.' Mrs Carter took out a large handkerchief and blew her nose roundly. A tear escaped from each eye and she mopped them ineffectually. 'It's not that. Dad would have been ever so proud of him, getting to play for England. But Vince has been getting into such bad company recently, gambling and drinking and I don't know what. I'm so frightened, Mr Ashcroft. He's been a changed boy since he did so well at Lord's last year. So distant. He used to tell me everything. And smoking. I keep telling him he'll ruin his health and his career, and he pays no attention. I don't know what to do with him. He hardly speaks to me.'

Mrs Carter was a large woman, and wept largely. Ashcroft said sympathetically: 'Do you know the reason for this sudden change in Vincent?'

She wept more loudly.

'No, no, I don't. It's since he met those South Africans. They're up to no good, Mr Ashcroft,' she said earnestly. 'Can't you stop them? Vince even said he was going to join those . . . those . . . rebels.'

She imbued the word with such intensity that Ashcroft smiled despite himself. Mrs Carter sniffed angrily.

'No, Mr Ashcroft, I mean it. My Ted refused to give anything to a cricketer's benefit if he'd been on a rebel tour. Bribery and corruption he used to call it, to help keep the Africans as slaves. He'd been out there, in the navy during the war, at Simonstown, and what he saw convinced him that those Boers were up to no good . . . And I agree. He was all for fair play, was my Ted. And now my Vince is going against everything Ted ever stood for.' She broke down and sobbed in real earnest. Ashcroft made soothing noises and thanked his lucky stars he had not sent Light, who was terrified of a woman's tears.

As the sobbing subsided, he made himself at home in the kitchen and brewed a fresh pot of tea. Mrs Carter dried her eyes and accepted a cup with a shaky hand.

'Oh, no Mr Ashcroft. You shouldn't. It's very kind of you. Thank you very much.'

'Not at all, Mrs Carter. Now I want you to tell me all you can about those South Africans.' She dried her eyes.

'I've never met them. I wouldn't have them in my house. All I know is that they met Vince last year and they seemed to like him. He's very young, of course, and I think they flattered him – said he was the best fast bowler in this country for twenty years and was sure to play for England, and so on. Then they took him away for two or three days when he'd hurt his ankle and couldn't play – Essex gave him the time off – and he came back, I don't know, somehow different. He wasn't my boy any more. He did say he wasn't going to see Hermann and Hennie any more. He said he was digusted, but I could never get him to say why. Then this year they came back when he was chosen for England and took him out to dinner at the Savoy. It was very grand, he said. He showed me the menu, but I couldn't understand a word of it.'

'What about his disgust?'

'He seemed to have forgotten that. He was full of this offer they made him to go to South Africa on a three-year contract. They promised him the earth – a house and a car and more money than you could ever dream of. Something like fifty thousand rands a year and a hundred thousand signing-on fee. I can't remember if that was rands or pounds. All he said was he could buy me the cottage Ted had always promised me when we retired.'

Her eyes filled with tears.

'I don't ever want to move from this little house. It was Ted's and mine. Vince showed me this brochure, all glossy colour and sunshine and naked girls. I suppose they would attract him, being a young man. I told him that money wasn't everything, but he said he'd only have a few years at the top as a fast bowler and he was going to make all he could out of it. I asked him what he thought his father would have said, but he just laughed and said I was old-fashioned, like his dad. And now this has happened. Tell me, Superintendent, is there any hope for him? He looked so frightened – terrified – on the television when that man died. I know he's done something wrong.'

Ashcroft forestalled a fresh flood of tears. 'I'm sure things aren't as bad as you think, Mrs Carter. As Vincent is the son of a policeman, you can rest assured we will do all we can to help. Perhaps you can, too. Have you got that brochure? And anything else that you can show me.'

'Why don't you come and look at his room and see for yourself, Mr Ashcroft? It's all to help him, isn't it?'

She led the way up the narrow stairs. It was the smaller of the two bedrooms, not more than 12ft by 10ft, with mementoes of a schoolboy past tacked onto the walls and a small collection of tiny cups on a narrow chest of drawers. Ashcroft took the brochure Mrs Carter so disliked from one of the drawers, and looked methodically through the others and the small fitted wardrobe. Tucked under a pile of white flannel trousers and shirts he found a plain envelope containing a first-class South African Airways ticket to Johannesburg, dated the following September, and £500 in new South African rand notes. A scrawled note said: 'Some pocket money to help you settle down. All the details later.' There was nothing else. He showed them to her.

'Thank you very much, Mrs Carter. This is not illegal, much though we may deplore it. Vince is perfectly within his rights to accept the money and go, though I doubt, like you, if it would be in his long-term interests. After what has happened in the last few years I doubt whether he'll ever play for England again after this season, if he does decide to go. I'll try to talk to him, but whether it will make any impression, I don't know. I have to see him in a professional capacity in any case. All I can say to you is I don't think he's done anything very wrong, just foolish. And I have overstepped my mark in telling you that much.'

But as he drove back up the A12 he reflected that young Vince Carter might well be in trouble up to his neck. How much had he taken from his South African friends? How much had he known about their motives? Had he known the dead cameraman, Phillips? Old Bill thought he had the outline of the plot, but there was a great deal of detail to be filled in. He must certainly speak to Carter, but there were a number of things he had to do first. He switched on his radio.

'Ashcroft here. Any messages for me, please?'

'Yes sir, but would you please conform to radio procedures. Over.' The girl's clear voice sounded as if it was speaking in a lost cause.

'Sorry, my dear. What are they? The messages, I mean. Not the procedures.'

'Detective Inspector Thomas wants you to call him direct, sir. He says it's important. Detective Sergeant Light says his morning at the betting shop was very profitable. That's all, sir. Over.'

She sounded disapproving.

'What's the latest score? At Lord's.'

'This is not an answering service, Chief Superintendent,' the voice was severe. 'But the last I heard was England all out for 195 at lunch. Over.'

'Ye gods,' Ashcroft groaned. 'I shouldn't have asked.'

'No sir. Over and out.'

He picked up the car phone, which he found much more congenial than the impersonal radio, and tapped out Thomas' number. The Inspector sounded keen and very much on the ball.

'We've found the flat they used, sir. On the fifth floor. The owners went away for the weekend. A Mr and Mrs Smithers. They answered an advertisement in the personal column of *The Times* from a Mr Foreman who wanted to hire a flat overlooking Lord's for a day. It was all fixed up a month ago. Mr Smithers likes to watch the cricket himself, but the offer was too good. A hundred down in advance and another hundred at the end of the day. This

Mr Foreman came round at nine in the morning as arranged and picked up a spare key. The Smithers went sailing with their son and daughter-in-law, and didn't get back until late. They stayed the night in Brighton and didn't hear any news until this morning. They thought in the circumstances there might be something fishy about their Mr Foreman, so they called the Brighton police and came back in a rush. The flat was immaculate, the spare key had been dropped, as arranged, through the letterbox, and an envelope had been left on the desk with £200 in tenners and a note typed on Mr Smithers' typewriter merely saying thank you. No signs anywhere of any fingerprints, apart from the Smithers', of course, but Forensic are going over the flat with a toothcomb for any traces of a weapon having been fired. Something may turn up.'

'Smithers all right?'

'Right as a bell, sir. He's a civil servant, in charge of the American section of the Passport Office at Petty France. He admits the temptation of making a couple of hundred tax free and no questions overruled his natural caution, and in any case is full of remorse. Says he'll give the extra hundred to charity.'

'What's the description of Foreman?'

'A big man, very well dressed. About 6ft, heavily built but not fat, dark, greying at the temples, short back and sides, heavy black moustache. About 50. Grey lightweight suit, expensively cut. Grey silk shirt, plain maroon tie. Black shoes, expensive leather. Germanic accent. Said he was working for *Der Spiegel*, photographing a series on the Englishman at his pleasure. What more typical a scene than Lord's? He said he'd take a chance on the weather, and of course it was perfect. Smithers is a good witness. We've got a photofit ready to put out the moment you give the go-ahead.'

'Good. I'll see the Press as soon as I get back, say in an hour. Make it an hour and a half, because of the traffic.'

'Very good, sir.'

'Anything else?'

'Sergeant Light's gone off to Claridges to see Mrs Viner. She must be quite something, sir. He went home to change first.'

'She is, Thomas. Quite something. And she might give us a great deal of trouble, if Light's not careful.'

'There's something else, sir. Forrester, the BBC man, has been making a few inquiries, and he's come up with the name of a sound technician who knew Phillips well. He's called Price, and he was regularly paired with Phillips until last year when they came back from a tough trip to Angola. Forrester doesn't know the details, but apparently Price refused to work again with Phillips, and the feeling was mutual. Price is coming back today from working in Wales, and I've got a WPC from Shepherds Bush at the BBC to bring him along here.'

'Interesting. What was he doing in Wales?'

Thomas laughed. 'Nothing there, sir. He's been down there for a week, shooting a feature film on the Air-Sea Rescue Service. When Phillips was shot he was hauling up a man picked out of a rubber dinghy in a force nine gale.'

'Spare me the weather report, Thomas. But well done. You sound a little harassed. Is anything worrying you?'

'Only what might happen if our man decides to kill somebody else.'

'If he does, there's not much we can do about it until he tries. But I am perfectly confident that he will not try again. Keep that photofit under your hat though. I want him to stay in this country until I know who he is and where he is. If we look as if we're getting too close he'll be gone like a jack rabbit.'

'Have you any ideas yet, sir?'

'No, but I know who has, Thomas. I'll see you in an hour.' He replaced the telephone in its cradle. Thomas could not see that his index and forefingers were firmly crossed, but he did note that Old Bill had not asked for the latest score, even though play had been in progress for an hour since lunch.

England's fortunes on the field would have given Ashcroft little satisfaction. In the players' luncheon room in the loftier reaches of Lord's, the back-to-back team tables afforded a strong contrast in attitudes. Mrs Betsy Smith, the cook, who had presided over the appetites of more internationally renowned cricketers than possibly anyone in the world, had never watched a game of cricket, but was known among a few fortunate cognoscenti as the best forecaster of a result in the business. Which was why James Cockburn ('pronounced Cock, old boy, not like the port') of *The Times* frequently staggered his opposition by the accuracy of his prognosis. Betsy, as

143

she was known only to those few intimates, made her judgments on the basis of the amount of food left on cricketers' plates. She had overwhelming faith in the quality of her cooking, and the only time she went spectacularly wrong was with the Sri Lankans, many of whom were vegans, a fact she hadn't known beforehand. Still, as James Cockburn wrote ruefully at the time, most of the others were wrong then, too.

This day the gloom at the England table was palpable. Roland Anderson, serving out the tenderest of Betsy's honeyed ham and the most subtle of fresh salads, did his best to raise his team's spirits, but even his experienced urbanity was not proof against what could only be described as a collective inspissated depression. Broadbent was too furious with the performance of his middle order batsmen to do more than sit and glower and sip at his orange juice. He was waiting until they could get back to the dressing-room to give them what he would describe in his blunt Yorkshire way as a 'proper roasting'. Even Alexander and Spencer, the mainstays of the team's spirits in adversity, had little to say, sitting together and exchanging few words. Vince Carter, who usually came back for more at least twice to gladden Mrs Smith's motherly heart, picked over his ham and thrust it away untouched.

The Australians, however, were still on the high engendered by the morning's success. In recent years it had often been their team which had been swept aside. Now they were promising to do the same to the old enemy in the best place of all, the home of English cricket. They bubbled and joked, stuffed their plates full and came back for more. No one noticed the lonely figure of Cousins, the manager, who sat at the corner of the table and looked sick, until George Viljoen, the most experienced member of the side apart from Imrie, came over to him and asked: 'Feeling crook, Griff? You don't look so chipper. Better get back to the hotel and have a rest up.'

Cousins smiled weakly.

'Thanks George. I'm OK. Touch of the sun, that's all. I'll be all right.'

He wondered if he would have the courage to tell Detective Chief Superintendent Ashcroft what he knew. And would he live long enough to do so? He had never been so grateful as when he and Ashcroft had found that Du Plooy and Van der Merwe had booked out of the Churchill Hotel the previous evening. But he had never felt so scared as he had been when he was told of Phillips' shooting, and he had stayed that way.

He summoned up the courage to eat a little ice cream, which made him feel better, and to stay with the team until Imrie and Comberton went out to open the second innings. Then, sending his excuses to the police, he called a minicab and was driven quietly back to his hotel.

He missed another treat for the Australian fans, and another scarifying of English pride. Buoyed by their morning of success, the Australian batsmen quietly began to consolidate their first innings advantage. Imrie's objective was to build a lead of at least 400 by sometime after tea on the Monday, and then bowl out the home side in the four remaining sessions on a wearing pitch.

By the close of play, he and Comberton had gone a long way towards achieving that end. They went steadily, even boringly at first, wearing down an already uncertain opening attack. Carter seemed unable to regain the fire he had shown on the first day; Spencer bowled competently as ever, but without any penetration, while the spinners spun their hearts out on a pitch suddenly seemingly made of concrete. Only 25 runs were scored in the first hour, and only 35 in the second. But after tea, on another blameless evening, both batsmen began to open out. Imrie found scope for his favourite leg-side glances and on-drives, while Comberton exploited the cut and the pull. By the time stumps were drawn Imrie had progressed to 83 and Comberton to 69, and neither had given an appreciable chance or even missed a playable ball. They strode in together briskly, acknowledging the cheers of the crowd, while the England side straggled off raggedly, scarcely bothering to give the opposition the conventional applause.

As several Sunday newspapers reported, it seemed that the death of the Australian captain had turned the hearts of the Aussies into iron, and the legs and arms of the England team into rubber.

England v Australia (Third Day)

A.B. Prettyman	b Walters	51
B. Coetzee	c Imrie b Smart	49
D.A. Spencer	c Rose b Smart	26
P. Alexander	c Martin b Smart	12
P.Q. Mandell	not out	21
J.G. Woodman	lbw Smart	3
C.J.A. Bowyer-Smith	c Jones b Smart	2
V.J. Carter	b Smart	0
	Extras	23
	Total	187

Fall of wickets: 4/127, 5/127, 6/141, 7/159, 8/163, 9/166, 10/187

Bowling	O	M	R	W
N. Walters	18	6	24	3
M. Martin	10	0	43	1
G. Jones	9	2	57	0
S.S. Smart	13.2	5	40	6

Australia (Second Innings)

*J. Viner	did not bat, dead	0
B.V. Imrie	not out	83
C.B. Comberton	not out	69

Extras 4

Total (for no wickets) 156

Bowling	O	M	R	W
V.J. Carter	12	0	43	0
D.A. Spencer	10	0	44	0
A.B. Prettyman	14	3	32	0
P.Q. Mandell	12	1	33	0

*Footnote: David Randall records in his *Great Sporting Eccentrics* the following entry in the scorebook for the Quaid-I-Azam Trophy final in Karachi in 1959:

First Innings

Abdul Aziz retired hurt 0

Second Innings

Abdul Aziz did not bat, dead 0

Chapter 6

The Third Evening

A large number of column inches, accompanied by photographs and 'action sketches' were devoted by the Sunday newspapers to the killings at Lord's. Two of the more sensationalist papers carried front-page leading articles calling for 'this Test of blood to be abandoned out of respect for the dead'. The accompanying copy, however, showed scant respect for dead or living, or even the simple truth. One picture dominated all the papers. An enterprising photographic agency had made a still of the dramatic close-up video shot taken by Phillips of Vince Carter, tears streaming down his face at the announcement of Viner's death. Most of the papers flanked it with pictures of the two dead men, with such headlines as 'Triangle of Death'. And they all, with differing proportions of accuracy and invention, ran 'in-depth' articles on the lives and characters of the three.

Probably because there was not much to say about Carter, who after all had not yet had time at 21 to build a career of triumph or disaster, and because too much had already been written about Viner, the concentration of interest was on Phillips, whom the *People* called 'The Mystery Cameraman', because so little was known about him. They all made much of his Rhodesian background, and the *Mail on Sunday* sleuths had ferreted out the fact that he had served in the Selous Scouts, Ian Smith's 'dirty tricks' brigade during the war leading up to Zimbabwe's independence, and advanced the theory that a vengeance squad had been sent to Britain to 'get him'. The *Sunday Mirror* had got wind of this 'exclusive' in El Vino's before publication and, furious at having missed it, ran a hastily contrived knocking story, claiming that 'senior Scotland Yard sources who declined to be named' had discounted this theory on the grounds that it was now so long after the event that time had healed the wounds of the past.

More interesting to Ashcroft, who had the first editions on his desk at Lord's before Light returned from Claridge's, was the account in the more restrained *Observer* of Phillips' Rambo-like image as a BBC cameraman. According to colleagues, he was a man who had lived hard, driven hard and played hard. He would go anywhere, do anything, at any time. He was highly praised by Richard Ponsonby, the current ace war reporter, for his willingness to keep filming in any circumstances. 'While I get the glory,' he told the *Observer* magnanimously, 'it's cameramen like Dave who face the bullets to put me on screen. I shall remember him.' Forrester had added a sober tribute to Phillips' ability as a sports cameraman, 'See picture, Page 1', but somewhat less forthcoming was Jonathan Leofric, the correspondent who had spent three months in the Angolan bush on Phillips' last dramatic overseas trip. He was 'unavailable for comment', according to the BBC Press office. Ashcroft remembered that he was waiting for Price, the sound recordist from that trip, to arrive from Shepherds Bush. He wondered whether 'unavailable' meant Leofric was away working, on leave, or had merely not wished to speak ill of the dead.

He was pleased to see that his Press conference had not made much space in the first edition. 'Detective Chief Superintendent Ashcroft, who is in charge of the investigation, said he was satisfied with progress. He declined to say whether any links had been established between the two dead men. But he confirmed that the police believe that both were murdered, and that Jack Viner, the Australian cricket captain, had not been killed by Vince Carter's bumper. "I can't say any more at the moment, but it is only fair to Carter and his family to relieve them of any anxiety on that point." He had nothing more to add at present. Asked if he was fond of cricket, Mr Ashcroft, who was wearing an MCC tie, replied: "Very". We can reveal that Detective Chief Superintendent Ashcroft was a keen club cricketer in his youth, and actually played for Middlesex Second XI before joining the police force. He scored a duck in his only match.'

He smiled wrily. Trust Thomas, the expert in diversionary tactics, to find the right smokescreen to cover up the fact that he had nothing to tell them. Following his instinct, Ashcroft had not released the photofit of the man who had rented the Smithers' flat, nor had he hinted that such a man existed. At his request and at the Yard's expense, the Smithers had returned to their relatives in Brighton for a few days, sworn to silence and a day and night watch was being kept on the whole block of flats from which the bullet had come. There was no news yet from the forensic experts that any traces of firing had been found in the flat, and there was still the faint possibility that the whole episode was a red herring.

He wondered about Vincent Carter. The silly young blighter had obviously fallen for a combination of flattery, bribery, alcohol, sex and blackmail, but Ashcroft did not think, as Mrs Carter did, that the boy was three-quarters of the way down the primrose path and knocking on the gates of hell. It would do no harm to let young Mr Carter sweat for another day or two. Then possibly a private word with Roly Anderson or his county captain might be sufficient. After all, you didn't want England's best fast bowler for years to land up in jail.

'Hullo, sir.' Light's cheerful voice jolted him from his reverie. The Detective Sergeant was patently brimming over with news.

'Wait a moment, Amber.' Ashcroft held up a hand. 'Don't rush it. Start from the beginning. And take it slowly.'

Light was pleased with himself. To spend two hours in the company of a beautiful and intelligent woman was stimulating enough in itself, but the story Julie Viner had to impart threw a new light on the case and a spotlight of certainty on Ashcroft's suspicions. It also broadened the whole scope of the investigation. At first, Light said, she had been hesitant.

'This isn't what I expected,' she said, looking round at the Claridges' luxurious furnishings. 'I thought I'd be sitting at a desk in some police station and having my statement taken down in shorthand. And talking to someone, well, excuse me, higher than a sergeant.'

'Don't worry, Mrs Viner. That will happen yet. Detective Chief Superintendent Ashcroft will be seeing you tomorrow, and you can't get much higher than that. He doesn't like taking statements and gets me to write it all down. Then he'll have time to digest it before he sees you. It's just routine.' He hoped this flagrant misrepresentation of his chief's attitude to police work would be forgiven. 'Where would you like to start?' He smiled.

One of his former girlfriends had said his smile would melt the stone heart of one of Nelson's lions. Julie Viner relaxed.

'Did you ever see my husband bat?' she asked.

'I'm afraid not,' Light admitted. 'I'm not a follower of cricket.'

'He used to wait, and watch, and never seemed to hurry. But before you knew it the runs would be flowing from his bat. I don't think he ever hit a six, but everyone says that he was beautiful to watch.'

'They tell me he never wore a helmet. Why was that? I understood all batsmen had to wear them these days as a precaution against being hit on the head.'

'It's not compulsory, and a few players – just a few – refuse to wear them. Jack said that a helmet was more dangerous than being without it. And a visor just added to it. He said he felt like a horse wearing blinkers when he tried one on. He couldn't see properly, hear properly, or react properly once he did see the ball. His reaction time was about halved, he reckoned. He was never hit by a bouncer before in his life. His eye was so quick. He just swayed out of the way. That's why I knew immediately that he'd been murdered. There isn't a bowler in the world, including the West Indians, who could hit my Jack like that. Somebody shot him, didn't they? Just as the ball was being bowled? Don't worry, Sergeant. I shan't break down.' She breathed deeply. 'I think I'm what they call a fatalist.'

'Why do you think he was murdered? Have you any idea who could have done it?'

'I reckon I know why. Who isn't so easy. That's up to you to find out.'

'Tell me what you think.'

Mrs Viner rose and moved across to the Sheraton bureau. She unlocked a black briefcase, brought it across the room and laid it on Light's lap. Her body rippled under her dress. Light thought she moved like a cat.

'It's all in there.'

'Tell me in your own words.'

She settled herself in her armchair, hands folded neatly in her lap. Only the slight flick of one thumb against the another betrayed an inner tension.

'Start at the beginning. When you met him.'

'My pa is a goldminer, and my ma is an Abo. I reckon you know that. It doesn't matter over here, I reckon, but it's pretty important in Oz. They live in a shack in the bush about ten miles from Townsville, in the Northern Territory. Pa could have made a good living, but he's bone idle. Reckon that's why he married Ma. She does it all for him. But he made enough to send me away to school, so I could read and write, and a few other things. Ma was ill and I'd been sent for during my exam term. I said Pa was a lazy bastard. I was 17, and I resented it. I didn't mind helping Ma, but he'd've had his arse wiped for him if he could've saved lifting his hand. Am I boring you?'

'Go on, please.' Light could have watched and listened to her all day. Her skin, like her voice, was liquid gold.

'I'd done the chores, but Pa had been impossible, and he fetched me a clip across the ear for something I said. Normally I'd've bashed him back, but that day I just hauled off and went walkabout for a bit. It was bloody hot – probably about 110 – and I was sitting on a tree wondering whether to run away back to school when this bloke came riding up on a pony. He said, "Mornin", miss. Hope I ain't disturbin' you." I said no, I was just thinkin', and he said could he join me. I didn't say anything so he came and sat on the log beside me and we both stayed there for about an hour, just thinking. Then he said: "I'm 19 years old and I'm going to captain Australia at cricket. Will you marry me?" And I looked at him and he looked like a man who would do what he said, so I said yes. We didn't even know each other's names.

'We went off and told Ma and Pa, and packed a few things, and I got up behind him on the horse and we rode into Townsville and got married. I guess we became acquainted on that ride.'

'You must have had a rough time at first.'

'Oh, it wasn't too bad. Jack's mum and dad were furious to begin with. Mr Viner called me an Abo whore, but Jack just stood up and looked at him, and made him take it back and apologise. He didn't hit him, but Mr Viner knew that if he'd said another word Jack would have killed him. He took a long time to get riled, but when he did, nothing could stop him. Anyway, we couldn't live at Jack's father's ranch after that. It wasn't only me, but Jack's ambition to play cricket. The old man said it was a cissy game. His idea of sport was to shoot a few roos or go shark-fishing off the

Reef. So Jack made him give him the money he was owed for helping on the ranch since he was 15 and we came over to England on that. We went to Lord's – they were full up, but someone suggested that Lancashire were looking for players after Clive Lloyd left and they didn't get Botham. So Jack went and saw Roly Anderson, who was skipper then, and he put us onto Larraby in the Lancashire League.'

She smiled as the memories flooded in.

'They were wonderful people. We didn't know if our money would last and I was pregnant. They found us a little two-roomed flat for £10 a week, and we didn't know until much later that the club was subsidising it for another £10. But Jack did them proud. No one has ever scored so many runs in his first season in the League. He even got a century in his first match. They were so good to us. Lancashire wanted him to sign on midway through the season, but Jack wouldn't let Larraby down. So we stayed to the end of the season and Larraby won the League. My baby was born a week later, and they staged a benefit concert for us and raised £3,000. That's why he was called Larry.'

'Did you have any racial problems?'

'Not really. There are lots of different colours in Manchester, and in any case nobody knows what an Abo is. Anyway, the next year Jack joined Lancashire, and we called our second son Trafford. He did just as well, and then a scout asked him to join New South Wales during the English winter, so it looked as though his career was set. But there was always me.'

'How d'you mean? Forgive me, Mrs Viner, but you would appear to me to be an asset for any husband.'

'Oh, no. I was raw in from the outback, and shy, and for the first few years I had babies to look after. So I didn't mix. Jack was a good-looker, and the girls were always after him, and when he began to be noticed by the Press it got worse. Whenever he was photographed there were girls hanging on his arm, begging for an autograph or a kiss. Then one national rag ran a story about his little Abo wife and the two half-caste kids at home, along with a picture of a blonde with her boobs hanging out kissing him. I could take it for myself, because I knew Jack, but when I read that about the kids it made me spit. Jack rang up Roly that evening and told him he might be late on the ground the next day and drove

153

down to London. He found the reporter in a pub. I don't know exactly what happened, but the man was found by cleaners the next morning trussed up like a chicken in the doorway of St Bride's Church. There was a label round his neck saying 'Father, forgive me, for I know not what I do'. He hadn't been hurt, and he refused to make a complaint. I heard later he emigrated to South America. But he never wrote about cricket again.

'That article did me good, though. It shook me up. I stopped hiding myself away and decided to help Jack. Roly's wife, Elizabeth, helped me. She gave me elocution lessons and made me take classes in dancing and deportment. I liked them. Then one day she said: "Why don't you have a shot at modelling? With that skin you'll be all the rage." It amused me, that what had always held me back should now be an asset, but what she said was right. I made a lot of money, but the actual modelling bored me, so I began designing my own clothes and showing them privately to the cricketers' wives here and in Oz. Now I design clothes and I'm fashion buyer for Keneally's in Sydney. And the boys are at Wincaster. That's like your Eton.'

She apologised for rambling on.

'But I'm coming to it. It sounds like the classic success story – rags to riches and all that. Well, I suppose it is, but it's been hard work all the way, for both of us. And now Jack . . .' She rallied. 'It was after that business with the reporter that Jack began to take real notice of race things. We made friends with Geoff Broadbent, who was then living just over the Pennines, and his wife, who's a South African Coloured girl. She's beautiful. Belinda, her name is. Geoff met her when he was coaching in Cape Town before the ban. I suppose it was natural that we were drawn together. We used to meet at matches and talk a lot. People seem to think I don't like Belinda, but they're wrong. I once had a row with her about her persuading Geoff to have a vasectomy, but we got over that years ago. You can't really blame her. I couldn't, once I heard what happened. She's had much more to put up with than I have. She can't even go back to her family any more. When she was engaged to Geoff a gang of white kids would chase her down the street. They treated her as though they owned her, like a slave. She had never seen some of them before. Then one day they caught her and took her into the church where she and Geoff were hoping to be married and raped her. Seven of them. She tried not to tell Geoff, but he was sent letters. Vile letters. So he took her to the police and complained, and showed them the letters as proof. All the policeman said was, "Did she like it? You've got no case here. They all do it, these Coloured bitches. Better take it to your toy policemen in England."

'When Geoff told Jack about it, I never saw him so angry. Even with the reporter. We talked for hours that night, until the dawn came up. Most of the time they were raging at not being able to do anything about the injustices. Geoff seemed to accept the situation, hopelessly somehow, without ever agreeing with it, but Jack thought about it for weeks. I knew he had something in his mind. He bought all the newspapers. He read book after book. Then one day he sat me down and told me his plan. It was about three years ago.

"Julie," he said, "I'm going to fight these bastards. It's not true that we can't do anything." He said that the root of race hatred today was in South African apartheid, and it had to be fought at the root. One of the ways apartheid was keeping itself alive was through sport. The bans and boycotts had worked to some degree, but not nearly as effectively as they could have done because of two things: the hypocrisy of both governments and the governing bodies of sport.

"Take cricket," he said. "It's at least made some moves against players who've gone to South Africa. But there are so-called rebel tours going on all the time, both ways, and nobody takes a bit of notice. Rugby's even worse. They seem to go out of their way to encourage double standards. Look at athletics. A little girl makes nonsense of the laws of England because she can run a bit. Johannesburg is open house to world tennis players, but the best have so much money anyway that the bribes don't attract them. There's a nominal ban on golfers, but they all trot over to Sun City to gather in millions in Krugerrands. If the money's right, the boxers fight, black or white. The only sport that has upheld the Gleneagles agreement has been association football, and that's because soccer has never caught on with the whites in South Africa, and there isn't the money in it. One attempt was made to get a rebel tour over there from Britain, but the Football Association stopped it because they were afraid of the South Americans chucking them out of FIFA."

155

'Jack said the trouble was that the South Africans were able to split world sport organisations with their money, and they could work in secret with their government's backing. He said Western international sport was divided among itself. Each government said one thing and did another. He knew South Africa would destroy international sport if it was allowed to continue in this way. And he was going to do something about it.

'He said the secret of all successful campaigns was knowledge, and apart from cash the most powerful weapon apartheid possessed was surprise. Often competitors for an event would already be in Pretoria or Johannesburg or Durban before the Western authorities were aware it was happening, their fares paid, their hotels paid, and their pockets full of rands. Often there were other bribes too, and blackmail.

'What Jack was going to do was to compile a complete dossier on apartheid's impact on world sports, starting with cricket. It was not going to be public, but he hoped to build up a complete picture of the way Pretoria operated, and so be able to forecast what they would do next. He would list not only every player who went to South Africa, but also how they were recruited, and by whom, how they were paid and how much. He wanted names, addresses, telephone numbers. He began with the official Diplomatic Lists, and employed press-cutting agencies to keep him informed of any official changes. People he could trust in the counties, like Badger, would send him snippets of information from Britain. Sometimes, and most valuable, a player himself who had been approached would give him information. Or a guy back from Pretoria would talk in the bar.

'I helped, of course. I kept the files for him and helped with the finance. All our spare cash goes on the project. We bought a small personal computer and I've stored all the information on discs. Most of it concerns cricket, of course, but the files are beginning to build up in other sports. Jack said he was starting to make out definite patterns of action by Pretoria. Lately he's been saying that they were working up to something big. They're going to try to destroy international cricket and rugby by staging two simultaneous world championships, with fortunes offered to the competitors merely for entering, and prizes of up to a million pounds for the winning teams. If that works, they believe they'll have finished the Commonwealth Games, which are on their last legs anyway; and then their next target will be the Olympics. It's all in there.'

Julie Viner pointed to the briefcase.

Light said: 'It sounds impressive. But what use can this be to us? I'm sorry, Mrs Viner, but the information is not about illegal activities, however reprehensible they may be morally. There's nothing to stop the South Africans offering anything they like to a sportsman to compete in their country.'

She said simply: 'I thought you would say that. But Jack's dossier contains the names and addresses and the aliases of more than half a dozen South African sporting agents operating in this country. Most are here illegally, or are using false names and documents. Some of them are former BOSS agents.

'There is also a file of threats which have been made against us in the past year, including death threats against both of us and our children. Our computer has been destroyed twice by burglars and all the tapes in the house stolen. Luckily from the start we've duplicated everything, but they know what we are doing. Our own police in Sydney have been sympathetic, but they seem to think we've been bringing it on ourselves. Jack made me promise that if ever anything should happen to him, I would take the whole thing at once to Scotland Yard. I've been scared every minute they might trace me here, even in Claridges. I should have given the file to you this morning, but I was even suspicious of you. But the porter said he knew you both.' She smiled faintly.

'Thank you, Mrs Viner. Have any of these threats been made in this country?'

'Not in that file. But just before you arrived I received a telephone call.'

She opened the briefcase and took out a small tape recorder. It had a small sucker microphone attached by a slim wire. She moved the 'play' switch and a hollow but distinctive voice spoke: 'Room 317? Good afternoon, Mrs Viner. You know what happened to your husband? I shouldn't go near the window, Mrs Viner. Or open the door. Or speak to the police. Good afternoon, Mrs Viner.'

Light moved swiftly to the telephone. She said: 'I checked with the desk. The call did not come from outside. It must have been an internal call from another room at the hotel. I thought I would die,

157

Sergeant Light. Just then they rang up from the desk to say you were on your way up. They said they were sure it was you. But I still don't know how I opened that door.'

For the first time she showed signs of panic. Light did his best to reassure her.

'Nothing will happen to you, Mrs Viner. I think it's highly unlikely the caller is staying in the hotel. We'll check, but there are plenty of public telephones here he could have used, and be well on his way by now. Don't worry. We'll move you somewhere safe and give you protection. Right away.'

He telephoned Detective Inspector Thomas, who promised to take care of everything. Suitable transport and escorts would be on their way within ten minutes. Would Light be sure to keep the tape of the threatening phone call? And go through the guest list with the hotel detective and the manager? 'And tell Mrs Viner not to worry,' said Thomas. 'I think she should go down to Selsdon for a day or two. We can keep an eye on her there. She'll be safe enough at an exclusive ladies' health establishment with a couple of WPCs to keep an eye on her. OK, Amber?'

D. I. Thomas was as good as his word. Within 30 minutes Mrs Viner was on her way to Surrey in a police car, accompanied by two experienced woman constables, the hotel had been searched for suspicious persons without result, the guest list had been checked and found 100 per cent kosher, as the house detective put it, and Light had headed back through the evening rush-hour traffic to Lord's, the briefcase containing Viner's files and the threatening tape on the car seat by his side.

As Light was finishing his narrative, a constable knocked on the door and showed in a black-haired man of about 30, with a thin hooked nose, dark brown eyes and a deeply tanned skin. Ashcroft waved a hand to bring Light to a halt in mid-sentence.

'This is Mr Price, Amber. Manny Price. He's the BBC sound man who's been good enough to come up from Wales to help. I know he won't mind if you join in. He was about to tell me of his adventures in Africa. Please go on, Mr Price. You joined Phillips in Johannesburg, you said. You hadn't met him before?'

'No, sir.' Price had a thin voice that almost lisped its sibilants. 'I'd heard of him, of course, because he had quite a reputation. It was my first tour overseas – we do three or six months at a time in

South Africa and it's turn and turn about. I had done overseas trips before, of course, but only for a few days. I was looking forward to it, and to working with Dave. Only it didn't work out like I'd imagined it would.'

'How was that? Didn't you get on?'

'It wasn't exactly that. We got on OK, working. He was good all right, even if he did know it all. I suppose he did. He'd a lot more experience than me anyway, and he'd already been in South Africa for five months. He was virtually a Rhodesian as well. Then Dick Robinson, the staff reporter, went on long leave, and we got a temporary replacement, Colin Crick. I thought he was all right, if a bit liberal to send to a place like Johannesburg. You can only work there if you conform to the government's idea of a good reporter – do everything they say, don't try to break their censorship, don't talk to the wrong blacks, and so on. Dick used to get by with sarcasm – some of those Afrikaners haven't got much between the ears. But he's been in the game a long time, much longer than Dave, and he knew his way around. The new guy was wet behind the ears, and Dave gave him one hell of a runaround.'

'How, exactly?'

'There's no way a television reporter can work if the cameraman won't co-operate – if he takes the wrong shots, poses him badly for into-camera pieces, runs out of film at the wrong moment. Dave even tried to blame a couple of breakdowns on the sound, until I made it bloody plain I wasn't standing for that, experience or no experience. We had quite a ding-dong about it, and I told him to give the young guy a chance. He said he couldn't stand parlour pinkoes. In fact, Dave was way out to the right of Genghis Khan. He spoke Afrikaans and he knew all the Afrikaner coppers, even the Security Bureau lot. It was a great help in some of the tight spots, and because of it we often got to places the others – CBS, ITN, the Germans – weren't allowed. But I somethimes wondered if he hadn't tipped them off once or twice when we'd come across something useful.'

'So you weren't a very happy crew, then?'

'No, and it got worse when we went on a trip into Angola.'

'I remember that,' said Light suddenly. 'You got ambushed and had to walk for a month. You all got some sort of award.'

Price was contemptuous.

'Yeah. It must have been for walking. The film we got was crap.'

'You said relations between you got worse,' Ashcroft prompted him.

'They did, Super, they did.' He seemed reluctant to say any more, but Ashcroft pressed him.

'Mr Price, I know you don't want to speak ill of the dead, but I assure you we do need to know. Please tell us what happened. From the beginning. How was the trip arranged?'

'Well, Dick had been trying for months to fix up a visit to Angola. You can do it from Pretoria, when Jonas Savimbi and his Unita guerrilla bunch are doing well. It's not so easy when the government in Luanda are squeezing them. When that happens it's common knowledge that the South Africans send a deep raiding party, or some bombers, to kill a few Angolans, and Cubans if they're lucky. Then you can't go in, in case you spot them. That's how it was first proved that they were operating in Angola at all – an ITN crew spotted the troops by accident. All Savimbi's gear comes from Pretoria, and a lot of his food too. It's all part of the South African policy to keep the blacks fighting each other – a bit like the United States arming both sides in the Arabian Gulf to keep the oil price up – and they're doing it all the time. They've nearly destroyed Mozambique by sponsoring Renamo, and they're keeping the pot boiling for Mugabe in Matabeleland.'

'Keep to Angola, Mr Price.'

'OK, I guess you know the politics. Anyway, this trip suddenly came through, and we went on it. I don't know if Dave Phillips had anything to do with fixing it up. He seemed to know what to expect, but he wasn't very communicative with Colin and me. We flew to Lusaka and were picked up at a hotel there by two Unita contact men in the middle of the night. They drove us in an old Land Rover for more than two hours through the bush to a sand airstrip where we were bundled into an rickety Dakota. It was about 40 years old and rattled like a set of castanets, but it took off all right. There was just us and the pilot. He was white, but he didn't speak to us, not that we could have heard him.

'We landed – quite a good landing – at another strip in the bush. None of us had a clue where we were, but we were met by another Unita man, in camouflage uniform. He said his name was Jerry, and welcomed us. The platoon meeting us was about a mile away, and would be with us in less than half an hour. He went to tell them we had arrived all right, the plane took off and we were left alone, with our kit, on the edge of the airstrip. It wasn't pitch dark. There was no moon, but the stars were shining like they only do in Africa. There were crickets, too, lots of them. It was like being in a rattle factory.

'Suddenly, there was an explosion and a hell of a lot of shooting broke out somewhere over on our right. There was no way of measuring how far away it was, but we could also hear some shouting, faintly, so it couldn't have been a long way off. We were shit-scared, naturally, and made ourselves as small as we could under a thorn bush. The firing lasted about 15 minutes and then stopped as sharply a̅s̅ it began. We didn't dare move, and decided to wait for dawn, which was only about an hour off, but before it got light Jerry came back and told us the platoon had been ambushed and the vehicle mined. They had fought the ambushers off, but they didn't know who they were. If they were government troops there would be more in the area, so it would not be safe to move until they found out. They would also have to try to repair their truck. It was the only one they had, and there was no prospect of finding another one. We were more than 100 miles from the nearest village. Dave swore at him in some African lingo, but he didn't seem to understand, and just said: "Wait there," and vanished again.

'When it was light enough to see, we took stock of our position. We had been told to travel light, and to bring all our gear in one rucksack apiece, so all Colin and I were carrying were the clothes we stood up in and a couple of shirts, a spare pair of trousers and a change of underwear. The rest of the space was taken up with film for the camera, my sound gear, a spare battery and a portable transformer which would work off a car dynamo to recharge it. Dave, who was more bush-wise than us, had two khaki safari suits and a wide-brimmed scout's hat, his camera and more cans of film. We each had four tins of those hard glucose sweets, which we'd been told would be appreciated by our Unita hosts. And Dave had an automatic pistol, and a box of ammunition. I think it was a Browning. He told us he was a member of a pistol club in Jo'burg. They're very popular there. He said he'd brought it for protection in the bush.

'It had been quite cool while the darkness lasted, not uncomfortable you know, but as soon as the sun began to rise it got hot, and it was obviously going to be very hot by the middle of the day. There was nothing to be seen around us, just the strip cleared of bush and the bush itself – thorn scrub and a few wisps of elephant grass, here and there a tree. Dave called one of them a marula. Everything was a uniform brown and totally flat. There wasn't a sign of a hill anywhere. Dave looked around and said, "M.M.B.A." We asked him what it meant, and he said, "Miles and miles of bloody Africa. It's what the settlers used to say in Kenya during the Mau Mau days." It was the only thing remotely funny I ever heard him say, but he didn't mean it as a joke. Miles and miles of bloody Africa was right.

'We had no food, of course, except the sweets, and no water, but we made a breakfast of some of the sweets, which quenched our thirst, at least. Dave took a few feet of film of us, for want of anything better to do, and we settled down to wait. It got bloody hot, and when we tried to get some shade under the thorn bushes we were bitten by ants. That was no joke, either. Colin began to get sunburnt, in spite of his hat. He's very fair-skinned.

'By midday we were beginning to feel very worried, but then Jerry turned up again with about 20 of his Unita comrades. They were all in some sort of uniform, but not all of them were armed. Three or four had bloodstained bandages, one limped on a sort of home-made crutch. They all had water bottles, and they gave us each a drink, but the only food they carried was biltong – that's strips of game dried in the sun – and hard biscuits.

'Jerry said it was impossible to mend the truck, and we would have to walk with them. How far? we asked. Where were we going? A few days, he said. Less than a week. We would march with the platoon to the main Unita force in the area, and they would send us by truck or Land Rover to see Jonas Savimbi.'

Price shuddered.

'We walked for 31 days. We didn't talk much after the first day, our mouths were too swollen with thirst. The Angolans were very good, even though Dave spent most of that first day cursing what he called fucking Kaffir inefficiency for landing us in this predicament. At the beginning he took film of the Africans on the march,

162

chewing biltong, sipping at their water cans. We got blisters, of course, all of us, but Colin really suffered. Dave had his army boots, so he was best off, and I had a pair of desert boots – brothel creepers – which were fine until the soles gave way, which happened after about a fortnight. My socks had given out long before. But Colin was in dreaful trouble. He had a pair of stout English walking shoes, but as the going was largely through loose sand they kept filling up with it and the grains rubbed the skin off his feet. In three days he was delirious with heatstroke and unable to walk. The Africans made a sort of stretcher on two long poles and we took turn in relays of four, two to each pole, to carry him, with one walking alongside trying to keep the flies off his face, which was peeled raw by the sun.

'We persuaded the Africans to change the routine, and we marched by night for as long as we could, building a sort of shelter for Colin with bushes during the worst of the day. The Africans found enough water from time to time to keep us going, God knows how, but three of their wounded men died on the march, and they suffered just as much as we did. Three or four times they shot some game – a springbok, I think, and one night a kudu, which was much bigger and gave us all fresh meat for two days. Another night they caught a bush pig and roasted it over the camp fire.

'After a week we asked Jerry, who seemed to be the senior of their two officers, where his unit was. He shrugged his shoulders and said they must have moved on. We would have to march on to battalion headquarters. Where was that? He wasn't sure, but he thought about a week's march. We tried to get him to draw a map, starting with a rough outline of Angola in the sand, but he had no idea of what we meant. All he knew was a smattering of English, how to handle a weapon, and how to stay alive in the bush. They all could. Without them we three would have died. One of the troops found a particular bush and made an infusion of its leaves in his billycan. He made Colin drink some, but it was very bitter and he spat the rest out. That night, he ran a very high fever and suddenly broke into a furious sweat, and then collapsed back on his stretcher. I felt his pulse, which had been alternately very fast and very slow, and it was not strong, but even, and he was breathing more easily than at any time in the past three days. The stuff

163

broke his fever, but it did nothing for his feet, which turned septic. The only thing we could do was bathe them when we could get a little water and try to keep the sun off them during the day. My great fear was they would turn gangrenous, and in desperation I took to using urine on them.'

Price looked round the Committee Room and shook his head.

'It says something, doesn't it, when the only thing you can do for your friend is to piss on his feet and stuff your fingers in your ears to cut out the sound of his screaming.'

'What was Phillips doing?'

'Marching. And cursing at the slow progress. I suppose in the first few days we made about 10 miles a day, dropping to about five at the most. I don't know when I threw my gear away because I couldn't carry it. I know the generator went first, then the spare batteries, then the recorder. Dave held on to the one can of film he'd taken but when I ditched the batteries he threw the camera into the bush. He resented Colin. He said Colin was placing all our lives in danger.'

'What did you say?'

'Colin was lying on his stretcher, either unconscious or in delirium, I can't remember. None of us had much left in us at all. I just said I thought we had to do our best to carry on. We were sure to find help soon. Dave said: "Not with that bloody dead meat holding us back. Why don't we leave him in the bush here for the lions?" I could not believe that he meant it. I said: "Don't be so bloody silly, Dave. You must be out of your mind." He said: "Look at the bugger. He's half gone already. It'd be easier to put a bullet in him." And he snatched out his gun from his haversack and pulled back the sleeve to cock it. I yelled, "Dave, don't!" but my legs seemed to be rooted to the ground. I shall never forget his eyes. He was utterly ruthless. He lifted the gun and pointed it at Colin and I could see the knuckle of the trigger finger tightening. But before he could fire Jerry slashed down at his arm with his rifle barrel. The gun went off, but the bullet missed. The gun spun away to the ground and Dave grabbed his arm and swayed. "Christ," he said. "You've broken my fucking arm."'

Price grinned.

'It all sounds pretty dramatic, and I suppose it was. I was pretty far gone myself. I'm a Jew, and I'm not at all religious, but I remember thinking that what Dave had said when he was hit was right. Jerry didn't look much like Christ, but he'd saved Colin's life and he'd saved Dave from murder, and in fact he saved us all for the next day we found the Unita army and a doctor. There was a supply plane going back to somewhere in South Africa but we didn't know anything about it. The doctor shot us full of dope and we woke up in hospital in Jo'burg. Dave had even lost the film he shot. They saved Colin's legs, but he was back in hospital the last time I heard. Nobody said anything and the Beeb looked after us bloody well. Even when I refused to work with Dave again they didn't say anything. I think they put it down to mental strain, which I suppose it was. I haven't told anybody all this before, and it's a bit of relief to get it off my chest.'

They asked him one or two questions, but he had little more to say, except that Phillips had been a bloody good cameraman anyway, and nobody should die that way. So they thanked him and let him go, and Light briefed Ashcroft on his eventful afternoon with the beautiful Mrs Viner.

Together with D.I. Thomas they studied the neat lists of names divided by sport and country, each with its address, most with telephone numbers, and alongside comments on role, personality, activities where known, aliases and family details. Piece by piece, it built up to a picture of a formidable organisation which had put down roots in every Western sports-playing country. Each network had its cells, responsible to the centre, and each cell had its contacts among sympathisers, in governments, civil service departments, big business, sporting bodies and even trade unions. There were lists of principals, agents and sub-agents and their links with South African diplomatic missions in various capitals.

Cricket provided by far the most complete picture of a world-wide web, but a similar pattern was beginning to emerge in ten other major sports. How these networks were financed was not apparent, but among the firms involved were some of the biggest multinational names in industry, banking, agriculture, mining, armaments and space. It was an impressive piece of detective work, but as Detective Inspector Thomas pointed out in his sceptical Welsh way, there was no proof here to satisfy a policeman, an attorney general or a jury, of criminal activity or even intent.

'There's plenty of guilt by inference,' he said. 'But if any of that was published there'd be the biggest libel case in the history of the courts.'

'Maybe, if it were done individually,' said Ashcroft. 'But if it were published as a whole I doubt if anyone would sue. If these facts were made known, they would ruin the reputations of at least a dozen individuals and half a dozen major companies. The information is far more damning than the lists the anti-apartheid movements have been able to give to the United Nations. It would certainly wreck the network itself, because the police forces of half a dozen countries would be obliged to look into the activities of the people named, if only to satisfy themselves they were in the clear. Let me give you an example.'

He turned the pages over and pointed to two names in the British file under cricket. They came immediately after a number of contact names in the South African Embassy.

'Du Plooy, Hermann. 52. NFA. Travels widely under own name as world sales director, Rand Mines and Minerals. (Firm does not exist.) Uses best hotel addresses. Avoids SA embassies, but hirer and external paymaster of rebel tours, so must have access to cash and travel facilities. Operates with Hendrick Van der Merwe (q.v.) in Britain, Australia, N.Z. and twice seen in Caribbean. Ex-Major, SAAF (Intelligence). Reputation: violent. Politics: far right. Good organiser. Personal: divorcé (15 years); suspected homosexual, sadist. NB: see Berger, General Herman (alias).'

'Phillips, David Peter. 39, single, but lives with former prostitute at 4, Shire Heights, Chalfont St Giles. BBC cameraman, much sought after. Recruited by Du Plooy (q.v.) in Johannesburg. Known pervert (see attack on J.V.). Born Rhodesia. Politics: anti-African, but otherwise unknown. Served Selous Scouts during UDI war. Member, several rifle and pistol clubs. Claims judo Black Belt. Fine shot. Suspected home base and scout for dP and vdM. Always flush with cash. Drives new BMW. Dangerous.'

Ashcroft said: 'Libellous, as you see, in both cases. But would either sue? And would we fail at least to investigate? Publication would be the most dangerous thing for them, and for the organisation for which they work. It's inconceivable that the South Africans had not got wind of what Viner was doing, and if he was right that they are about to launch this major drive on world sport, they would not stop at murder to prevent publication. I believe that is exactly what they did, and they had the ideal instrument in Phillips. He was a man they already knew to be ruthless, and to have had experience of killing, and worse, in the Selous Scouts. He was a willing recruit in Johannesburg, and was already working for them, and almost certainly being paid by them to maintain a base in England. He had worked himself into the periphery of the cricket scene as a television cameraman, and was an expert shot. He had good cause to dislike Viner intensely, if hate is not a better word. He certainly would have no compunction in killing him. And what better place to eliminate Viner than at the Lord's Test match? Think of the publicity worldwide.'

Light stirred.

'You can just imagine them adding "Sport is Safer in South Africa" to their brochures. But why all this elaboration? Why not just shoot Viner, as they did Phillips the next day? And why shoot Phillips anyway? He'd done the job for them.'

'I think you used the right word. It was elaboration, but it had a point. A rifle would have made a noise which would have attracted instant attention. It would have been impossible to conceal, and Phillips would have been forced to leave his camera unattended to fire it. Fixing up a gadget like the one he made was relatively simple for him, and in any case it looked like just another piece of TV equipment. He took a chance on the ball-bearing being found, of course, but it might easily have been dropped by a small boy. Phillips probably planned the whole thing, once he'd been given the target, and took great enjoyment in doing so, particularly as the South Africans paid. He might well have got away with it, if he hadn't been so greedy, if he hadn't been such a good cameraman, if that pompous idiot Brownley hadn't been quite such a good doctor, or even if Broadbent and your Brigadier hadn't noticed that Viner was on his way down when he was hit by the ball.'

He looked at both his listeners.

'I don't think there's any mystery about why he was killed himself. Whether we caught him or not, his usefulness to them was finished. If he got away with it, there was no guarantee that in the future he might not have talked. After all, he was an unstable character for all his expertise. And his behaviour in Angola will have got back to Pretoria. Anyway, killing him would avoid paying him any more, and presumably they'll have already arranged to sell the house and make a profit on the whole exercise. In spite of her hopes, I can't see your Miss Sharon Smith suddenly becoming a lady of property. But she does know too much. You'd better get on to Chalfont, Amber, and make sure she doesn't become another statistic. I hope it's not too late. I'd forgotten her.'

They waited while Light dialled the Chalfont number.

'Detective Sergeant Light here, Scotland Yard. May I speak to the DO, please? Oh, he's popped out. Is that WPC Clarke, by any chance? With an E? It is? Good. Are you well? Good. I'm calling about Sharon Smith. Has anyone been up to the house today? I'm a bit anxious about her welfare. Oh, I see. There's someone up there 24 hours a day? Good. Would you alert them that an attempt may be made on Miss Smith's life in the next couple of days? Don't alarm Miss Smith. Just tell her to be careful. You've done so already? Oh. Thank you.'

He returned to the table, slightly pink. Thomas grinned at him.

'With an E, eh? Nice, is she? Sergeants get all the luck.'

Light ignored him with dignity, and spoke to Ashcroft.

'It seems all right so far, sir. They've got a couple of men up there permanently. And Sharon Smith knows how to take care of herself.'

'I wouldn't be so certain, Amber. We've no real proof yet, but I think it's time we put the net out for Du Plooy and Van der Merwe. And I must arrange to see the South African ambassador. That will probably spoil Sunday morning for both of us. Thomas, I want your team to check out every name on this list, and get Sydney on to doing the same. Stick to cricket. Don't worry at the moment about the other sports. We want current whereabouts for the past few days and any unusual activity over the past, say, six months. Put a general call out for information on Du Plooy and Van der Merwe, but don't say what we want them for. Warn they may be armed.'

'Save them for me, Thommo,' said Light.

'And you, Amber, will be seeing your former lady friend. Where and when are you meeting her?'

'Green Park, sir. On the deck chairs.'

'Watch your back, Amber. We shouldn't have let those two run loose. Too much rope, but it may hang us rather than them.'

'I'm sorry, sir, but I can't think that they're all that much of a threat. They're only two Boers, after all.'

'That's the classic mistake we British have been making ever since we tried to take on Kruger. Never underestimate an Afrikaner, Amber. He may be arrogant, but he's nowhere near as thick as he sounds. Remember, it was an Afrikaner who made the world's first successful heart transplant. Van der Merwe may not be too bright, but Du Plooy has plenty of brains behind that bluster. He's been operating this business now for five years, and that's all we know about, without raising any of our suspicions. He may be getting arrogant, but the death of Phillips looks as though it might be the first real slip he's made. I wonder why?'

'Maybe he was under pressure to speed things up. Maybe Pretoria wants to launch this sports offensive sooner than we think. Or maybe,' Light added with a flash of inspiration, 'Phillips had ballsed things up for him, with all that elaboration we were talking about. I didn't think he recognised me as a copper at the Waldorf, but what if he did? And so soon after Phillips killed Viner. Perhaps he thought we'd got on to Phillips and he'd grassed on the whole deal. Or was threatening to grass. Maybe they're planning something else that Phillips knew about.'

'All those points may be valid, separately or collectively, Amber. There is also the possibility that Phillips' death was intended to be read as an ANC revenge for the killing of Viner.'

'Or is just that,' said Thomas drily. 'But I can't see it. We all know Viner was on the blacks' side, and the public know that, to some extent, but I can't see any black group in this country having the organisation to set up a hit like this at such short notice. And they couldn't have known that Phillips killed Viner. It's not even been announced yet. No, the blacks are out.'

'We're going round in circles,' said Ashcroft. 'Let's all get some sleep while we can.'

The joint proprietors of the Fontein Hotel, James and Helen Merrifield, were justly proud of what they had achieved in the few years since they had successfully evaded Mr Mugabe's constraints on the movement of money from Zimbabwe. The Fontein was not exactly a private hotel, and certainly not a public house, but it was luxurious and private behind high hedges in that part of Hampstead known as Millionaires' Row. The house itself did indeed belong to a millionaire, owner of vineyards and gold mines, who found it prudent these days to remain in Stellenbosch and find his amusements in Swaziland; but who had proved very amenable when it came to renting the house as an hotel to an organisation of which he had never heard, but of whose objects he thoroughly approved when they were explained to him by General Berger. He even donated the nominal rent to the organisation, the Friends of World Sport, and only jibbed when he received the bill for the conversion of the building into an hotel – £250,000. It wasn't the money, he explained to General Berger, but the exchange controls. 'Don't you worry your head one little bit, Frikkie,' General Berger said, showing him the sort of look he used to terrorise the terrorists. 'Just give me the cheque in rands and I'll fix it.' The millionaire, who never made out cheques, only signed them, called his Indian accountant, and handed over the money without further demur.

A quarter of a million pounds made a good job of turning a Corbusier-built, 16-bedroomed mansion into a hotel accommodating some 50 guests which, by some curious coincidence, needed a manager and manageress at just the time the Merrifields were leaving Zimbabwe, or Rhodesia as they both preferred to call it. The palatial rooms had been divided into three and even four comfortable bedrooms, each with its own lavatory, bath or shower. The more expensive of the rooms even provided a bidet. The interior had been decorated in creams and greens, and the furnishings came from Heals. There was a handsome dining room which, at a pinch, could seat nearly 100, but was rarely needed unless a special function was required. There was a steady turnover of guests, the clientele growing by word of mouth, but the basis of the Fontein's modest prosperity was the regular if unobtrusive use of its premises by the Friends of World Sport and, in particular, by a Mr Du Plooy and a Mr Van der Merwe.

The Merrifields could never remember quite how they came to hear of the opportunity to run the new establishement. They had written off to a London address more in hope than expectation at the time of the Lancaster House conference, and were thrilled and delighted to receive a joint offer within a month. They sold up

170

their four-star Fontein Hotel in the Vumba Mountains and were equally pleased when their new employers agreed without opposition to their choice of the same name, Fontein. It was no more than confirming their run of luck when General Berger discreetly helped them to launder their money across the international financial restrictions and land them in London with most of their capital intact.

Now James Merrifield ran the restaurant and the bar, while Helen managed the hotel and supervised the menus with cool efficiency. They were never intimate with their guests, who nonetheless seemed to like the unobtrusive service and excellent food, cooked to perfection by a large black member of the Tangwende tribe, who had joined the Merrifields 20 years before in Rhodesia and begged them to take him with them to London when they left. His brothers would kill him, he said, for 'selling out' to the white man. The Merrifields conferred, and as M'pika had proved a first-class cook and, in addition, had learned more than a fair smattering of English, they concurred. More strings had to be pulled with their international contacts, but they managed to provide M'pika with a British passport under the name of Peter Empick, sold their hotel to South African Breweries and flew out to London.

The Fontein did not make them a fortune, but provided a comfortable enough living. M'pika discovered English beer and a laughing Matabele girl from Muswell Hill for a wife and to help in the hotel. Apart from them the Merrifields gave a bed and pocket money to university students, sons and daughters of old Rhodesian and South African friends and business acquaintances, in return for help with waiting and cleaning and general assistance around the hotel. As a system it worked well and cheaply, and it kept them in touch with the past they regretted so much.

Other memories had come flooding back some winters before, when a big man with an iron-grey moustache and a vaguely military air tapped at the little window labelled 'Reception' and asked for a room for a week. Th receptionist signed him in, and that night he had come in brushing the first snow of the winter off his officer's camel-hair and shivering. He demanded a large whisky in the harsh English of the Afrikaner and leant on the bar in a characteristic attitude.

171

'Good God, it's General Berger,' Jim Merrifield said, without inflexion. In the halcyon early days of UDI, General Berger had been a frequent and demanding paying guest at the Fontein in the Vumba, and for a terrifying two weeks, he had been seconded from the South African Army to be the commander of a field unit of the Selous Scouts, who had requisitioned the hotel as a base for 'operational purposes'. The Merrifields later learned that their activities included the public rape and massacre of five nuns, reported in the government press as the fiendish acts of black nationalist terrorists.

'No, Merrifield, I'm not General Berger. My name is Du Plooy, the same as on your register.'

'Very well, Mr Du Plooy. What can I do for you?' Merrifield added after a pause: 'Sir?'

'Since I retired from the army I've been travelling around the world as the representative of several South African firms. I've been looking for a place in London to act as a base. I don't want to maintain a flat and a staff, but I want to rent two rooms – I need sometimes to accommodate a business acquaintance – on a permanent basis. I might be flying in at any time of the day or night without notice and leaving again equally suddenly. Can you accommodate me?'

'It depends what you're prepared to pay.'

Du Plooy had it worked out.

'You charge £50 a night bed and breakfast, or £250 per week. For two using the same room you charge £350 per week. I propose a compromise. I shall pay you £20,000 for the two rooms, cash down in advance, provided they are available to me at any time that I arrive, without notice. Any extra meals and liquor I shall pay cash for. Is that agreed?'

Merrifield blinked. It was a very good deal, tax free, for him.

'All right, Gener . . . sorry, Mr Du Plooy. Provided my wife agrees.'

And so it was decided, and the arrangement had remained for four years on the same basis, with Du Plooy insisting on raising the rate each year in strict line with inflation. It was tacitly understood between them that the Merrifields asked no questons, but often they lay awake at night wondering exactly what form of business he was engaged upon, and concluding that it could only be sanctions-busting, probably, in view of Du Plooy's former army connections, to do with arms. It was no business, they agreed, of theirs. He used them exactly as he had said he would, and in fact hardly troubled them, staying in all a maximum of eight weeks out of the 52 in a year and only occasionally requiring the use of the second room. He did not ask for his money back.

A year ago, Du Plooy had booked the entire hotel for the two weeks covering the Lord's Test the following summer, including the use of the dining-room all day on the Sunday, for an international body called 'Friends of World Sport'. He explained that the members were an elite group of sports-loving people drawn from many different countries, and they would be in London for the Test match, some to enjoy their favourite game, others to sample the English sport for the first time. They would also, on the Sunday, require the dining-room for their yearly conference, just a couple of hours in the morning and possibly, if the election of officers proved contentious, a short while in the afternoon as well. The Merrifields agreed, accepted £25,000 in crisp £50 notes, and promptly booked a Christmas holiday in the Solomon Islands.

'It's funny, Hel,' said Merrifield that night as they laid up the dining-room for 45 breakfasts. 'Du Plooy said they were coming in from all over the world, but apart from a couple of Americans and Germans, I'd swear they were all Cape Dutch. It's more like a military exercise than an annual outing. And they want a blackboard and chalk for the meeting tomorrow. More like a briefing than a meeting, if you ask me. Reminds me of that time in the Vumba.'

His wife frowned. 'Don't. But they are an odd lot. Grace, the girl doing the top floor, said she was sure she saw a revolver poking out of one of the cases in 43. And they've got some peculiar baggage. Different shapes.'

'I shouldn't worry. They're probably some obscure sporting implements, like hurling sticks or stoolball bats. This is a sporting convention, you know. They're behaving themselves, at any rate. No complaints on that score. And they're drinking the bar dry. Of lager, anyway.'

'If they are up to anything, it's nothing to do with us,' Helen said briskly, putting the last salt and pepper pots into place with a decisive bang. 'It worries me sometimes, how we've come to rely on Du Plooy and his money. But apart from the tax-free bit there doesn't seem to be anything wrong. It's not as if he's drug-running or anything like that.'

'Not that we'd know if he was, although that Van der Merwe he brings back sometimes looks as though he'd been doped. Oh well, it takes all sorts to make a world. I haven't seen either of them for a day or two. But that Schuster, the German, says Du Plooy'll definitely be here for the meeting tomorrow. I expect that'll mean he'll be in later tonight.

'It's none of our business. Come on, love. Let's go to bed.'

As she was drifting off to sleep, she thought she heard her husband say: 'There's another funny thing. They've been at Lord's for three days, and I haven't heard one of them say a word about the killings. It's very odd . . .'

Chapter 7

Sunday

Bart Imrie woke with sun streaming brightly through his open window on the top floor of the Waldorf Hotel. It had been a warm night, and although he had thrown off the covers he had been perspiring. His mouth was dry. It always was after a few beers. There were a couple of cans still beside his bed, but he felt more like a cup of tea. They used to send up pretty young maids in little black dresses with short skirts, and the tea came steaming hot in a pewter pot, with two biscuits on a plate. Nowadays a black plastic electric kettle stood on a shelf, and you popped a tea-bag or coffee-bag into a thick white cup and added the boiling water. Then you added this white powder if you wanted cream, or opened a tiny plastic holder of milk. Sugar used to come in a bowl in little lumps. These days it, too, was encapsulated in plastic. Imrie made some tea. He swore as his fingers ripped the top off the milk container too rapidly and most of it squirted over his pyjamas. He added what remained to the teacup and took a sip. It tasted of plastic too, so he abandoned it and turned to a can of lager. It was warm, and flat, and tasted of tin, so he went back to the tea and wondered why he was feeling so low. Thank God it was a rest day, except there was that bloody sponsor's lunch party.

He ought to have been on top of the world. Here he was, leading an Australian team which had got the measure of the Poms, and at Lord's, too. He knew there would be pain later over Jack's death, the poor bastard, but all that seemed to be shut off from his real world, the world of the little red ball, the sweetness of the timing that sent the ball to the boundary, the thrill of the wickets going down, the roar of the crowd. He knew that he had taken over the team at a crucial time for Australian cricket, when the slow improvements brought about by Viner over the past few years had to be consolidated if the fickle public was not going to lose all interest in the game at Test level. He knew he'd done well, too, after that appalling beginning. He'd forever remember Jack going down onto his stumps, his own shock and disbelief when the announcement came. We were saved by Collie Foster, he remembered, and Charlie Comberton. And then that amazing session when he'd seemed to have the golden touch. What a bit of luck the boys bowled like that, especially Sissie. It was all bluff, really. There was nothing in the wicket. The Poms talked themselves out. They didn't seem really interested. Look how easy it was for Charlie and me there yesterday. But that Carter, he was half the bowler he'd been on Thursday. Two, three yards shorter and no swing. The lads reckon he's still shell-shocked about poor old Jack. So was Griff.

That was what was nagging at him. Griff Cousins. Imrie hadn't seen the manager after the game, which had been annoying when Australia had had their most successful day in the field for years. It was odd the manager had not been there on the steps to congratulate him and the team, but the physio, Doc Wright, had told him that Cousins had been feeling crook and buggered off early back to the hotel. Imrie didn't like the man, but he supposed he'd better find out how he was.

He swung his legs out of bed and dialled the manager's room number. No reply. He was either out to the world (which was always possible) or had already gone down to breakfast. Imrie showered slowly, dressed in shorts and an Aussie gold T-shirt and strolled down the stairs. He disliked lifts. At Cousins' door he knocked, softly at first, then more loudly, calling out the manager's name. A door opened along the corridor and a bleary face looked out.

'For Christ's sake stop that bloody row. It's the middle of the night. Oh, sorry Bart.'

'It's OK, Charlie. Have you seen anything of Griff?'

'No, and I don't flaming well want to. 'Night.' The head disappeared.

Imrie grinned and knocked again. He tried the door, but it was locked, so he went down to the hotel reception desk.

'Have you seen Mr Cousins this morning?'

'No, sir.' The girl checked the rows of pigeon-holes. She picked out two letters. 'It looks as though Mr Cousins hasn't been back since yesterday morning, Mr Imrie. His key's still there, and these letters must have come yesterday. There's no post on Sundays.'

'Do you know if he came back at all yesterday? He felt crook at Lord's and said he was getting a taxi to come back some time during the afternoon. I'm a bit worried, miss. Have you another key to his room so I can have a look to see if he's there?'

'I'll get the manager, sir. He's got the pass-keys.'

But Cousins was not in his room. His bed was made and did not appear to have been slept in, and the room had not been disturbed since it had been tidied up by the maid the previous morning.

'Shit,' said Imrie, scratching his head. 'The bloody manager can't just disappear. I expect the little bugger hung one on last night and is sleeping it off somewhere. Unless he went whoring.'

'Would you like me to inform the police, Mr Imrie?'

'No, no. He's probably pissed out of his tiny mind somewhere. If we tell the cops it'll get into the Press; this tour's in enough trouble as it is without having stories of drunken managers to add to it. He'll turn up. He's done it before.' And indeed Imrie's mood was much more one of anger than concern. Cousins' absence would place a much heavier load on the acting captain than was necessary. There was this lunchtime party for the Universal Life Insurance Company on the lawns at Hurlingham. If Cousins didn't turn up then Imrie would have to make a speech, and he would rather face a battery of West Indian quickies on a bad pitch than do that. Trust the little sod to let them down.

When the coach came to take the team to Hurlingham the manager had still not returned to the hotel.

Imrie's opposite number in the England side, Geoffrey Broadbent, had no reason to wake up in a good frame of mind. On the face of it, he had far more to worry about than Imrie. His team were in bad shape: they had failed to break through the Australian second innings and the way they had bowled and fielded the previous day it seemed they would not do so, in this match at least. Broadbent sat on the open window ledge trying to work out when and why his authority seemed to have slipped. He'd always been in control of himself and his team before. Perhaps it was when he dropped that catch off Carter's bowling, or the shot he played to get himself out in the first innings. A captain must set an example, and these were two examples of bad cricket. Or perhaps it was his handling of young Carter after he had hit Viner. Bloody bad luck, that. Carter had bowled superbly in that first innings burst, though, but yesterday he bowled crap. Pure crap. Said he felt ill, but there was nothing wrong with him. Silly young sod. And Spencer's not helping, with those snide cracks.

Broadbent breathed the air deeply and refused to let his thoughts mar for one moment his enjoyment of the morning, his coffee, or the anticipation of crisply fried bacon, sausages and eggs which lay in wait for him in the dining-room downstairs. There was very little traffic at that time of a Sunday morning and there was a slight heat haze beginning to form over Regent's Park. It was going to be another corker of a day. He hoped there would be plenty of ice at the Hurlingham party.

He donned a dressing-gown and padded along the corridor to the room Carter shared with Bowyer-Smith, the second youngest member of the team. Bowyer-Smith was in the shower, singing, not very tunefully, the Eton Boating Song but Carter was lying in bed under a sheet with his hands behind his head, staring at the ceiling. His eyes were bloodshot and encircled by dark rings and a half-smoked cigarette dropped from his lips. Broadbent leaned over and took it out, dropping it into an empty beer can. It sizzled quietly and died. The smell of stale smoke intensified.

'Faugh!' Broadbent wrinkled his nose. 'This place stinks like a brewer's armpit. Come on, lad.' He twitched the sheet from Carter's recumbent form. 'You're coming with me. Shower, shorts and Nikes. Five minutes. Downstairs. By yourself. That's an order.'

Without waiting for any response, he went back to his own room, changed into running gear and went down to the foyer. When Carter appeared somewhat more than five minutes after, but suitably clad, Broadbent led him into the morning air without speaking and set off at a fearful pace into Regent's Park. Alternating 50-yard sprints with a hard miler's lope he soon had Carter panting and straining for air, but he drove him on relentlessly round the Zoo, past a lake and out into the park again. They passed a few early morning joggers, all too occupied with their own fitness to recognise a couple of cricketers. Suddenly beyond endurance, Carter stopped, sank to his knees and began to retch, agonisingly. Broadbent dragged him to his feet and bent him bodily over the parapet of a little bridge, holding him firmly while Carter emptied the contents of his stomach into the water below. When he had finished, Broadbent half dragged, half carried the lad to a convenient public bench.

He took off his tracksuit top and hung it over Carter's shoulders and watched. After a while the heaving shoulders steadied and the sweat began to dry on the queasy forehead. Carter took his head out of his hands long enough to say, over his shoulder: 'Sorry, skip.'

'Sorry? Sorry? I should bloody well think so.' The Yorkshire accent was very pronounced. 'If you're man enough to be picked for England you've got to be man enough to keep youself in shape. You bowled like a dream on Thursday, and like a wanker's auntie yesterday. Now I don't know what's bugging you and I don't want to know unless you feel like telling me. But you're going to get it under control, or you'll be finished. Now I'll tell you what you're going to do.'

Carter stared miserably at him, but said nothing. He looked as if he was about to vomit again.

'You're going to jog back to the hotel with me and have a long, hot shower. Then you're going to eat breakfast – eggs, bacon, the lot. And then you're going to get into that Mini of yours and drive straight down to St John's Hospital in Chelmsford. Your mother's in there.'

'Mum? Mum? What's she doing in hospital?'

'As far as I know, Mrs Carter has fallen and broken her collar-bone. She'll be going home tomorrow, but she wants to see you soon. She tried to telephone you last night but you were too far gone. I promised to make you get in touch with her today. Chelmsford's not that far.'

'OK, OK, I'll be there. But what's the rush, if Mum's not badly hurt?'

'Apparently she is very anxious about you, and has something urgent to tell you. She wouldn't leave a message. Roly Anderson asked me to have a word with you.'

'I said I'd be there, didn't I? But what about the party? Roly said we'd all to be there.' He was like a truculent child.

With difficulty, Broadbent kept his temper.

'You're excused. And that reminds me. No drinking. No smoking. You've got 24 hours to put paid to that hangover and whatever else you've got. You'll pull your weight tomorrow or I'll guarantee you'll never play for England again.'

They jogged back to the hotel in resentful silence, but Broadbent noticed that when an hour later Carter appeared showered, shaved and smelling of talcum powder, he ate with a young man's appetite of the bacon, eggs, sausages and mushrooms and followed up with toast and quantities of marmalade. Afterwards, looking more purposeful but still worried, he left quickly without speaking to anyone. Broadbent could only hope he was heading for Chelmsford.

By the time Broadbent had finished his coffee and reported to Anderson what he had done, Carter had passed through Stratford and was hitting 80 mph on the A12, foot flat down in the fast lane and cursing the coast-bound holiday drivers who insisted on sticking to the legal limit. The Mini shrieked in protest, but kept going gallantly and rolled Carter through the gates of St John's Hospital, Chelmsford, just 45 minutes after leaving the hotel.

He was directed along a series of old-fashioned corridors to the intensive care unit, where he was greeted by a stiffly starched sister who ushered him into a bright white cubicle the size of a prison cell with the words: 'You've got ten minutes, Mr Carter, and you mustn't tire her. Ring for the nurse if you think she needs help.'

'But, Sister, what's wrong with Mum?'

'Hasn't anyone told you? I'm sorry. She had a severe stroke and fell down. She broke her collarbone against a table. Her left side is paralysed and she may have another stroke at any time. She can just speak, but not very clearly. She has been asking for you all the morning.' The sister made him feel he had been neglecting his duty, which he resented, but all his belligerence melted when he saw the shrunken figure of his mother, lying lumpishly but motionless in the white sheets. Only her eyes were alive. He bent to kiss her and smelt the sour smell of sickness. Her hand clawed for his, and he strained to hear her whisper, word by word: 'Tell. Me. Truth.'

It was the eyes, really. He hadn't meant to tell her anything, to add to her distress. He had never realised his mother's strength.

All his life it had been his father who had been the master, the big man impressive even without his policeman's uniform, something akin to God with it on. After he died there was an emptiness for both of them, and he had never considered his mother could fill the gap for him. But he looked into her eyes and knew she was past distress, past shock, and he told her everything. In terms of human wickedness it did not add up to very much, and the telling took only nine of the ten minutes he was nominally allowed, but for Vincent Carter it was catharsis. As he spoke it was as if a mountain was slipping from his shoulders, freeing his mind and body from the guilt that had been weighing it down for days before he bowled the ball after which Jack Viner died.

He saw clearly for the first time not only how foolish he had been, but how he had been duped, starting with the flattery, then the drink and the pot, and then that first, perverted, experience of sex. He saw how he had been inveigled into betting on himself to deliver that bumper at Viner, and why he had been paralysed with guilt afterwards. He felt as though he were a small boy again and he felt a man, at last. He stood up and kissed his mother, who smiled at him with her eyes and gripped his arm tightly with her good hand.

'It's all right now, Ma. I know where I'm going. Thanks to you.' He knew he had three jobs to do. The first was to tell Detective Chief Superintendent Ashcroft and Detective Sergeant Light everything he could. The second was to help England win the Test. And the third was to find the man who called himself Du Plooy. The first would be easy, now, but the other two more difficult. He said his thanks to the bossy sister and surprised her into unaccustomed silence by kissing her on the cheek. 'Well!' she said to herself, watching him stride out of the ward. 'Before and after. It might have been a different man.'

Detective Chief Superintendent Ashcroft enjoyed a less rewarding Sunday morning. Promptly at 10.30, as arranged, he was ushered through the reinforced steel doors of the South African Embassy in Trafalgar Square and into a large room heavy with polished mahogany, a portrait of Cecil Rhodes, and dark brown ceiling-to-floor curtains. In the few minutes in which he waited he was

181

struck by the silence. No whisper of Trafalgar Square's tourist bustle on a beautiful midsummer Sunday forced its way through the bullet-proof glass of the windows, and his feet sank noiselessly into the pile of the carpet. He had the feeling of being anaesthetised from the outside world in an atmosphere purged of everything more polluting than the odour of furniture polish. He found his pipe, still blackened and encrusted from his abortive efforts to smoke it, and held it in his hand, somewhat comforted by the pungency of the stale tobacco although he could see no matches with which to light it. He had the feeling he was being watched.

He did not have long to wait. Although he heard no door opening, a tall elegant man with grey hair, dressed expensively all in grey, materialised at his side, holding out his hand.

'Good morning, Chief Superintendent. I am sorry to have kept you waiting. Langstrom, First Deputy Secretary. I am sorry the Ambassador is unable to see you himself, but I have his authority to give you our fullest cooperation. So far as we can. How can we help?'

The lips smiled, but the grey eyes in the spade-shaped face stayed as cool as Ashcroft's own. The accent was pure Oxford. Ashcroft remembered the name.

'Thank you, Mr Langstrom. Balliol, wasn't it? Fencing and rugby football. An unusual double blue.'

A genuine smile this time.

'Thank you. Rather, should we say, a blue and a half? You were a cricketer, weren't you? Worcester? A little before my time. Now, Mr Ashcroft, I believe you have a problem, and we may be in a position to help. Is it in connection with the unfortunate incidents at Lord's? I was there with the Ambassador on Thursday. We were rather surprised that the match had not been called off.'

'There was a great deal of discussion, of course. But it was decided that on the whole it was better to carry on as normally as possible. Mr Langstrom, the investigation so far indicates that a South African national either committed, or is responsible for one if not both the murders at Lord's. The names we have are Hermann Du Plooy and Hendrick Van der Merwe, who purport to be salesmen for a non-existent firm called Rand Mines and Minerals. In general their activities appear to have been devoted to attracting cricketers to play in South Africa, but until now they do not appear to have overstepped the laws of this country, except possibly the immigration laws, and we are investigating that aspect. Murder is quite another matter. We believe them to be dangerous and we are investigating that aspect. Murder is quite another matter. We believe them to be dangerous and we are urgently seeking them, to help in our inquiries. In the first place, are you aware at the embassy of their presence in Britain and the purpose of their being here?'

'I will make inquiries, Mr Ashcroft, but to the best of my knowledge the answer is in the negative. You may rest assured that this embassy would not condone any activity that was against the laws of your country.'

'If they were to seek asylum in the embassy, would you grant it?'

'That would depend on the offences they were alleged to have committed. If the Ambassador was to deem it a political prosecution, then I presume the matter would be for resolution between the two governments. But if the persons concerned were wanted on a charge as serious as murder, then we would have no hesitation in handing them over for the due processes of the law to take their course. We would not hinder you in any way. In some ways, Chief Superintendent, there is a higher regard in my country for the laws of others than perhaps is the reverse case.'

Ashcroft ignored the thrust.

'Thank you. I take it, then, that the embassy has not been supporting financially or in any other way the activities of Messrs Du Plooy and Van Der Merwe? They seem to operate very freely with cash in spite of your country's rather strict laws in that respect.'

There was a tiny twitch of muscle at the side of Langstrom's mouth.

'Come now, Chief Superintendent, you would not expect us to admit anything so harmful as breaking our own laws, let alone yours, would you?'

'Such cases have been known,' said Ashcroft mildly. 'If you should hear of anything that might assist us in our inquiries, I would be very grateful if you would ring me either at New Scotland Yard or Lord's.'

'Of course. This embassy does not approve of unofficial operations and does its best to discourage them.'

183

Langstrom escorted him to the front door and unexpectedly accompanied him out onto the steps of the embassy. The sun struck them with welcome warmth after the air-conditioned chill of the building, and the bustle of Trafalgar Square washed over them.

Langstrom shook Ashcroft's hand formally, bowing slightly so that his face came closer to the Superintendent's.

'I am told that the Fontein Hotel in Hampstead is a good watering hole.'

He pressed Ashcroft's hand and vanished behind the silently closing door.

It was a beautiful day, and Ashcroft did not hurry as he walked down Whitehall and along to New Scotland Yard. He had always regretted the move from the Embankment and the cosy Victorian pokiness of the original Scotland Yard, preferring its desperate inconvenience to the glass-partitioned modernity of Victoria Street.

He found Light waiting with some impatience. The Detective Sergeant's hunch had paid off, it seemed. He was early enough to have found a couple of free deck chairs in Green Park and he carried them as far from the main throng as he could, finding a half-shaded spot and setting up camp with a Thermos of coffee and two cups. He waited half an hour, sipping his coffee and watching London disport itself in the sun, and was beginning to get bored when a weary voice said: 'Hullo, Amber. Don't get up.' Renee dropped into the deck chair and accepted the plastic cup of coffee with a sigh.

'I can't be long. He's gone to a meeting or something. He nearly killed me on Thursday night.'

Light studied her. Renee Hodge was still a good-looking woman, although the bright sunlight betrayed the lines beside her eyes and her ultra-blonde hair. Her figure retained all its attraction for men, and she had no hesitation in displaying it and her exquisite legs. Light said suddenly:

'Why didn't you stay on the stage, Renee? You'd have made a bomb.'

She sighed again.

'I know, dear. That's what I'm always told. But I couldn't act, I couldn't sing and I wasn't a very good dancer. It was second line of chorus for me and a lot more energetic than my other job.'

She laughed. Light said: 'D'you see anything of Sharon Smith these days? She gave you your first job, I remember.'

'Yeah.' The Cockney-American was laconic. 'Waving my pussy at fat businessmen. The lunchtime letch, they called me. She's pulled out, the last few months. Don't know where she's gone. Some rich daddy, probably.'

'You haven't heard from her?'

'Well, there was a message a couple of weeks ago. She told Hermann she wanted a couple of girls for a blue video party, somewhere in the country. You know the sort of thing. Booze, a bit of pot, then lay this guy for the cameras. Good pay – a couple of hundred plus another one for exes. That's not my scene now. I try and stick to one guy who can afford me.'

'How long have you been with Du Plooy?'

'About six months, on and off. It's a good deal. I can do what I like when he's away, so long as I'm available when he's in England. He's fixed me up with a nice little flat just off Charlotte Street and he comes there. He keeps his clothes there.'

'Did he know about the offer from Sharon?'

'Oh, yes. It was him that asked me to find the girls. When I heard the price I said to him, joking like, that it'd be worth a day off. He didn't like it a bit. You can't have a laugh with Hermann. No sense of humour.'

'Did he hit you?'

'No, but I thought he was going to. I'd never thought a man like him could be jealous. Not like that. "I'm paying you, and you'll bleddy stiy yar." ' She managed a tolerable imitation of the Afrikaans accent.

'Is he kinky?'

'Not so's you'd notice. It's funny. He doesn't seem to like sex all that much. He's very straight-laced about it. I've often wondered if he wasn't the other way a bit, and likes me around for the respectability, so to speak. There's that Hennie. I'm also a good way of getting him in with the cricketers. They always flock around us girls like bees round a honeypot.'

'Do you know what he's doing with them?'

'He says he's laying on these rebel cricket tours, but I think there's a lot more to it than that. He doesn't say very much, but I

185

know he wants to buy up every top sportsman in the country. And he's got the money, too. A whole suitcase full. He brought it to the flat once.'

'I suppose he went to the Test match on Thursday?'

'Yes he did, in the afternoon. He said he had a headache in the morning and watched it on the box.'

'Did you watch it?'

'No, not really. I can't stand cricket. But I did see that man fall down, when the ball hit him.'

'What did Hermann say when that happened?'

'Nothing. Just . . .'

'Just what?'

'Well, he sort of smiled, and went to the telephone. He shut the door so I couldn't hear what he was saying, but I know he phoned South Africa, because he couldn't get through on direct dial and had to get the operator to help. Then I could hear him shouting "Is that Pretoria?" But what was funny was when he'd finished the call he came back and insisted on making love. Real sex, like a bull. It'd never been like that before. And he kept saying "Stuff the English. Stuff the English," all the time he was doing it.'

'And then?'

'Then Hennie called and they went off to the Test match together.'

'Did you hear any more of what he said on the telephone? Come on, Renee, you're not going to tell me you're not inquisitive?'

'Well,' she admitted, 'I did try a bit, but he would have been so angry if he'd caught me. There was something about a meeting. At some hotel. I think he said the Fountain, or something like that.'

'Do you know the date of it?'

'No. I think he said Sunday, but which Sunday I didn't hear. I think he said they expected quite a few people there. Fifteen, or it could have been fifty.'

'And Friday?' he asked casually, but she was not deceived. 'I know what you're trying to do, Amber. You think he shot that BBC man, don't you? Well, I'm not going to help you. Hermann and Hennie went off to Lord's again in the afternoon and I haven't seen them since.'

'Not even at night? Isn't that unusual?'

'No, not really. He's had these meetings before and he's stayed in the hotel.'

'Have you any idea what these meetings are?'

'Something to do with sports, and cricket. They don't say much, and he never tells me anything. But . . .' She paused, and Light thought it better not to push her. After a while she said: 'It's just that I got the feeling that this meeting was much more important. Hermann has been, well, different. Sort of on edge. He gets very angry with Hennie, and he's spent hours on the telephone. All over the country, and abroad. It'll cost him a fortune.'

'How do you know where he's been phoning?'

'I don't. But when you've got nothing to do but sit and count the clicks when he dials, you can't help noticing.'

'Renee, have you noticed anything else recently?'

'Well, he had some pretty heavy parcels delivered. He said they were equipment for this meeting. They were covered in red seals and looked terribly official.'

'What shape? What size?'

'They were just boxes. Two were about two feet across, I suppose. The third would have been about three feet long and about a foot square.'

'When was this?'

'It must have been about two weeks ago. He took them all away the day after they arrived. He even apologised for their having been sent to the flat, which was odd for Hermann. He usually doesn't give a monkey's for what I think.'

That was about it. They sat in the sun for a few minutes, each of them busy with their thoughts. Light asked a couple of desultory questions and then got up to leave. He handed Renee a brown manila envelope, which she slipped into her handbag.

'It's been nice talking to you,' she said with a faint smile. 'Just like old times.'

A thought struck him.

'Renee. I wouldn't stay in that flat if I were you. We've got an alert out for Du Plooy and Van der Merwe. Suspected murder.'

She was shaken, but her streetwise experience told her not to be surprised.

'I can't believe it. No, yes I can. I mean, Hermann wouldn't hurt me, would he?'

'If he knew I was a policeman, he would have done just that. You didn't tell him, did you?'

'Course not. I'm not stupid. Hermann doesn't like police.'

'Is there anywhere you can go?'

'Your flat?' she asked with a flash of spirit. 'Or is that out of bounds these days? It didn't used to be.'

Light flushed.

'Come off it, Renee. I'm serious.'

'So am I.' A pause. 'You're just trying to frighten me. What's he done, anyway?'

'At the present count, illegal entry, currency smuggling, drug ditto, conspiracy to defraud, procuring and murder. Is that enough?'

'I think I could go to Sharon for a bit anyway. She'll have plenty of spare rooms now.' She made a little 'oh-oh' sound.

'Renee. So you do know where Sharon lives, then?'

'Yes,' she admitted reluctantly. 'Sorry, Amber. But I wasn't there when they set up Vince Carter. Honestly I wasn't.'

Another pause. For the second time Renee knew she had said too much. Light grinned at her.

'I think you'd better come down to the Yard and make a statement.'

They walked past Buckingham Palace to New Scotland Yard and found Ashcroft ensconced at his desk. Detective Inspector Thomas was there too, the shadows under his eyes deepening in the hue from lack of sleep. His industry and that of his team of detectives had borne fruit.

'It's coming together very well,' he told Ashcroft. 'We've had checks run on all the names on Viner's list that look halfway relevant. That's about 55, mostly in this country but about a dozen in Australia, more in South Africa, half a dozen in the States and Canada and a couple of real beauties from Ulster. One from each side, just to keep it neat. The rest of them from all over this country. The funny thing is they're all – those of them we can trace – quite legit, except the Irishmen, who are both rogues with records as long as your arm. GBH and upwards. They're the odd ones out. The Brits seem to be mainly businessmen, though there are two private airline pilots, one or two trade unionists, a parson and a couple of scoutmasters. Not more than a parking fine and a drunk driving between them. The Aussies seem to be much the same, and so do the Springboks, though I don't suppose we'd be told any different. The Yanks seem OK too, but Miami are checking. One of their senior officers thought he tied a couple of names on the list with ones he's got stashed away in a desk drawer, so he's going to confirm. A connection with the KKK or the John Birch Society, or something. If he's right, he'll come over direct.'

Thomas waved at the telephone on the desk as his Welsh sing-song paused for breath. As though by magic it rang at that moment. Ashcroft picked it up and indicated that Thomas should listen in on the extension.

'Ashcroft here. Detective Chief Superintendent. Can I help you?'

'Sure can. Miami here. Hank Freeburg. Captain.' The voice sounded ironic. 'You the guys making an inquiry about the Jaybee Society?'

'That's right.'

The voice did not stop, riding over any question.

'Arnold B. Tewson and Jeremy Rubekker. Suspect Klansmen. Never proved. Hot-shot lawyers for Jaybee, now in mid-sixties, now retired. Two of the guys responsible for the Rhodesian Birch campaign in the sixties. The others on your list all hard right, which is no big deal over here these days. Clean records. Funny thing, they're all outta town. Tewson and Rubekker flew London Friday. They said they were going to a cricket match, for Christ's sake. Address: Fontanne Hotel, Hampstead. Could be the others were on same plane – People's Express from Miami. That do you, Superintendent?'

'Fine, thanks very much. I presume Jaybee is John Birch.'

'Right on. Say, what's this cricket? Like baseball, only fast asleep, I'm told.'

'Come over, Captain, and let us initiate you. We owe you a favour.'

'Sure. Be there tomorrow. Ciao.'

And he hung up, leaving Ashcroft gazing in some bemusement at the telephone. He relayed the gist of the information to Light. Thomas was already deep in the telephone directory.

'Plenty of Fountain Hotels, but none in the Hampstead area,' he reported. 'No Fontanne. A Fontaine in Mayfair, and one in Richmond.'

189

He ran his finger down the columns of names and back up again. 'Ah, that sounds better, Fontein Hotel, in Bishop's Avenue.'

He wrote down the number and passed it to Ashcroft.

'Hang on a moment.'

Two minutes later he had elicited from the duty sergeant at Hampstead Police Station that the Fontein Hotel was a comfortable establishment, rather like a private hotel, run by two ex-Rhodesians of good reputation.

'Very quiet, no trouble with the licence in six years. No call girls, or if there are they're the upper crust sort. Private dining-room, big enough for parties or small conferences. Small bar. £50 a night B and B. It's no doss house.'

'Amber. Quickly.'

But Light was already halfway out of the office.

'Thomas. Get a warrant. Fast as you can. Twelve men, back and front. But don't move until you hear from Amber. If he confirms it, the charge will be conspiracy to murder. We'll sort out who did what later. I'll wait here. I think we're probably too late.'

They were, but only by ten minutes.

The meeting of the Friends of World Sport had lasted only 90 minutes. The members had received their briefing and had all departed to their allotted points on the map by the time Light was standing in the neat cool foyer asking Jim Merrifield and his wife about their guests and, particularly, about Mr Hermann Du Plooy. The Merrifields told him all they knew, without reservation, but with a feeling that a lucrative source of income was about to be denied them.

'How did you come to know him in Zimbabwe? Rhodesia?'

'He came to stay at the hotel, which was a coup for us. He was a bit of a legend in the seventies. They say he used to take his leave from the South African Army and come to Rhodesia to relax by fighting a real war. Once people knew he stayed with us they used to arrive in droves just in the hope of catching sight of him. He'd got the helluva reputation with the Selous but he never gave us any bother. He helped us set up over here, Sergeant, and he's brought us a lot of custom since. We've always felt he was using us, but he pays well, and in any case we don't agree with sanctions.

190

We've never actually liked the man, but we hope he's not in trouble.'

Light said that if Du Plooy was in trouble, it did not seem to involve the Fontein. He asked if Du Plooy had ever used the hotel for assignations.

'Sex, d'you mean?' asked Mrs Merrifield. 'No. I told him from the start that if he wanted the place for that sort of thing, he could take his custom elsewhere. And he never has. He's used us more like a rented room.'

'Tell me about the Friends of World Sport.'

'We don't know very much. We think Du Plooy runs it. This is the first year they've been here. They booked in for the whole of the Test, but they all booked out this morning before the meeting. Mr Du Plooy explained that there was no need for a long meeting as they'd done all the business over dinner the night before.'

'Do you know what that business was?'

Jim Merrifield replied, 'No, except it had something to do with South Africa in world sport. You can't help overhearing a bit in a small place like this, though I don't like eavesdropping and Du Plooy was very strict that the meeting was not to be disturbed. No coffee or anything.'

'What did you hear?'

'Oh, a couple of them were waiting to pay their bills after breakfast, and one was saying to the other that at last the Friends were doing something really worthwhile. He said they'd be world-famous by the end of the Test match if they all played their parts right. But then his friend hushed him up and they didn't say another word.'

'Did you gather that there was anything wrong – illegal – in what they were planning?'

'I didn't, and I don't think Helen went near them today, did you, darling?'

'No, but they were all laughing and joking when they went out of the coach. One of them said it was the biggest laugh in history. They seemed in a pretty good mood, except the two Irishmen. I heard one of them say something about "bleeding cricketers" and the other something about the money being good, though. And they didn't go in the bus with the rest. I saw them go off down the road looking for a taxi. The rest all piled into the bus together and I waved them goodbye.'

'Where were they off to? Do you know?'

'No, I don't. It was some sort of tour.'

'Do you remember the coach?'

'Sorry, Sergeant, I don't. It was just one of those huge ones, cream and red, I think. I didn't notice.'

'And they're not coming back here at all?'

'No. I don't know when they'll be back. Mr Du Plooy's arrangement goes on for the rest of the year. He doesn't have to renew it until November. He doesn't have to say when he's coming, either.'

Light took descriptions and reported dispiritedly to Thomas and his squad, waiting patiently across the square in an anonymous minibus. Thomas, refusing to be depressed, sent two men into the hotel to look through the rooms, 'just in case' anything useful had been left behind, and radioed the Irishmen's descriptions back to the Yard for circulation.

'It's no use putting out a call for the coach,' he admitted cheerfully. 'If we stop and search every cream and red coach in London we'll bring the traffic to a halt for 50 miles around. That would be fun, eh?'

Detective Chief Superintendent Ashcroft did not think it would be fun, but he did not say so. Instead he spent the next five hours unsuccessfully trying to piece together the jigsaw of Hermann Du Plooy and the Friends of World Sport.

His deliberations were complicated by a number of interruptions. First there was Vincent Carter, demanding his presence as a Catholic might a priest for his confessional. There was not much Ashcroft could say to comfort him, beyond telling him that he had been a bloody young fool but if he was lucky he might just escape charges of being an accomplice to murder, using drugs and conspiring to defraud the bookmakers. But Carter appeared to regard Ashcroft, a senior policeman, as a substitute for his dead father, and merely talking seemed to benefit the bowler's spirits. A wearying business.

As soon as Carter left the telephone rang. It was the manager of the Waldorf Hotel, reporting that Mr Griffiths Cousins, the manager of the Australian cricket team, had been missing since Friday afternoon. The players had expected to see him at their lunchtime party with the sponsors at Hurlingham, but when he had not shown up Mr Imrie had decided to inform the police. He, the manager, had volunteered to do so. Mr Imrie was feeling tired after the party and wanted to rest, but would of course be available to the police if they wished to send someone round. Ashcroft, feeling as though he was on a roller coaster that was beginning to run out of control, detached Light and a detective constable to the Waldorf and added Cousins to Thomas' list of people the police wanted to interview.

Then there was the Press, with whom Ashcroft was as communicative as possible without saying anything significant; but before some of the more acute journalists began to point this out, he was able to divert them with the sensational titbit that the Australian manager had been missing for 48 hours and, yes, it appeared germane to the case of the two killings, as one Sunday sub-editor had felicitously dubbed it.

Ashcroft's satisfaction in being able to tell the journalists something they had not known first was somewhat marred by a call from Light at the Waldorf. He reported that Cousins had turned up in a taxi drunk and incapable of speech five minutes after the police had arrived at the Waldorf and was now sleeping off a monumental hangover. Light had caught the taxi-driver, who was waiting for another fare, and learned that Cousins had been dumped in his cab by a lady – 'Know what I mean?' – in Maida Vale, who handed over a ten-pound note and told the cabbie to drop his fare at the Waldorf and keep the change. Light sounded more than a little angry, but Ashcroft merely told him to give Cousins a couple of hours, then to wake him with a cup of strong coffee and notice of arrest if he failed to answer questions satisfactorily. In the meantime, Light was to carry on asking questions, particularly of Imrie and the Australians, to see if any of them could throw light on Hermann Du Plooy and his machinations. And when he had finished with Cousins, Light was to proceed to Selsdon and to ask Mrs Julie Viner about the Friends of World Sport, an assignment Light accepted with some alacrity.

Ashcroft told Thomas to redouble his efforts to find Du Plooy, and then had himself driven to Lord's. His MCC tie and his Chief Superintendent's ID gained him entry from a surly gatekeeper, and he strolled slowly across the turf to the square in the late afternoon light, letting his thoughts travel far and wide. The covers were not over the worn pitch. It was some hours to go to dusk yet, and no sign of a break in the perfect weather. Viner had stood HERE, he thought, taking up a batsman's stance and then correcting himself. No, HERE. Viner was left-handed, of course. Did that mean anything? No. Then what did? He was back to the basic question. What was the motive in all this? Here, in the still heart of Lord's, he again had the impression that there was a roller coaster out of control.

He strolled slowly to the Nursery End sightscreen, still pondering. To the right there was a roped-off area covered by a tarpaulin, where the blood had dripped from Phillips' shattered skull. That was a vicious, unnecessary murder, organised by a vicious mind; it was a twisted, convoluted mind that had planned the details of Viner's murder. Phillips the ruthless hedonist had manufactured the air gun, affixed his ingenious sight to the videocamera, and fired the ball-bearing that killed Viner, the great cricketer and anti-apartheid campaigner. But Phillips was dead, and there must be a logic to the two deaths. The long arm of coincidence did not stretch so far. It seemed obvious that Du Plooy had masterminded Phillips to kill Viner and then killed Phillips himself, or at least arranged his killing with the maximum of publicity. That was another illogicality. Why at Lord's, during a Test match? In any case, Du Plooy's involvement still had to be proved. Both men had served in the Selous Souts; both were used to gratuitous killing. Both men had an interest in sexual diversion, not to say perversion. It seemed obvious, too, that Du Plooy had been Phillips' source of funds; and that Du Plooy had access to unlimited money. That money must come from somewhere.

There, sitting on a bench in a stand at Lord's in the silence of a warm summer Sunday evening, Ashcroft began to formulate his theory. It was so outrageous that he did not believe it himself. But later that night he received a phone call from one Jim Merrifield, ex-Coventy CID, and he began to think he was on the right track.

Chapter 8

The Fourth Day

Six o'clock on a Monday morning is not a good time to be woken by the telephone. Ashcroft struggled from a deep but uneasy sleep and placed the receiver to his ear, shrugging on a dressing-gown as he did so.

He heard a click and the bleeping as the caller struggled to put a coin in the slot. Another click.

'Ashcroft.'

'Peter Langstrom here. Sorry to disturb you so early, but I thought I'd better ring you. I'm in a call-box and I haven't much time.'

'Go ahead, Mr Langstrom,' said Ashcroft, wondering how Langstrom had acquired his private number, which was ex-directory.

'I was not entirely frank with you, Mr Ashcroft. Du Plooy is well-known in our country for his exploits against the blacks under another name. But information has come to my notice which I think you ought to know. It is common knowledge to both of us that Du Plooy has recently been operating in the field of sports sponsorship and promotion. Not long ago he formed a body called Friends of World Sport whose aims and objects are to promote the interests of South African sport. I must emphasise that this is a project financed entirely by private enterprise, and is not supported by the state, although of course Pretoria is sympathetic. If you see what I mean?'

Ashcroft grunted. So far, this he knew. What Langstrom was saying was that he need expect no official help from the embassy in tracking down Du Plooy. In fact he would meet obstruction.

'The point which I think you should know is that Pretoria has latterly become concerned that Du Plooy has gone much farther than is acceptable. Our Security Branch is of the opinion that, in common with a number of our countrymen, the pressures on the South African way of life have affected him in such a way as to make his actions unpredictable. They feel that this Friends of World Sport may well conceal something really spectacular in world terms. A statement of defiance, perhaps. Welcome as this might seem to be to my government, many of us believe such a thing can only be counter-productive in terms of bad publicity to South Africa, especially when, er, deaths are concerned. Others among us do not feel this way, which is why I am telephoning you on my early morning walk. Stop him, Ashcroft, for Christ's sake! He's round the bend, and he's got a young arsenal. Two murders are enough.'

The last words were uttered with an intensity totally absent from the earlier measured diplomatic tones, and before Ashcroft could reply the line went dead. He replaced the receiver slowly, scratching his head. That was all very well, and he appreciated Langstrom's slightly paranoid efforts. But apart from emphasising the urgency of the search for Du Plooy, the call had added little to the meagre sum of his knowledge. He pondered his way slowly through a bath, a shave, dressing, breakfast and coffee, and then rang the incident room. The indefatigable Thomas was there already.

'Nothing much overnight, Bill. Cousins came to, eventually, and swore he'd been out on the town. He gave some vague address in Soho. Light checked, but found nothing and no one, of course, to remember him. Imrie's written a four-page complaint to the Australian Board of Control, but Cousins doesn't seem to care. I must say I think the feeling's mutual. Amber's having another go at him at the hotel this morning. Renee's gone to Sharon in Chalfont, who've been good enough to reinforce that little girl – I mean WPC – keeping an eye on both of them. Du Plooy hasn't been anywhere near them. Oh, and by the way, those two Yanks from the JBS are booked back to Miami via Frankfurt, which is a bit odd but good riddance, on a flight tomorrow. Not a smell of Du Plooy or Van der Merwe. That's it, I think.'

Ashcroft replaced the receiver, still pondering. His thoughts were interrupted again by the front door bell. A look through the fish-eye-peep-hole revealed Light and Julie Viner. Light looked flustered and angry. Ashcroft opened the door.

'Well, Amber?'

'Sorry, sir.' Light had himself under a tight rein. 'Mrs Viner insisted on speaking to you personally. And urgently. She would not tell me her reasons. She says it's a matter of life and death.'

'Come in, both of you. It's too early to be standing on the doorstep. Good morning, Mrs Viner; you must forgive my state of attire. Amber, you know where the coffee is. Whatever the urgency I will not meet it unshaven and in my pyjamas. Nor before breakfast. I shall be as quick as I am able.'

He shambled off, showing no inclination to make haste, while Light busied himself making coffee. Julie Viner sat still and silent in Ashcroft's big wing armchair. He handed her a cup of coffee and returned to the kitchen, where he busied himself with bacon and a frying pan. He knew Ashcroft's breakfast tastes, and Ashcroft without his breakfast grew progressively more difficult to handle as the day wore on.

Presently Ashcroft put his head round the door.

'Thank you, Amber. Very thoughtful of you. Perhaps you wouldn't mind producing a plate for Mrs Viner. Two eggs, if you don't mind. You'd better have some yourself, too. I gather you've had a long night.'

Light suppressed a snort; but he made himself some toast and the three of them ate the alfresco meal in silence. To his surprise, Julie Viner's appetite matched Ashcroft's, even to the suppressed but companionable burp after the last mouthful had been washed down with a second cup of coffee.

Ashcroft looked at her. The golden tan was underlaid with a tinge of grey, while there was the suggestion of a shadow under the brown eyes and the cream linen business suit was slightly crumpled. Nevertheless, she was still a very beautiful woman.

'Are you ready to talk now?'

'Thank you, yes.' She looked at Light. 'I am sorry about my behaviour at the hotel. Perhaps you will understand when I have told you what happened to me.'

Light nodded. His professional pride had been bruised by her refusal to confide in him rather than Ashcroft, but the snub had not damaged his inquisitive nature.

It was her fault, she told them, in not trusting the police to act speedily or decisively enough and in holding back vital information. Jack Viner had discovered the previous year that the Friends of World Sport were to use the Fontein Hotel, and during that summer Julie herself had stayed there, using her business name. She had soon struck up an acquaintance with the chef, Peter Empick and his wife, and without much difficulty had recruited them to the Viner cause of anti-apartheid. They had kept her in touch by letter, and although they didn't know what the exact plans were, it was obvious something big was planned for the period of the Lord's Test.

'Whatever it was, Jack said he would find out while he was over here and do whatever was necessary to stop it. I had a seat booked on Concorde to come in any case, which was how I was able to get here so quickly when they murdered Jack. I got hold of Peter on the phone on Saturday night and he told me about yesterday's meeting. He still didn't know what it was all about. I thought of trying to gatecrash the meeting, but Peter said it would be impossible. He said he knew Du Plooy in Africa and he was a very dangerous man.'

She had sat in the comfort of Selsdon Park thinking of her dead husband. It was midnight and fear fought with her inner fury and lost. She had picked up the phone again and dialled.

'Peter. I'm sorry to keep you awake. But I must get to that meeting. Make me a waitress. Anything.'

The deep African voice was grave.

'Madam, I have told you how bad that Du Plooy can be.'

'My husband is dead. That is all I know. You must help me.'

'You will not be able to get into the meeting. It will be useless.'

'Let me serve at the lunch. I might hear something. Men never notice waitresses.'

Eventually Empick agreed reluctantly to find her a waitress's uniform and to help serve the lunch. He could justify an extra hand, but he made her swear not to try to eavesdrop the Friends' meeting. It would be asking for trouble.

So it was that when the Friends of World Sport adjourned for lunch, the elegant Julie Viner found herself disguised in a short black dress with a tiny pinafore and a white cap on head, her long legs in black tights and a silver tray balanced on one hand, handing round the sherry. She quickly discovered she had been wrong in one thing. Far from being unnoticed, she was instantly the focus of male attention, most of it lustful. She ignored the repeated innuendoes and evaded the sly touching hands and tried to concentrate on the snatches of conversation she was able to catch.

'Another one, please miss . . . Ta. Oz eh? Lovely tan you've got. Is it all over?'

'. . . And I've got to get to Luton. Jan over there's for Birmingham . . . Where are you heading for?'

'Oh, I'm here. Man-to-man escort.'

'Lucky bugger . . .'

'Say, look at the crumpet . . .'

'Yeah, I could do with a piece of that . . .'

She felt a hand on the back of her thigh and forced herself to move on impassively.

'Hermann seems to have got it all fixed up. It'll be the helluva laugh, man.'

'Yah. Stuff those buggers at Lord's, eh?'

'Another drink, sir?'

'Rather have a nibble. Ha-ha. Give us a kiss.'

'*Gentlemen.*' Merrifield's voice rose fortuitously above the convivial voices. 'Lunch is served.'

Julie extricated herself from the groping hands and helped serve out the roast duck *à l'orange* and the strawberries and cream. She was in demand for pouring out the claret, of which there seemed an unlimited supply. She identified the chief groper and brushed her breast against his cheek as she leaned across to pour his fifth glass of wine. She felt his sharp intake of breath against the thin dress and drew back without haste, allowing her eyes to meet his briefly.

'He was an Afrikaner,' she told Ashcroft and Light scornfully. 'Dirk van Rensburg. A tobacco auctioneer, I think. He slipped me an envelope a bit later with £50 in it and a note saying "Red Rover in drive. D Reg. 2.30". I brought him a triple brandy and winked at him. It was like giving candy to a kid.'

Van Rensburg drove her to a country hotel somewhere in Essex and there threw her on the bed, tore off his trousers and passed out. When he came to a few hours later he was contrite, hungover and very sick. He also turned out to be a masochist, which made Julie's task very simple. With his willing co-operation she used his shirts to tie his hands and feet to the old-fashioned bedposts, made a slip-knot with his shoelaces and then tightened it round his testicles until he screamed for mercy behind the vest she had stuffed in his mouth. Then she thought of Jack and jerked the shoelace again, hard.

'Talk, you bastard,' she said.

Van Rensburg talked, and when he had finished, Julie Viner tightened the shoelace a last time and stuffed the gag back in his mouth. Then she took his car keys and drove back to Selsdon, arranging for a 6 a.m. call as a parting shot. Two miles along the road she stopped the car, got out and vomited at the roadside. When she reached the hotel at Selsdon Park at 3 a.m. she had found Light sitting in the foyer.

'We've had half the police forces in London out looking for you for 12 hours,' he said. 'Where the devil have you been and what the hell have you been doing?' He looked at her in sudden astonishment. 'And what the hell are you dressed like that for?'

Julie Viner looked at him scornfully.

'Sergeant Light,' she said, keeping her voice low. 'I've been doing your fucking dirty work. Literally. I am going to have a long bath, and an hour's sleep, and then you're going to take me straight to Superintendent Ashcroft. Oh, and by the way, there's a man in a bedroom at the Peldon Rose in Essex and unless he's been able to free himself, which I doubt, he should be able to help you with your inquiries. He's not a pretty sight.'

She stormed up the stairs and Light, bemused, ran for the telephone. The indefatigable Thomas was still there, and within 30 minutes two Colchester policemen were knocking up the landlord of the Rose at Peldon and demanding access to Mr van Rensburg's room. As the policeman told Inspector Thomas from the radio car: 'There was a right old mess, but no sign of Van Rensburg. Seems he packed a suitcase and scarpered.'

Ashcroft did not find the story Julie Viner said she had forced out of Van Rensburg of much assistance, except that it confirmed the urgency of apprehending Du Plooy and his henchmen. Van Rensburg had been a tobacco auctioneer for 20 years, working through the transition from Southern Rhodesia to Zimbabwe, and his experience had confirmed all the racial prejudices inherited from his father, the badly-paid manager of a tiny gold mine on the outer fringes of the Rand. Even in the acute agony he had been suffering Julie had heard the contempt in his voice for the 'Kaffirs', as he called all blacks. Like most Afrikaners, he was a great follower of sport, particularly cricket and rugby, and had been recruited by Du Plooy two years previously during a match between South Africa and the rebel Australians. The Friends of World Sport could not have found a more willing volunteer, nor Du Plooy a more pliant confederate. His total belief in the supremacy of the Afrikaner over all other forms of mankind was expressed in perpetual cliché. All British were 'Yaapjes' or 'Rooineks', Americans 'wankers', Indians and Chinese 'Asian bastards' or 'yellow bastards', whichever fitted the case. He was delighted, indeed proud, to be part of any scheme which he was told would further white South Africa's cause in its battle for survival in the face of world opprobrium, especially in the realm of sport.

So far his tasks for the organisation had been small ones, but of growing importance. He had brought over the barrel of the AK47 used by Du Plooy to shoot Phillips, merely one of a dozen couriers whose luggage contained the rest of the lethal weapon. In Van Rensburg's case the barrel had been cunningly hidden in the handle of a cricket bat, which he had been ordered to wave cheerfully as he strode, sweating, through the 'green route' at Heathrow without receiving more than a cheerful grin from the Customs men on duty. He had been given the cricket bat by a steward on the aircraft from Johannesburg, as arranged, and thought it had contained drugs until he handed it over to Du Plooy in the Fontein. He considered he had earned his spurs with the Friends at the meeting when Du Plooy detailed him to book flights in the names of Foster and Comberton to Frankfurt from Southend Airport, open-dated. A half a dozen other members were given similar tasks. At the meeting of the Friends had even been audacious enough to ask Du Plooy the reason for this curious proceeding.

Du Plooy had always worked on the 'need to know' principle. 'Never you mind,' he had answered in his guttural accent. 'Just do as I tell you. All I can say to you is that this is going to be the biggest thing in world cricket since W. G. Grace. Bloody Lord's will be laughing all over the wrong sides of their faces by the time I've finished with them.' Then he had ordered them all to book out of the Fontein, to go to their various tasks, and to find alternative accommodation for the night. They were all to report back to the Fontein by four o'clock the next afternoon, when further tasks would be allotted them; but in the meantime they were to make themselves scarce and in no circumstances to get into trouble. The South Africans would be flown back to Johannesburg by charter jet; the others would return by various routes to their own countries.

Voices had been raised, questions and complaints aired, all of which Du Plooy heard impassively, his arms folded, shaking his head.

'Who . . .?'

'Why the . . .?'

'What the bloody . . .?'

'How the devil . . .?'

A voice asserted itself, instantly stilling the babel.

'Mr Du Plooy. Did *you* kill that cameraman? Phillips?'

In the silence, Du Plooy stooped under the table, then rose slowly to his feet holding something behind him.

'Gentlemen,' he said flatly. 'I am not prepared to discuss the matter.' He produced a gun from behind his back. 'Unless my lawyer is present. Now, *voetsak*!'

The sudden crudeness of the Afrikaans dismissal shocked them all into movement, and they shuffled out, some still laughing nervously at what they preferred to think was Du Plooy's little joke.

A fine Monday morning in the middle of a heatwave in June is the best possible day to view Test cricket. The packed crowds of the first three days of the match have thinned to a comfortable gathering of cognoscenti, the bar service is quick and there is room to spread a sandwich lunch on an adjoining seat or two. But when Ashcroft reached the ground shortly after ten o'clock, he realised that Lord's this Monday was going to be different.

Queues for the turnstiles stretched right round the ground.

Uniformed police trying to control a seething mob outside the Grace Gates were forced to form a cordon to press back the crowds, allowing the members through. The England cricketers had to be escorted into the ground by a posse of police; and when the Australians arrived in their coach it took ten minutes and much swearing to clear a way through the crush. The mystery of the Lord's murders had caught the public imagination, and even after the gates closed 15 minutes before play was due to begin, a crowd of several thousand blocked St John's Wood Road throughout the day, feasting on titbits of information filtering through the gates and the recurrent bursts of applause that surged over the prison-like walls. And there was plenty of that. For the 23,500 packed inside were privileged to witness the greatest performance by an England fast bowler since Bob Willis knocked over the Australians with his eight wickets in 'Botham's match' at Leeds in 1981.

Imrie and Comberton resumed their second innings opening partnership with Australia leading by 279 runs, all their wickets in hand and two full days left for play – in any cricketer's eyes, a winning position. Imrie told his team in the dressing-room before they went out: 'If we don't stuff the bastards this time we deserve to be shot.' And Cousins, restored by a night's sleep to equilibrium if not favour with a team used to hard drinking, added unnecessarily: 'And you will be.'

However, they were not reckoning on meeting a Vince Carter from whose mind all sense of guilt had been expunged. The big bowler felt as though a physical weight had been lifted from his shoulders. Off a two-pace run in the loosen-up net he skimmed past Broadbent's ear with one ball and bowled him with the next, at which the skipper told him to ease up before he killed someone.

'Don't worry, skip,' he called back, to Broadbent's astonishment. 'I'm saving them for the other side.'

'You do that, lad,' said Broadbent.

Roland Anderson, who was watching, nodded. There was something about Carter this morning that he had not seen before. He thought: 'He's grown up,' and was not surprised when after the net practice the young man asked to see him alone and confessed all that had happened.

'If it means I never play for England again,' he said, 'I can't help that now. But I've got another innings to show what I can do.'

'Yes. You've got another innings. Jack Viner didn't have one, Carter. But I'll do my best to explain to the Board. They'll probably want to see you.'

'I know.' But the prospect did not seem to daunt Carter, who added: 'When you think you've killed someone, the world seems to be at an end. But it's different now. Cleaner.'

He went out onto the field and bowled Imrie with his second ball. The first pitched short and flew to the boundary off the shoulder of the bat over the head of Broadbent, at first slip, so fast that the captain retreated two yards and signalled for Woodman to move out of the cover field to take up position at fourth slip. The second, a bullet-like full pitch, hit the top of the off stump while Imrie was still shouldering arms. Imrie departed to generous applause for his 87 runs, but kicking himself that he had not translated his overnight score into his fifth Test century. As he passed a sympathetic Comberton, he told him: 'I blew that one, sod it. Take it easy, Shiner. Time for a ton. I'll declare at tea or 450 ahead, whichever comes first. Luck, mate.'

Foster, the next batsman in, began confidently enough with a push-shot into the empty off-side which yielded two runs and then 'Chinese cut' a four between his legs. A bye brought Comberton to face Carter, who was working up a fearful pace. He was late down to the last ball of the over, which reared just outside his off stump, taking the outside edge of the bat and giving Alexander a straightforward catch which he accepted gratefully. As the players clustered round to congratulate Carter, the bowler felt a glow of genuine confidence such as he had never felt before. He said to Broadbent: 'Can I have another slip, please, boss?' and Broadbent, beaming, was only too pleased to oblige him.

But Carter needed only the help of Broadbent himself and Alexander, with two more catches, to run through the rest of the innings by lunchtime, transforming an overnight average of 0/43 to 9/61, the best figures by a fast bowler in the history of Test matches. With the score at 184, Foster, who had garnered eight more runs off Spencer, drove at a Carter ball that left him a fraction off the pitch. The snick as the ball hit the outside edge of the bat could be heard even in the stands, and Broadbent took a stinging catch to his midriff, rolling backwards with the force of

204

the ball and landing like a puppy, arms and legs pointing sky-wards, the ball clutched triumphantly in his right hand.

Carter carried on his run-through to haul Broadbent to his feet and hug him, soccer fashion, and was in no way put out when he was told, in broadest Yorkshire, 'not to piss about, lad, get on wi' it.' He waited impatiently for the next batsman, MacPhail, to settle at the crease and promptly unsettled him with a ball that reared off a length and whistled past the ducking helmet. MacPhail took a turn round the stumps to settle himself a second time and then, as Carter was accelerating in the middle of his run-up, stepped back from his crease swatting at an imaginary fly. Carter's answer to the ploy was classic: a fearsomely fast yorker which sent MacPhail's middle stump flying so far that Alexander, the wicketkeeper standing nearly 15 yards behind the wicket, caught it. That was four wickets for Carter now, and with the crowd roaring him on with every ball he knew he was bowling faster and better than he had ever done.

Smart offered some brief resistance, driving hard and looking more confident than any other batsman, but after conceding a straight-driven four to the pavilion rails, Carter 'held one back', as the reporters say, and gratefully accepted a simple return catch. From then on it was nothing but a procession of batsmen trailing to and from the pavilion as Carter ran through the last four wickets for only five runs, the roar of the crowd growing more hysterical with every success. And when he spreadeagled all three of Martin's stumps to close the innings at 215, the crowd converged onto the field from all sides as the team formed a posse round Carter, lifted him onto their shoulders, and carried him in triumph to the pavilion.

In the confusion, Broadbent thrust the ball into Carter's hands, shouting in his ear: 'Keep that, lad. It'll be something to show your grandchildren.' As they struggled through to the pavilion, Carter shoved the ball deep down into his trouser pocket. The entire Australian team crowded onto the players' balcony to applaud him and the packed members, including Detective Chief Superintendent Ashcroft, rose to do the same.

In the dressing-room, Broadbent deliberately chose to insert a note of realism into the euphoria. As the flurry of congratulations died down, he said soberly, 'There's the hell of a long way to go still. Vince here's turned the game round our way but we've still got to find three hundred and thirty-eight to win. That's a bloody lot of runs.'

'Oh, I don't know, skip.' Spencer was an eternal optimist. 'We've got a day and a half to try and if we all get a few we'll make it. I'm due for a ton myself,' he added cheerfully, drawing the derisive attention of those who had been clustering around Carter.

'Huh. Listen to him. Who hasn't had a ton since last Christmas?'

'January,' said Spencer, very much on his dignity. 'Port o' Spain.'

'Jammy one, that.'

'Bloody hard work. It was 100 degrees!'

'Come off it, Monkey. Two quickies broken down and only a tweaker left! A ten-year-old could have scored a hundred on that day.'

'Why didn't you, then, Cagey?'

'Run out. By Chopper.'

'That was your fault, Cagey. Halfway up the bloody pitch on my call . . .'

'Balls to that. You never even call your auntie . . .'

The chaffing bandied about between the players until they trooped upstairs for lunch. Carter was relieved to be alone with his own thoughts for a minute or two. It was almost too much, this return to the heights so suddenly after being so low. But he basked in the warmth of their praise and their friendship, and knew that although it was only a game, this was his life. But there were still two things he had to do.

The Test was, as the Press said, boiling up to a classic finish. Carter's success with the ball had put fresh heart into a team which on Saturday had looked already beaten. But Broadbent knew that England still had a hill to climb.

In the event, the England batsmen, led by Prettyman, made a highly respectable start. Keyed up by Carter's success, they went out determined to build a believable challenge. Although Prettyman looked the more confident of the opening batsmen, his partner Williamson, grimly determined to get behind the line and playing every ball as though it was made of TNT, stayed for an hour and a quarter until the shine was off and he was bowled by

Jones. Prettyman, belying his name with twelve fours thumped through the cover field or either side of long-on, made 73 before stepping down the wicket to Smart and steepling a huge catch which Walters did well to hold right by the Nursery End sight-screen. Prettyman and Graham had put on 95 for the second wicket, and Graham went on to his own half-century before stumps were drawn. It was, said *The Times*, mixing its metaphors, a fair springboard from which to launch a bid for victory on the fifth and last day, but if the wind was set fair for England they had to beware the sudden squalls to which English batting was always only too prone. Much, said *The Times*, would depend on the batting form of the captain, Broadbent, who would have to show the sturdiness and application of his animal namesake, the Badger.

There being no developments to report on the double murder hunt, Detective Chief Superintendent Ashcroft called off his scheduled Press briefing and looked forward to a comfortable dinner with Dr Heatherington, whom he liked very much, and to a peaceful night's rest. He was wrong again on both counts.

Australia (Second Innings) continued
Overnight: Australia 310 and 156/0. England 187

J. Viner	did not bat, dead	0
B.V. Imrie	b Carter	87
C.B. Comberton	c Alexander, b Carter	84
P.C. Foster	c Broadbent, b Carter	14
R.P.D. MacPhail	b Carter	0
S.S. Smart	c and b Carter	15
G. Viljoen	c Alexander, b Carter	2
B.F. Rose	lbw Carter	5
N. Walters	c Alexander, b Carter	0
M. Martin	b Carter	0
G. Jones	not out	0
	Extras	8
	Total	215

Fall of wickets: 1/156, 2/162, 3/184, 4/184, 5/207, 6/210, 7/212, 8/215, 9/215

Bowling	O	M	R	W
V.J. Carter	23.2	7	61	9
D.A. Spencer	14	2	60	0
A.B. Prettyman	22	3	53	0
P.Q. Mandell	12	1	33	0

England (Second Innings)

A.B. Prettyman	c Walters b Smart	73
F.A. Williamson	b Jones	12
P. Graham	not out	52
B. Coetzee	not out	3
	Extras	12
	Total (for 2 wickets)	152

Fall of wickets: 1/43, 2/138

Bowling	O	M	R	W
N. Walters	11	2	39	0
G. Jones	12	0	49	1
S.S. Smart	9	0	36	1
M. Martin	10	5	16	0

Chapter 9

The Fourth Evening

Vincent Carter spent an hour of the afternoon's play soaking away his stiffness in a warm bath and another hour on Doc Wright's treatment couch, his efforts of the morning having put even his young fit body to the test. Then he dressed in slacks and sweat-shirt, with a windcheater on top, and packed up his gear, confident from the manner of England's second innings that he would not be needed again that day. A couple of Lord's Old Faithfuls had club-bed together and sent him a bottle of Bollinger '74 in an ice-bucket, and he asked Doc Wright to borrow some glasses from the bar for the team at the end of play. Then he settled down with the other players on the balcony to watch the batsmen nibble away effectively at Australia's lead and to sign the ever-growing pile of autograph books sent up to the dressing-room.

'What's up, Vince? You're far too serious for a man who's just broken a world record.'

'I'm still thinking about Jack.' It was true, in a way, but not with the self-destroying bitterness that had previously clogged his every thought.

They stood up to applaud the players into the pavilion, and Carter uncorked his champagne to a round of cheers. One or two cricketers had cameras, and a blurred shot of Carter filling the glasses appeared the next day in one of the more lurid tabloids with, inset, a picture of him weeping on the field the previous Thursday. The captions read curtly: 'Then' and 'Now'. Someone came in with a pile of telegrams of congratulation; from someone else more bottles of champagne arrived and within twenty min-utes the dressing-room turned into a shambles of naked bodies, raucous laughter and cigar smoke. Anderson, the manager, sought Carter out and had a word in his ear.

'Wrecker Imrie would like you to go round for a few minutes, if that's OK with you.

'Right, Mr Anderson. Reckon I'm safe?'

Anderson grinned. 'He's guaranteed your return, but I'm not sure about your safety. It depends if you can take Foster's lager on top of champagne. Don't be too long. And don't get too tight. We've got the interviews to do yet and I've promised you to throw you to the wolves.'

'Oh shit.'

'Don't knock it. You never know when you might need them. And Vince.'

'Yes, boss?'

'Bloody well done.'

'Thanks.'

He strolled round to the Australian dressing-room, amiably fielding the congratulatory pats and plunging straight through the doorstepping Press and cameramen with a 'Later, guys!' before they could stop him. The room appeared to be in very much the same state of milling disarray as England's, but as he stepped through the door an Australian voice shouted above the row: 'He's here!' and the entire team turned in unison and began to clap. From the victims to the victor it was as sporting a tribute as could have belonged to Roy of the Rovers, but nonetheless welcome and moving for that.

'Come in, cobber, and make yourself at home.'

'That was a great piece of bowling.'

'Shit-hot.'

'Jesus mate, how d'ye do it?'

'Drink up. You deserve it.'

Yet another glass was thrust into his hand and suddenly Carter found himself seated on the table, with the Australians grouped round him, plying him with champagne but apparently otherwise oblivious to his presence and running through the amazing day ball by ball.

'And then you shook me up with that bloody bouncer first ball and I thought "I'll fix you," and pulled out on the run-up to the next ball. I was trying to give you a hernia, but what did you bloody do? Ripped my sodding middle stump out, that's all. Bloody beaut yorker.'

'Bloody great.'

'Bloody marvellous.'

211

'And then I thought I'd got you when I put you through the covers, you bastard, but you went and held it back. Oldest trick in the book and I fell for it.'

'Did you . . .?'

Between-times Carter was aware of the dressing-room attendant plucking at his sleeve.

'Mr Carter. Mr Carter. The manager wants you.'

'God. I'm meant to be talking to the Press,' he said with some thickness of vowels.

'Fuck the Press,' said several Australian voices, loudly. 'You're talking to us. Let 'em fucking wait.'

'Right, tell them to piss off. Have another drink, Vince. You screwed us this afternoon. It's our turn to screw you.'

Carter closed his hand round the cricket ball in his windcheater pocket and slowly brought it out.

'Would – would you guys mind signing it?' He was slurring, slightly.

'Sure. Give it here. Where's a bloody pen?'

A ball-point was produced from somewhere and they crowded round to sign the ball, still only slightly battered. More drinks appeared; time wound on and in the television interview room Peter Proudfoot gave up waiting for him and 'went without him' to talk to a willing Broadbent, backed up by Anderson, who had himself been told to 'frig off' when he tried to use his influence to drag Carter to the interview by sheer force.

In an increasing haze Carter heard Smart's voice, high above the others.

'Hey, I got it, fellers. Let's kidnap him. Let's make him ours for the night. What d'you say?'

A chorus of assent.

'Better ask the victim. Eh pal?'

'Well, er . . .'

'Grub's good. Company's better. Girls prettier. C'mon, then.'

Carter gave in with good grace which owed a great deal the mixture in his brain of euphoria, champagne and several 'tubes' of lager.

He genuinely wanted to avoid the media, and his intelligence reckoned slowly that the opposing camp was about the last place they would look. He held up his cricket ball, covered with signatures.

'So long as you don't try to nick my ball,' he said.

There was a roar of laughter.

'Nick your ball?' said Jones. 'No, we'll have your balls for breakfast.'

With much Mirth, they made their plan as they dressed, swiftly now. The half-hearted protests of Cousins were swept aside and he was sent down to make sure the coach was ready. Carter was given an Australian cap and surrounded by the big Australian fast bowlers, also wearing caps. Imrie, entering into the spirit of the thing, opened the dressing-room door suddenly and led a solid phalanx of laughing cricketers, whooping and shouting, out and down the stairs like a rugby scrum, arms linked and brushing aside Pressmen, television cameras, TCCB officials and autograph hunters.

The coach was waiting massively on the roadway outside, its door swung open. The Australians, Carter in their midst, piled into it, still laughing, and plumped down into the seats. Carter found himself towards the back, by the window. Next to him was Smart, grinning with delight at the success of his ruse. Next, he said, or rather shouted, they would try Carter – a proper kangaroo court, he said – for his slaughter of the innocents.

The security man jumped in and took his seat in the front beside Cousins, the driver touched a control, the door swung smoothly closed and the coach moved off into St John's Wood Road.

Imrie, on the other side from Carter, looked out of his window.

'Where the hell are we going?' he said suddenly. 'Hey, Griff,' he called, 'ask the driver where he thinks he's going?'

The coach had turned left off St John's Wood Road and was heading for Swiss Cottage, instead of right and for the Marylebone Road.

Cousins stood up and turned to face the players.

'It's OK, lads,' he said, pitching his voice so they could all hear him. 'It's just a little extra sponsorhip deal I fixed up with some charity outfit. We'll only be there an hour. It's only about ten minutes drive away. We'll be back in the hotel by eight-thirty.'

'Christ, Griff, don't we get a flaming moment of our own?'
Other voices took up the protest.

'What charity, Griff?'

'It's not in our contract.'

'I'm too bloody bushed.'

'Me too.'

'Turn the bloody coach round.'

The manager held up his hands against a tide of protest that
looked like expanding into a full-scale mutiny.

'Now hold on, fellas. Hold on. It ain't so bad. I know it's a bit
off, but they're a good bunch. 'Sides, I wasn't going to tell you this
till afterwards, but there's a hundred apiece in tenners for each of
you afterwards. Straight up. It'll be a great party.'

Imrie was still suspicious.

'But what's the charity, Griff?'

'It's a bunch called Friends of World Sport. It's just been
formed to promote friendship in sport all over the world. Something to do with an instant reaction to Jack's death, you know. I
couldn't say no, and I didn't want to tell you until the end of play.
Anyway, we're nearly there. Turn up here, Fred,' he said to the
driver and the coach swung into a long wide road lined with trees.

'Up on the left about 100 yards. By that big tree.'

The prospect of £100 in their pockets seemed to have mollified
any Australian resentment. In the back seat Sissie Smart turned to
Carter, slumped next to him in an amiable haze and whispered:
'Sorry chum. But we'll get you a hundred smackers as well.'
Carter, who had heard only the words 'great party', did not care by
now whether they went to town or Timbuctoo, grinned rather
foolishly as the driver swung the coach into a curved drive
between great rhododendron bushes that instantly hid them from
the road. Led by Cousins, the Australians tumbled out, grumbling
half-heartedly.

James Merriweather greeted them at the double doors of the
Fontein. More acute observers might have noticed that his smile
seemed tense, his bonhomie brittle.

'Good evening, gentlemen. Welcome. Welcome. The Friends
are meeting in the dining room. Very pleased to see you all. Well
played. Straight through, gentlemen. Cloaks on the left.'

Carter excused himself and peeled off into the gents. As well as

214

needing relief for a bursting bladder his head felt light and his eyes bleary. He filled a basin with cold water and plunged his head and face into it, letting the cleansing coolness seep into him. As he combed out his damp hair Smart put his head round the door.

'Come on, Vince. Come and get your lolly, if you don't want to get left out.'

'OK. Just coming.' He put on his windcheater, feeling as he did so the weight of the cricket ball in its pocket. His fingers fastened on its familiar roundness. It was somehow reassuring.

The large room appeared occupied with the usual official party scrum, but Carter noticed at once that it was a 'men-only' thrash. Most of the guests were drinking champagne, and Carter took a glass for himself from a full tray beside the door. There were several small tables with chairs dotted around, and a large table at the head of the room, with something bulky at its centre holding up a white sheet draped like a tent.

'Funny lot,' Smart said at his elbow. 'They don't seem to know what they're here for. And none of 'em seem to have been at the match today. They didn't know about your record. Never mind, we'll soon be back at the ranch.'

'Gentlemen, please.' Merrivale appeared at the door, 'General Hermann Berger.' He stood aside like a butler and through the door, in full-dress uniform complete with four rows of medals, walked the man they knew as Hermann Du Plooy. He strode to the large covered table and stood facing them, removing his cap slowly and placing it under his arm. He made an impressive figure.

Imrie broke the silence.

'Say, Hermann, what is this? Fancy dress?'

'No, Mr Imrie, this is not fancy dress. I have a proposition for you. But first, let me show you this!'

On the word, he whipped the sheet from the table, revealing a mounted golden globe the size of a football, with the map of the world etched delicately on its face. He touched it gently and it began to rotate silently.

'You are privileged to see, gentlemen, the championship trophy which will be awarded by the Friends of World Sport to the winning team at the Word Sporting Jamboree in Johannesburg next year. I have also an envelope here for each of you in

215

compensation for having lured you here under, shall we say, slightly false pretences. I would like you to examine the globe as you collect your envelopes. Then I have something else to show you here.'

He placed his hand on a long box and continued. His voice took on a sort of chant, as though he had learned what he was saying by heart and was addressing a platoon of recruits to the South African army . . .

'If you were thinking of walking away with the globe, I should warn you that it would take two strong men to lift it. It is made of solid, 24-carat gold and weighs over one hundred pounds. The plinth and mounting arm are solid platinum and weigh about the same. The fulcra at the poles which act as the bearings are two diamonds each of several hundred carats. All these valuable elements are produced, of course, in South Africa. At current prices the objet d'art at which you are looking is valued at about ten million dollars – the richest prize ever offered in sport.'

'Sounds like fool's gold to me,' Imrie said in his dry Australian way. No one moved. 'What's it got to with us? We're not going to South Africa. We're going back to the Waldorf.'

He turned his back on Du Plooy and began to walk to the door. Du Plooy's voice rang out like a whip-crack.

'Stand still!'

Imrie stopped in mid-stride and swung round. His face was livid.

'No man speaks to me . . .'

He stopped. You do not argue with an AK47 when it is pointed at your stomach from ten feet. The fury died from his face but his eyes were bleak.

'Sit down, Mr Imrie. Sit down everybody and listen to what I have to say.' He gestured around the room with the barrel of the automatic rifle. The team sat down, too astonished to be scared.

The man in the general's uniform continued his speech: 'I am sorry to be so dramatic, but please understand that I have used this weapon many times and am considered an expert at long and short range. We have no intention of harming you, but I must insist that you accept our invitation to compete for the Friends' Globe. In each of these envelopes is £100, as promised, and a draft on a Johannesburg bank for $100,000 in whichever currency you may choose. You will have no problems with taking the cash out of South Africa. I can assure you. If you decide to stay, the money will be doubled, in South African rands, of course.'

There was not a movement in the room. It was as though they were holding their breath, waiting for the spell cast by the gun to break.

Imrie said: 'You must be mad. There's no way you can hijack the whole Australian team in the middle of a Test match in England.'

'Not mad, Mr Imrie. Just practical. I promised to deliver an international team to the Jubilee, and I have chosen you. No one knows where you are. We have ten private hire cars outside to drive you all to Stansted Airport within five minutes. Each of you will be escorted by one of us, to whom I regret you must be handcuffed until we are in the aircraft. For your information, you are officially a group of illegal immigrants being sent back to Australia.'

Unnoticed at a side table, Vince Carter shoved his hands deep into the pockets of his windcheater and leaned forward in his seat, his eyes intent on Du Plooy. He was utterly sober. The mists had been blown from his brain by the first shock of Du Plooy's appearance, and a mounting anger fuelled by cold calculation had taken over his whole being. He had no fear, no thought beyond one: 'When?'

On the other side of the room, Imrie said: 'We're not going. You can't shoot the lot of us. You're bluffing.'

'No bluff, Mr Imrie. Your escort is waiting for you at the door.' He jerked the gun up. 'Move!'

In one smooth movement, Vince Carter stood up and threw his autographed cricket ball with all his force.

When Carter bowled at his fastest with a straight arm it was calculated later by a computer that the ball travelled at an initial speed of 95.6 mph. As a fielder, he was accurate enough to hit the wicket-keeper's gloves over the stumps from 60 yards eight times out of ten, with the leverage of the bent arm giving a 'muzzle velocity' to the ball of at least 125 mph. The average man's brain reacts to a physical threat instantly, but takes at least three-fifths of a second to transmit a response to his muscles. It took under half of that time for Carter's cricket ball to travel the 15 feet from his hand to Du Plooy's face where it struck the bridge of his nose with the force of a cannonball.

Imrie leapt for the AK47 as it dropped from Du Plooy's lifeless hand, but froze once more as Ashcroft's voice from the door said: 'Thank you, Mr Carter. Don't bother, Mr Imrie. We have everything under control. Light, get the ambulance men. Or the undertaker, if more appropriate.'

Chapter 10

The Fifth Day

A cloud no bigger than a man's hand grew into a tiny blip unnoticed on a meteorologist's chart and by Tuesday morning the drought had broken and the rain was blanketing the green grass of Lord's Cricket Ground, steaming up the windows of the Press room and confining the teams to their dressing-rooms. Inside speculation was equally divided between whether the rain would stop in time and the pitch be fit enough for the match to be finished and the whereabouts of young Carter, who had not been seen since he had brought the melodramatic events of the previous evening to such an abrupt and violent close. Such speculation was mirrored closely among the members in the Long Bar, the private boxes and among the few hundred super-keen fans who gathered forlornly in front of the Tavern. In fact, Carter was at the moment was fast asleep in Light's flat. Light had been detailed to whisk him off and keep him out of the way of the Press until the whole of the Friends' plot could be unravelled, a task that had so far taken all night and most of the early morning. Ashcroft had promised a Press and TV conference at midday, and there was still much to do.

Ashcroft, Light and Thomas were very tired. In all they had arrested 29 people, and each one had been charged with conspiracy and questioned. Lawyers had had to be contacted, statements meticulously recorded, the newspapers and TV to be accommodated and angry or anxious relatives placated.

'I don't know.' Thomas leant his head on his hands and rubbed his eyes. His Welsh sing-song sounded more like a dirge. 'D'you think we're going to make this conspiracy charge stick? All they're saying is that they joined this phoney outfit in good faith as a reputable organisation with perfectly respectable aims, whether you agree with the politics or not, and this paranoid schizo deceived them. Even that bloody fool Van Rensburg thought he was helping in the biggest put-down on the British the world had ever seen. It was all a joke, he said. Joke? Hah! The only bloody joke was when the Colchester boys caught him at Mersea trying to hire a bloody paddle boat to take him across the channel.'

'Don't worry, Thommo,' said Light, 'if it's not conspiracy, it's accessory before or after the fact. After all, Van der Merwe will go down for life and we've got Du Plooy, or Berger or whatever he calls himself, even if he doesn't live to stand trial. The rest are small fry. Talking of frying, I hope the judge does just that to Mr Cousins. He was in it up to his dirty neck.'

Ashcroft turned from the window.

'At least we won't be troubled by the business of diplomatic immunity. South Africa House has washed its hands of the whole thing. They've never heard of the Friends of World Sport or a Jamboree. The official word from Downing Street is that both were figments of a madman's imagination. Although how they're going to explain away a hundredweight or so of gold, platinum and diamonds I don't know.'

Light looked at him.

'There are too many things I don't know, either, sir,' he said. 'I think you took a helluva chance, if you don't mind my saying so. If Merrifield hadn't been able to nick the firing-pin out of that AK47, that bloody madman would have shot Imrie and half the Australian cricket team, as well as a fair slice of the Met. And your career, Bill,' he added, forgetting the proprieties in his warmth.

Ashcroft declined to notice.

'What's the time, Amber?' he inquired mildly.

Light, checked in full flight, looked irritably at his watch.

'Ten fifteen. Why?' He added: 'Sir.'

'I think you'll have the answer to your question in one minute,' said Ashcroft; and at that moment PC Evans put a large head round the door and announced: 'Mr Merrifield's here, Super. Says you're expecting him. Can I send 'im in?'

'Please do.' Ashcroft got to his feet, which made Light stare. It was an honour reserved for the Commissioner himself and (possibly) royalty. He was also smiling.

'Come in, Jim. Thanks for coming. I think you've met Inspector

Thomas and Sergeant Light already, but they don't yet know that you were formerly a Detective Sergeant in the Coventry CID.' He turned to the others. 'Jim worked with me on that Keith case I told you about. It had a considerable Midlands connection. He wasn't called Merrifield then. Old habits die hard, eh Jim?'

'You old bugger,' Light muttered to himself.

'What's that, Amber?'

'Nothing, Sir.' He couldn't help feeling resentful. 'So you knew all along? You might have told us.'

'No, I didn't know anything, Amber. There was the South African connection from the moment you mentioned Peter Stuyvesant cigarettes in Carter's case, and it became a certainty when you ran across Du Plooy – Berger – in the Waldorf. The role of Phillips was central to the case, of course. He had to die because he was the one element that linked the whole scheme together. But what that scheme was I did not begin to see until Friday evening after Phillips had been killed. And even then I didn't believe my own theory. I could not imagine any sane man dreaming up a plot to kidnap an entire cricket team in the middle of a Test match. It was the cricket element, I suppose, which made it so unbelievable to me. We're quite accustomed to madmen hijacking Jumbo jets with 500 people on board, and even ships with a couple of thousand passengers. So why not a cricket team? Even a Test team, if you wanted to discredit the whole British Establishment.' he paused. 'I suppose you might call it the laager mentality, eh Jim?, It breeds delusions of many kinds. At any rate, when both Mrs Viner and my contact at the South African Embassy mentioned the Fontein Hotel, we were lucky to find Mr James Merrifield in charge there. You carry on, Jim.'

Light thought the lines round Merrifield's eyes made him look much older than his professed 45. Merrifield spoke slowly.

'It's all coincidence, or luck, or whatever you call it. When I resigned from the CID I didn't actually leave it all behind. It was some obscure department of the Foreign Office, I was told, which was looking for a likely sleeper, as they called it, to make a new life in Ian Smith's Rhodesia after the unilateral declaration of independence, and report back from time to time. There was a number to ring, but I never used it, but from time to time someone would come and stay at my hotel and identify himself, and I'd pass over

221

what scraps I'd been able to pick up. I think I was quite useful before the Lancaster House agreement, disabusing the FO and the Government of their delusions about Joshua Nkomo's power and so on. I also gave them quite a lot on Gerber, or Du Plooy as you know him. He was a real bastard during the war out there. I thought he was mad then. He once killed a patrol of six armed Zanu men with a knife and his bare hands.

'At any rate, the FO were quite happy for me to come back after Zimbabwe got its independence, but they still kept tabs on me even though they gave me an official letter of discharge. No pension, of course. I told them about Gerber and his arrangement to keep permanent rooms with me, and that I thought he was up to something, but I never found out what. Even after Sunday's meeting which you lot just missed I had no idea. Gerber's a cunning cruel sod, and ruthless. So I thought I'd better come out of the closet again, and that night I rang Bill to tell him about the second meeting that Gerber had booked for last night. Bill told me what he was afraid of, and asked me to look for any weapons, particularly an automatic rifle. I found the AK locked in a cupboard, so I took out the firing-pin and left it where it was. You know the rest. But I still thing you were taking a chance, Bill, that Gerber wouldn't have another gun. Or that none of the others would be armed.'

'No. Gerber was a one-man band. He would never trust anyone else with any responsibility in his schemes, let alone a gun. When Phillips showed signs of independence, Gerber killed him, deluding himself that he was furthering his cause by such public slaughter. I expect he saw it as a sort of execution. Once the AK was made safe, I had no worries on that score. He could not have tried to hold thirteen or fourteen young men with a hand-gun or a knife, and we were going to be there, anyway. I had to let the hijack go to the Fontein, in order to net Gerber. He obligingly fell into his own trap.'

Ashcroft stood up, stretched, and stared again across the cricket field to the grey and white covers over the pitch glistening with moisture, at the long pipes leading off to the outfield to fan-shaped areas of rainwater spreading into the grass. As he gazed, shaking his head slowly, the disembodied voice of the Tannoy boomed hollowly across the dripping ground.

'Ladies and gentlemen: The umpires have decided that there can be no more play today, even if the rain were to stop. The match has therefore been abandoned as a draw. Thank you for your loyalty and persistence which we hope will be rewarded at Edgbaston in two weeks' time . . .'

The voice droned on. Up in the stand to his right Ashcroft could see the hospitality boxes packed tight behind their wide glass sliding picture doors. He wondered how many excuses had now to be drastically amended now there was no longer a match to attend. He sighed. There was much to do. He turned.

'That's about it,' he said. 'You'll wrap it up, Thommo? Amber? I'll see to the wolves. You'll want to get away, Jim.'

'Yes Bill.'

'OK, Sir.'

'And Amber?'

'Yes, Sir?'

'Don't worry about Mrs Viner. I have spoken to Anderson, and she will be going to stay with them for a day or two in the Pennines. She'll be all right. I shall drive her up tomorrow myself.'

'Yes, Sir.' Stolidly. The old devil, he thought.

'Oh, and Amber. There was a telephone call for you. A WPC from Chalfont. She wants to know if its all right to call off the watch on The Heights. I said you'd ring her yourself. She seemed anxious to speak to you personally.'

Light waited until the room was empty. As he dialled the Chalfont number he wondered if WPC Clarke would look much older in a dress, over a candle-lit table.